Like a Summer Song

Simran is an engineer from Delhi College of Engineering. After a two-year stint with BCG, she pivoted to a career in marketing. But at heart Simran is a storyteller chasing inspiration in everything life has to offer.

Simran is also a spoken word poet and mental health advocate who is always up for swapping stories over numerous cups of tea.When not crafting compelling tales or spearheading strategic campaigns, she can be found on her yoga mat practising a Surya Namaskar or compulsively creating her next travel itinerary.

Follow her on Instagram @simran__dudeja, where she talks about her life, travels, adulting struggles, favourite books, movies and everything that catches her fancy.

Like a Summer Song

Simran Dudeja

NU VOICE
PRESS

First published by NU VOICE PRESS 2023
An imprint of Hubhawks Pvt. Ltd
www.nuvoicepress.com

ISBN: 978-81-963184-7-5

Typeset by Saanvi Graphics, Noida
Printed at Thomson Press
Published by Nu Voice Press

"For those of you who love romantic stories, this is it."

–**Ajay K Pandey** Bestselling author of *You are the Best Wife*

To my Nanaji, from whom I get the literary gene, he would've been the proudest grandfather if he were with us today.

Author's Note

Dear reader,

The first draft of this book that you hold in your hands was conceptualised in 2020, during the peak pandemic when the world slowed down and we were exiled to our own company with more mental and physical room to reflect and confront what we truly want.

So, to adjust to the new normal of unending *work-from-home* in my then-first job, fresh out of campus, my small self-care routine would be to take a sunset-watching break while sipping on tea, sitting on the front porch of our former Jaipur residence. I would simply quieten my mind and witness the stunning pink skies of the pink city slowly change colour. And in those meditative moments, a poem would reveal itself to me. You will find those poems preceding every chapter of this book.

These poems are journal entries written by these characters, intended to give you a peek into their subconscious thoughts in the form of free verse.

I often think of poetry as an epiphany; it arrives on its own terms, but it's always when you genuinely need it. While the entire manuscript has undergone rigorous rounds of editing and proofing, I wanted my poems to be spared by the editor's sword. For these are nothing but unfiltered streams of my pure consciousness, which I extend to you today. This book is now yours. And I hope that you will keep it safe.

Like A Summer Song Playlist

Kahin Toh (Jaane Tu Ya Jaane Na)

Tears in Heaven (Eric Clapton)

Here Comes the Sun (The Beatles)

Daylight (Taylor Swift)

Tu Hi Hai (Ali Zafar)

Late Night Talking (Harry Styles)

Cruel Summer (Taylor Swift)

Rewrite the Stars (Anne Marie & James Arthur)

You Are in Love (Taylor Swift)

We Fell in Love in October (Girl in Red)

Ain't No Sunshine (Bill Withers)

Keep Driving (Harry Styles)

Unsteady (X Ambassadors)

Sign of The Times (Harry Styles)

Love You Like A Love Song (Selena Gomez)

Capital Letters (Hailee Steinfield)

Can't take my eyes off you (Frankie Valli)

Perfect (Ed Sheeran)

Love in the Dark (Adele)

Sleep On the Floor (The Lumineers)

Cold Mess (Prateek Kuhad)

I've Got You Under My Skin (Frank Sinatra)
Say Yes to Heaven (Lana Del Rey)
The Way I Loved You (Taylor Swift)
Say You Won't Let Go (James Arthur)
Hold Back the River (James Bay)
Stubborn Love (The Lumineers)

Prologue

“This doesn’t have to be our story, you know?” he said.

She lifted her gaze and rested it on his face, looking at the soft lighting of the room falling on his sharp jaw.

“There are multiple parallel universes existing in space at this point in time. And our lives would look so different in each of them,” he said, holding her gaze.

Her hazel eyes pierced through him, as if searching for a hope to alter their current reality.

“I think in an alternate universe, we’d be living in a large house in the countryside with a rusty fireplace and a big backyard,” she said, arching her eyebrows.

“We’d have three children and two dogs. We’d do gardening, barbecue evenings, and lay in the warm afternoon sun on cold winter days of December eating oranges,” he chuckled and paused to gauge her reaction. “And spinach and corn sandwiches too!” he added. The corner of her lips had curved into a reassuring smile.

“Or…” he continued, “We could simply be a couple of twenty-something artists trying to make a name for themselves. You’ll write, I’ll sing, and together we’ll make it work.”

“I’m listening,” she said, looking at him, this time more intently.

“We’ll hit the road with nothing but a backpack on our shoulders and go on tours across cities, performing for large crowds in stadiums or cosy home gigs. We’ll drink mulled wine, listen to records, make art, travel, and live each day like it’s our last.”

"I can picture us doing that," she finally said.

"You can?"

"Yes!"

He could see a distant sparkle in her eyes.

He brushed the back of his fingers softly on her damp cheeks. A shudder went through her. She let out a deep sigh, feeling galaxies swimming in her stomach, as his skin came in contact with hers.

"Dhruv," she whispered.

"Hmm?"

"With you by my side, I find the courage to dream."

"I love you, Vaanya!" he said and pulled her in a bone-crushing hug. His breath trailed off on the valley between her neck and shoulders, making her skin tingle into goosebumps.

"I'll always love you, Dhruv. In every universe..."

"Vaanya!" his grip tightened around her waist, before he pulled away.

"But you know what's the best part?"

"What?" she asked.

"In every other universe, we'll be together," he said with a calm on his face. "We'll always find each other."

"Our souls will recognise each other," she added.

"Every time."

He smiled, and said "Coffee?"

"Sure," she laughed at his strangely charming ability to segue from a deeply consuming conversation to an entirely different topic.

Dhruv walked over to the kitchen to make them some coffee. Still cold from being drenched in the rain earlier, Vaanya sneezed in a shrill voice.

"Are you okay?" he popped over from the kitchen and offered her some fresh clothes.

She put on his old loose shirt and the cologne gave her a feeling of warm familiarity.

In the kitchen, the coffee had begun to brew, slowly and gently. Bubbles began forming in the pan as the concoction of water and milk boiled. The strong aroma drew her in.

She stood at the doorway and watched him pour the coffee into mugs as he subconsciously added one-and-a-half teaspoons of sugar into hers– just how she liked it.

"You still remember?" she smiled.

"Like the back of my hand," he answered in a heartbeat.

Nestled on the couch, with the same playlist from years ago playing in the background to keep them company, they began sipping the steaming hot coffee from ceramic mugs that slowly melted the icy years of separation with its comforting warmth.

His gaze rested on her, and he wondered how she looked just the same, after so many years. Her big, hazel eyes stared back into his deep metallic ones.

She leaned forward to place her supple lips on his. He grabbed her waist, and kissed her back with intense vigour to make up for all the lost years. And just like that, their world stopped spinning for a moment.

Suddenly, a harsh noise began to unsettle him. He felt dizzy. Eventually, the noise forced him to open his eyes, just to see the long queue of cars behind him, honking loudly, and poking him to move forward. On the road, and probably in life too.

He let out a deep sigh and hit the steering wheel with his cold hands, regaining consciousness, hoping that it wasn't just a dream.

The traffic began crawling, but his heart was still stuck somewhere on Carter Road, in the rain, on the damned and dreamy streets of Mumbai, with her. The song that brought an upsurge of memories kept playing on the car radio -

"Kahin to hogi woh, duniya jahaan tu mere paas hai.

Jahaan main, jahaan tu aur jahaan bas tere mere jazbaat hain!"

He revved up the car engine and continued driving home when suddenly his phone rang.

"Where are you, Papa?" A small voice on the other end of the phone reverberated in the car as he picked up his nine-year-old daughter's call.

Dharya, who had accidentally stumbled upon her father's journal.

Chapter 1

Tears in Heaven

I can smell winter in the air
The petals of the rose
I gave you on the last day of July
Fall mercilessly
Remembering your foggy breath
Meandering its way to mine
Through the smoke between us
As we drifted through the city
Hand in hand
Gushing with the blowing August wind
You lit a cigarette
And I smoked with you
Under the warm glow
Of the slipping September sun
Bringing with it an everlasting October

I can smell winter in the air
As November creaks
And a chill runs down my spine
“The rose petals shudder
And so do I

—DHRUV

"At the end of the day, love never goes to waste. We're put in this world only to love and learn. Later in life, you'll look back and realise that, despite the pain and confusion, you were simply getting closer to your destiny," Mrs. Malhotra said to her son who had stumbled home drunk again, in the dead of the night.

"I don't know what I am doing, *Ma*!" he slurred. A dishevelled boy, with an unkempt beard, and a face damp with half-dried tears, rested in his mother's lap.

A goddamn year had passed, yet the twenty-one-year-old Dhruv Malhotra continued to walk deliriously into bars, filling the void she had left in his heart with alcohol, cigarettes, and the company of strange women.

The morning after another bizarre and blurry night, he woke up with a splitting headache, as his eyes adjusted to the light. When an hour of staring at the ceiling and drinking two cups of black coffee did him no good, he sat on the floor in his dimly lit room, clutching his guitar and journal close. He began pouring his grief into writing a song, but even creating new music reminded him of her. How they had spent so many afternoons in his basement studio recording covers of their favourite Coldplay songs, after which she would drag him to the terrace for smoking a cigarette while watching the sunset; unaware at the time that just like the memories of her, this carcinogenic habit would be hard to get rid of.

To most of his friends and his parents, he looked almost unrecognisable. A thick beard covered his gullible boyish face, making him look jagged and intimidating. He spent most of his time holed up in his room. The only time he would leave the house was to hit the gym. His social circle diminished, and his grades began falling quickly.

Less than a year ago, an innocent faced Dhruv was everyone's favourite. Lead guitarist at the college band, an impressive academic record with straight As, a tall physique with broad-shoulders, a lofty sense of confidence and a sharp wit. He had everything going for himself. Until he met the stunning Anisha Singhania.

She stepped into his life like an uninvited storm. He had enjoyed getting soaked in the pouring rain, but before he knew it, he had been struck by lightning.

In the summer of his pre-final year at his Engineering college, Dhruv was conducting auditions for the college band, when a tall and attractive girl with chestnut hair walked up to him.

"Hey, I'm Anisha," she extended her hand.

"Hi! I'm Dhruv," he responded softly and shook hands with her. He couldn't help but notice the manicured nails, polished with a deep black colour.

"I have heard a lot about you," she said with a strikingly odd smile.

"Oh, is that so?" he appeared visibly embarrassed.

"Yeah, I've heard people say how you're the best guitarist this band has seen in years. I sing a little myself. So, I was wondering if I could join the band too."

"Thank you, that's very flattering... You're welcome to the auditions."

"Thanks for the warm welcome!" she tilted her head to look at him from another angle. "My turn is in half an hour, so I thought it'd be a good idea to get to know one of the finest seniors in college."

"That's really kind of you. I'd love to catch up, but I'm sorry, I need to focus on these auditions right now," Dhruv shrugged and excused himself.

"No worries. It was nice talking to you."

"All the best for the audition, Anisha," he said with a placid smile.

Anisha went back and sat on one of the empty chairs in the opposite end of the auditorium.

He tried to focus on the auditions, but his gaze sprinted in her direction every few minutes. A couple of times, she caught him stealing glances at her and returned an alluring smile.

Half an hour later, it was her turn. And for some reason, Dhruv was excited about her performance. As her name was announced, she walked up to the stage with her gaze fixed on Dhruv, and sang 'Girl on Fire' by Alicia Keys.

"She's just a girl and she's on fire
Hotter than a fantasy
Lonely like a highway
She's livin' in a world and it's on fire
Filled with catastrophe
But she knows she can fly away"

Dhruv was spellbound. Her deep husky voice was sexier than her perfect curves. And up there, she was literally 'on fire'.

Back home that night, Dhruv was busy working on a new song with his best friend, Arnav. Suddenly, his phone vibrated to notify of Anisha's follow request on Instagram.

"Who is it?" Arnav enquired.

"Well do you remember that girl, Anisha, from the auditions today?"

"Yeah, the hot chick who sang, 'Girl on Fire'?"

"Yep. It's her follow request."

"Dude, I saw how she was talking to you. She is totally into you."

"Let's not jump to conclusions. It's just a follow request."

"That's her move."

"She could simply want to be friends. But she sure is hot though."

"Well for starters, you don't look like a pig yourself."

"Way to make a guy feel good about himself," Dhruv smirked.

"Okay fine. You're smart and a great musician. And you're kinda rich too. Bottom line, you're quite a catch, so go for it!" Arnav said sarcastically while grabbing Dhruv's phone from his hands and checking out Anisha's Instagram profile.

"Well, my parents are rich," Dhruv said, focusing on the keys of the piano.

Arnav rolled his eyes and continued stalking her profile.

Dhruv looked at him with a slackened expression and accepted the follow request.

In less than five minutes, his phone buzzed again. This time it was a message from Anisha. He opened his DMs to a, *"Hey! How're you doing?"*

"See? So, what happened to Mr. Righteous, let's-not-generalise-and-jump to -conclusions?" Arnav gloated. "Say this to her and I bet she is going to fall harder for you. Save your intellectual content for her!"

"As you say, sir!" Dhruv resigned to his friend's comments.

"Good! Now you have fun with your new and smoking hot endeavour," Arnav smirked, bidding goodbye.

"See you tomorrow buddy," Dhruv shrugged, ignoring Arnav's remarks, and got back to his phone and checked out Anisha's profile. Her display picture was a stunning portrait of her clicked on some exotic beach. She was wearing a pair of cute denim shorts and a bright pink bralette that subtly exposed a tattoo on her back. It caught Dhruv's attention before another message from her popped up on the screen.

"Hey! Are you there?"

Dhruv opened the chat window to text her back.

"Hey! What's up?"

"Nothing much. Was listening to some classical jazz."

"Oh, I love Frank Sinatra. 'Fly me to the moon' is such a classic."

"You do? I thought only girls dig those kinds of songs."

"I am a huge fan of Sinatra and a lot of other artists from that time. I think if you're passionate about music, you tend to appreciate good work, irrespective of the genre or the artist. Besides, those are classics."

"Oh, I think I am talking to a proper musician here," she added a few blushing emojis to her reply.

"Haha come on, you're embarrassing me."

"You know what's better than a passionate musician?"

"What?"

"A modest one."

"Hahaha! Is that so?"

"Oh, it is so. Anyway, who's your favourite artist or band?"

"Umm apart from Sinatra, I am a huge Coldplay fan, but I love Eric Clapton and John Mayer too."

"Ahh, 'Tears in heaven'!"

"Oh, it transports me to another world every time I listen to it. In fact I was planning to do a cover of it tomorrow."

"Really? If you don't mind, can I join? Like I won't sing, but I can help, you know?"

"Yeah, sure. That'd be nice."

"Perfect, when and where?"

"Umm... tomorrow, my place, around six?"

"Sounds great. I can't wait!"

"Great, see you then. Also, I forgot to mention, you were terrific today. I mean Alicia Keys is phenomenal, and you did absolute justice to her."

"Did I? I thought I blew it."

"Are you kidding me? No, you had the whole crowd going crazy over your voice."

"Oh really, you too?"

Dhruv didn't know what to say, so he let her comment slide and replied with a laughing emoji.

The next evening, she came to his place and they had a lot of fun recording 'Tears in Heaven' in his basement studio. Although the actual recording didn't take more than half an hour, they spent the remaining two hours hanging out in his room and talking about everything; college, the band, music, career plans, and even dream cities.

"I don't want to be tied to one place," Anisha said. "I want to travel the world. Go to every small and big city and perform on every stage. Let my voice be heard loud and clear. Everywhere."

"Sounds like a fancy plan. I hope you're able to create this life for yourself."

"What do you want to do?"

"Umm. I am not too sure. Dad wants me to go to a business school. Although, they won't be happy with anything but the best. And then once I have my MBA degree, he'd rather have me join the family business. Try to digitise things and expand to newer markets."

"You just told me what your dad wants. I had asked, 'What do you want?'"

He looked at her and let out a deep breath.

"Well, I want to build a life of my own."

"And what does that life look like?"

"I don't know. Simple yet meaningful, and fulfilling. Something I can be proud of."

"That's so abstract."

"Yeah. I guess. It's not just about what I want to do for work, but the impact I have in this life. I want to have meaningful relationships and experience life from different lenses. Travel, but not just to see the world, but to experience cultures and to learn about people and what drives them."

"Your plan sounds so fancy and existential at the same time. How do you do it?"

"Hahaha, I don't think it's a plan. It's just something I hope I get to do."

"Hmm"

"Have you watched *Before Sunrise*?"

"No."

"In that movie, Julie Delpy says this line to Ethan Hawke, and it hits me so hard every time I think about it, 'Isn't everything we do, a way to be loved a little more?'"

"Wow! That's deep," Anisha stood there, looking at him intently for a few minutes.

"Why so serious, Ms. Sighania?" he said whimsically, to lighten the air.

"Just trying to process your depth, Mr. Malhotra."

"It's not that serious man," he chuckled, "I mean, I am decent at math so maybe I can work at a bank," he chuckled. "Buy and sell stocks. Work on deals. Maybe."

"You're such a terrific musician. Why don't you want to do something with your talent?"

"I don't know. I guess I don't want to play for the world. I want to keep this only for myself."

She took a moment to absorb his ideas and then suddenly stood up. "Can we smoke?"

After that day, they began to hang out often. Anisha became a regular visitor at the Malhotra house in Sainik Farms. They would talk for hours, order food, and watch movies. One evening when Anisha was unusually quiet, they went up to the terrace and sat on the uneven concrete floor watching the sun-set behind the horizon, staining the sky blood red.

"I was sixteen when my dad died," she stared into nothingness as she spoke, and it seemed as though words came out of her mouth without her consent. The shadow of her hair falling on her bony face danced on her cheek as slight darkness began to set in.

Dhruv was surprised at her sudden confession. She never told him much about her family and was unusually reserved when it came to her parents. But that day, she looked uncharacteristically sad as she continued talking.

"It was cancer."

Dhruv looked at her, not knowing what to say, as she stared at the drab mesh-like figure created by the dilapidated rooftops of neighbourhood houses.

"My mother always used to ask him to quit smoking. But, it was as though he loved cigarettes more than he loved any of us. You know, I loved him the most. When he passed away, I was a total wreck. I began hating him for choosing the filthy carcinogenic addiction over his family. I was so mad at him, that I stopped eating, studying, everything. Can you be mad at the dead?" she asked, but Dhruv had no answers. He had barely processed Anisha's confessions. He had no idea she cloaked such things behind her cheery demeanour.

"It was the third of September, I clearly remember. Ten days after Dad passed away. We had barely even sorted out his belongings. My mom would spend hours just sitting in his chair, hugging his old white shirt.

"In the evening of the same day, I drove to the small cliff ten kilometres south from our Goa house. I barely knew how to drive, but anger makes you do strange things. Before leaving, I had grabbed the last pack of cigarettes from dad's belongings and so at the cliff, I stood by the sea and lit my first ever cigarette. I still don't know why I did it.

"I think I did it partly because I was mad at him and wanted those cigarettes to consume me in the same way. And partly because I felt it was the last thing that connected me to dad, the one thing he couldn't give up. I embraced it as a part of my life. Every time I smoke now, it reminds me of him. And I hate it. But I also love it. And I miss him," she completed her monologue and lit another cigarette. Dhruv held her hand and drew concentric circles on her skin with his index finger.

She kept smoking, her eyes fixed rigidly on a broken stool lying in the corner. The black crows cawing on the thin wires between electricity poles created an eerie atmosphere. He looked at her, and he couldn't help but think that the more he got to know her, the more of a mystery she seemed to him; but one that he was quickly spiralling into. She held the cigarette between her index and middle fingers and stuck out her hand in his direction. He stared into her dark eyes and accepted the cigarette. Without exchanging a single word, they sat there smoking late into the evening, until the entire place got bathed in darkness. Suddenly, he felt her smoky lips on his. Her hands slowly traced his body, and he could feel his lips slowly brush against hers. She tasted like coffee and cigarettes. His hands grazed her inner thigh, and they got lost in each other's smoke-stained breath.

For a whole year, Dhruv dated Anisha. Since that momentous evening on his terrace when she opened up about her childhood, things quickly picked up between them. And before he knew it, every big and small thing about her seemed extraordinary to him. Her passion for music, her funky nails, and eccentric tattoos. Her habit of making jokes at the most inappropriate times and then suddenly shifting gears, to share a deeply personal childhood story and always lighting a smoke while she told it.

In a matter of a few months, Anisha's personality started rubbing on him like sandpaper. The usually quiet and absorbed-in-his-own-world Dhruv began going to parties and social events with her. They began bunking classes and hanging out at a *tapri* near college, smoking cigarettes, and drinking *adrak* chai. Later they would drive around the colourful lanes of old Delhi to explore the food scene, visit local pubs, art galleries, and old architectural monuments.

On her birthday, Dhruv planned a surprise terrace party at his place and invited all their friends. She walked in at midnight to see the whole place dazzling with fairy-lights, helium balloons and a big, customised cake that had a picture of her, singing at the band auditions.

"This is straight out of a dream!" she said and kissed him on the lips. "Thanks for being in my life."

They cut the cake, got drunk on cheap tequila, and danced the night away.

As their social circle expanded, they began getting more invites to parties from common friends, where they went as a couple. But often Anisha would just stay outside in the smoking zone and end up talking to a lot of new people. At another such party, Anisha struck a chord with someone she borrowed a lighter from.

"What are you doing tomorrow evening?" a man with a giant tattoo and broad built who lent her the lighter, asked her.

"Why?" she inquired bright-eyed.

"I'd love to take you out for coffee. I know a really nice place here."

She took a moment and smiled, as though assessing the situation.

"Is there so much to think about?" he smirked.

She laughed and rolled her eyes at his remark before finally agreeing. "An innocent coffee won't hurt anyone."

Dhruv attracted plenty of eyeballs too, but he usually kept to himself. He'd grab a drink and talk to a few people, before starting to look for Anisha and ensure she wasn't getting too wasted. Initially though, he appreciated how tactile she was, but eventually he grew jealous seeing Anisha work her way through all these social events, getting enormously drunk, and dance seductively with many strange men. At first, he thought he was being too skeptical and old-fashioned. So, he tried to shove his thoughts away, but then Anisha began lying to him about her whereabouts, drinking, smoking, and partying heavily. Dhruv was concerned, and hoped she would come around. And when he confronted her, he was only met with contempt and accusations of being an overprotective and jealous boyfriend.

He started feeling increasingly anxious when Anisha wasn't around. And ever since he had heard from a couple of common friends that Anisha got so wasted at a party, she puked for two hours straight, he started showing up at parties he wasn't even invited to, just to take care of her, drive her home safe and make sure she doesn't do something that she would regret later.

To an informal fresher's party hosted by the band, Dhruv who was in his final year and Anisha who was now a sophomore, were invited as seniors. It was at a coveted club in Vasant Kunj, near Dhruv's place, but he still went all the way to pick up Anisha from her hostel.

She was wearing a little black dress and high-heeled gladiators.

"Hi babe!" Dhruv smiled as she entered the car.

"Hey" she replied distantly as she adjusted the seat to make herself comfortable.

"You're looking stunning tonight."

"Thank you" she said with a bright smile. And then after assessing him from top to bottom for a full minute, she squinted her eyes and said, "You don't look too bad yourself!" laughing at her own remark, she fixed the collar of his shirt.

Like always she began touching up her make-up in the mirror.

"Eyes on the road, mister!" she teased him, as he looked at her, adoring her antics.

Just then her phone rang. Before Dhruv could see the screen, she quickly pressed the buzzer to put it on silent.

"Who is it?"

"Some sales call or something, been getting too many of these lately," she replied, visibly bothered, and threw her phone back in her clutch in a haphazard manner.

"Then why are you so flustered?" he asked, eyes fixed on the road.

"I am not flustered," she shot back. A tiny bead of sweat formed on her forehead.

He pulled a tissue and offered it to her. She looked at him for a second, and then took the tissue reluctantly.

"I think this new moisturiser does not suit my skin," she said, dabbing the tissue lightly on her forehead and cheek.

"There's water in the backseat if you want."

"No. I am good. Thanks."

After a few moments of awkward silence, Dhruv tried to lighten the atmosphere. "Did you hear about the auditions that happened last week?"

"Uh hmm..." she replied, still staring out the window.

"People were going on and on about the guy who sang 'Breathless.' What's his name? Avinash, I think."

"Well, good for him."

"I think the band is to see some great talent this year."

"Yeah. I guess."

"Anisha..."

"Hmm?"

"We met around the same time last year."

"Yeah"

"You know, we owe this relationship to the band."

"Maybe"

"Had you not come to audition, we probably wouldn't have been dating."

"I am still going to the same college. We could have met anywhere, Dhruv. Seriously, why are you so sentimental today?" she frowned and looked out the window.

"I was just being nostalgic. What's the matter with you tonight, Anisha?" he raised his voice.

"I don't know. I am sorry. I think I'm PMSing," she groaned and continued staring out the window.

"Okay. I am sorry. Do you want to stop on the way for a smoke or some tiramisu?"

"No. It's fine. Let's just go."

"No, seriously? Whatever makes you feel better."

"Honestly. Just getting there would make me feel better," she snapped back.

They drove the rest of the way without exchanging a single word.

At the party, they received a warm welcome. Dhruv was among the senior-most members of the band. A flock of junior boys and girls surrounded him.

After a while, as the chatter slowly faded and he freed himself from the crowd, he strolled around to look for Anisha. Making his way past big crowds of people dancing and singing loudly, he finally reached the smoking corner, where he'd hoped to find Anisha. But to his surprise, she was not there. He felt a little anxious and decided to get himself a drink to ease his nerves first. Meanwhile, he tried reaching her phone, but it was switched off, which fueled his worries. She never slipped away from a party without telling him. He didn't know what to do and ended up nervously downing four pegs of whiskey. He kept trying her phone repetedly and checked with a few people, but nobody knew where she was.

All the alcohol created pressure on his bladder, and he headed towards the loo. As he reached the restroom, he heard moaning sounds from the adjacent women's loo. A weird feeling rose in his stomach. He felt like he might throw up. Without thinking further, he pushed open the door.

Dhruv received the biggest shock of his life.

Anisha was kissing a junior from sophomore year. The loud thud startled her, and she jumped seeing Dhruv standing over them.

Dhruv couldn't believe his eyes. The abhorrent shock, coupled with the effect of three pegs of whiskey he had downed earlier, made him lose balance. He almost fell and held the door for support. Anisha was scared out of her wits and rushed to support him. But he shrugged her hand and stepped back, incapable of letting her touch him.

She saw a burning rage in his eyes that she had never seen before.

"Dhruv..." she cried and ran after him as he raced down the stairs.

The pain and fury gleaming from his eyes peered at her. Almost everyone at the club fell silent and gathered around to see what was happening – a drunk and shell-shocked Dhruv rushing out of the premises and a weepy, guilt-ridden Anisha chasing him down the parking lot.

But before she could catch hold of him, Dhruv was already speeding off in his car. The screeching sound of the tires on the road echoed in the deathly silence as everyone quieted down.

"Dhruv..." Anisha screamed in the middle of the street and wept inconsolably.

A whole week went by, and Dhruv didn't show up at college at all. He barely picked calls from any of his friends, and simply spent all his days and nights locked up in his room. Sometimes the sound of a guitar echoing through his room was the only signal that he was alive. Worried sick, Mrs. Malhotra called Arnav.

"Aunty, I've tried calling and texting him so much. But he barely responds," he told her over the phone. Next evening Arnav showed up at the Malhotra house unannounced and opened the door to Dhruv's room, only to see a bony figure lying on the bed in the darkness.

"Oh Hi…I didn't know you were coming," Dhruv got up, taken aback. His weight loss was apparent. With a thick unkempt beard, he looked shabbier than ever.

Arnav entered and switched on the lights.

Dhruv flinched. "Ah, switch off the lights," he groaned.

"No"

"Arnav…"

"Bro, you're a mess," he reprimanded, kicking him out of bed. "That's it. We're going out tonight. It's been ten days since you have shown your stupid face to any of us."

"Man, I don't feel like it."

"I don't care, buddy. If I want to hang out with my friend Dhruv, I will hang out with my friend Dhruv. Period."

"What are your plans?"

"Clubbing!"

"Ugh! I don't want to go to a stupid club."

"We'll get some booze, have some fun, meet some hot chicks and we'll get you over that bitch."

"You don't have to call her that," Dhruv shrugged.

"She is a bitch," Arnav's face stiffened.

"Arnav, please..." Dhruv tried to raise his voice.

"Okay, just go take a shower," Arnav resigned.

"Arnav please, I swear I would have come, but I just don't feel like going out tonight."

"Get your ass off this couch right now, trim your messy beard, take a shower, put on clean clothes. We're going clubbing tonight. It's settled."

Dhruv protested, but before he could make an argument, Arnav shut him up and said, "Listen, dude, your 'sad boy vibe' days are over. Enough of being this caveman. We're getting you cleaned up and out on the scene tonight. The world has too many beautiful people. And it's a shame you're holed up in your room behaving like some psychopath. Stop wasting away your youth and good looks, my friend. Carpe Diem!" Arnav smirked and Dhruv hung his head low in resignation.

"By the way, you stink," Arnav threw a towel on Dhruv's face.

"And don't forget to shave that god-awful beard," he added.

Half an hour later, he emerged out of the bathroom looking like the same old Dhruv again. The clean-shaven face highlighted his boyish features. On the inside though, Dhruv didn't feel any less miserable than before, but Arnav didn't give up on his friend. He forced him into the car, as they went on to pick up their other two friends from college, Rohan, and Sameer.

Rohan bought a new bottle of scotch. He raised a toast to Dhruv, "Here's to our boy and the return of his days of freedom and fun."

The night continued, hopping from nightclub to nightclub, drinking gallons of alcohol and meeting new women. Dhruv got way too drunk in an attempt to wash away Anisha's memories. The more they flashed across his eyes, the more he drank in the hope of it fading out into nothingness. At one point, he barely recognised anything or anyone. It was all a giant blur. Small fragments of consciousness kept escaping his mind like pieces of spatial matter gallivanting across the sky. He felt like he was getting pulled away into an expanding labyrinth and his sense of self slowly continued sinking to newer lows.

Later in the night, he ended up sleeping with a slick woman who he'd met at the club a few hours ago. The next morning, the memory of the night had almost vanished, but the hole in his heart had widened.

Chapter 2

Here Comes the Sun

Sunlight seeps through her skin indefinitely
Yet she keeps looking for light
In all the dark places

Brightening up every room she walks into
She is the sweet summer morning
To the endless winter night
Of my deserted heart

The universe stops and sings
A gentle lullaby in my ears
Each time her lips
Curve in my name

—DHRUV

"Please, Ma! What is the need for all this melodrama?" Dhruv shrugged.

But Mrs. Malhotra stood undeterred, with a silver *pooja thaali* decked with the ritualistic *diya,* marigold flowers, a tiny silver bell, a small bowl of curd and saffron. All this elaborate tradition, to wade every possible evil off her beloved son, on the crucial day marking the beginning of his business school education.

Despite a long and gruelling year that almost seemed like a blur to him, to everyone's surprise, Dhruv managed to get into one of the premier management institutes of the country. Luck and brains were by his side, hard work not so much - given his wretched state most of the year after things ended with Anisha.

Everyone except Dhruv was thrilled. Afterall, it had all turned out as per the grand plan chalked out for him – engineering first, followed by MBA, then joining the family business and taking it to the next level.

Dhruv had mixed feelings about how his life was going to turn out here, as he entered his dusty hostel room. He placed his bags on the floor and tried to breathe in, the entire place that would be his home for the next two years. Arnav had also gotten into the same B-school. Even though he was in Mumbai due to the sudden death of a relative and would join a week later, it comforted Dhruv to know that he'd have his best friend around.

To kill time until the first class, he decided to take a stroll across the campus and get the lay of the land. The campus had sprawling gardens and wide-open amphitheatres along with multiple little canteens that served things like hot tea and coffee, street style chowmein, sandwiches and omelettes. But the main gardens, located in the heart of the campus caught Dhruv's attention for their oddly inviting charm. A canopy of lush trees sheltered the area and even on the hottest day of summer, there was something particularly cool and calming about those gardens.

As he continued walking, trying to capture every sight with his bare eyes, he suddenly spotted a piece of paper lying near a wooden bench. He picked it up and saw a poem scribbled on the crumbled sheet.

Had we known
That the last time we pulled away
From each other's arms
Would turn out to be like the parting
Of a dried leaf from the willow tree
On a dreary autumn afternoon
Would we have tried and wrapped
Our dangling arms around each other
A little longer?

But don't worry, my love
Soon
We'll be together again
Our smiles and sighs will do all the talking
While we will just quietly watch
Our maddening love grow stronger
And reflect in our eyes

Soon
We'll dance chasing the colours of the sunset again
Stretching far into the vast horizon
While you play my favourite record on the stereo

Soon
We'll be on top of the Ferris wheel again

That will be glowing with the light
Of a thousand fireflies dancing around
So bright that our eyes hurt
And I know you'd grab me a piece of the moon
Like you always do

Your breath will again draw
Maps of our story on my skin
Gleaming under the pale moonlight

Our sleepy eyes
Heavy with daydreams
Hidden at the corner of our lashes
Will catch all these metaphors
Like a soliloquy poem

But promise me, you'll never think twice again
And I promise to build and rebuild
Every single breaking bridge
As long as it leads me to you

Because my love,
I have run out of places to run to
So, can I make you my resting place?

We'll curl around in the sheets
And get matching tattoos
While somersaulting across the sky again
Until you promise to stick with me after

I'll walk in wearing the cherry red dress you bought me in august
Carrying cherry blossoms on the tip of my tongue for you
And there'd be the Lumineers blasting through the room
When I jump into your arms that feel like a warm bed of sunflowers
Under the colours you stole, for me
From the rainbow

We'll sleep on the floor and make love on the roof again
I will shed like yellowwood leaves
On crimson sidewalks of estranged
October evenings
I will spill for you like milk
On a cold hard floor at midnight
Drizzle like honey
That dissolves itself
Completely
Trickle by trickle
Again, my love
The November rain will fall too hard
And so will I

He felt a mysterious connection to the poem. It was as though the poet could peek into his heart and voice all his feelings in verse. He kept the piece of paper in his wallet and headed back to his dorm.

Throughout the day, he couldn't help but think about the poignance of emotions in those words. It stirred something in him that he didn't quite understand. To calm his racing thoughts, he splashed cold water on his face and then grabbed his bag to make it to the first ever class of the MBA journey.

The brilliantly-lit, dome-shaped classroom was filled with students. The massive room emanated the sky-rocketing ambitions of the young people in it. A lost Dhruv walked in towards the very end of the room to find an empty seat. Just then, his eyes fell on the left-most corner at the back where a girl in a lilac top sat on an empty desk, reading a book. She looked radiant. Lost in her own self, as though the world around her had dissolved into insignificance.

Dhruv scanned the room and realised that she was one of only six girls who were present in the class. For reasons unknown to him, he felt a strange urge to go and sit next to her. He followed his instinct, and walked up to her.

"Hi! Is this seat taken?" he asked, calming every nerve in his body.

His voice drew her out of the almost meditative reading, and he instantly felt terrible to have disturbed her. She glanced up at him, and the first thing he noticed was her dark brown hair flowing till her waist, mischievously playing with her earrings that created a ringing sound as she moved her head to look at him.

Distracted and unable to process her gesture, he looked in her deep hazel eyes searchingly, as though they contained the answers to the questions troubling him for the past year.

She was a breath of fresh air. Like a nostalgic summer song that suddenly comes on the radio, offering relief from an endless loop of a trending song playing on your phone for days.

"Hey, no, it's not. You're welcome to sit," she beamed at him, interrupting his wandering.

Her voice was tender, but confident.

He felt as if the universe had stopped for a moment and whispered a gentle lullaby in his ears.

He moved closer and sat next to her. After a few minutes of awkward silence, he tried to break the ice and start a conversation.

"I am Dhruv," he said, stretching out his hand.

"Vaanya," she replied with a firm handshake.

"Nice name," he said with an air of confidence, but regretted instantly, realising how stupid it sounded as a conversation starter.

"Thanks!" she replied with a mild, expressionless face.

"You have a nice name too!" she said, not really knowing how to receive a compliment such as that, and immediately both laughed realising their inability to make small talk.

She arranged her books to make room for him and he settled next to her.

"I am usually better than this," he said self-assuredly.

"It's okay! We all have bad days," she said briskly, which made him laugh.

"That's a bit harsh!" he smirked. "But since it's the first day, I hope you can cut the man some slack?"

She chuckled at his attempt to humour her. Just then, the professor arrived and what seemed to be the beginning of a conversation, ended on an abrupt note. The buzzing lecture hall suddenly became silent, and only the coarse voice of the strict, grey-haired Microeconomics professor echoed in the room. The next hour passed with the two of them trying to focus on the price elasticity of goods, while stealing occasional glances at each other.

As the lecture ended and the professor walked out of the room, after bombarding them with tonnes of reading and assignments, Vaanya also scurried away, mouthing an uncaring 'bye' with a slight cordial smile.

The fast-paced college environment offering numerous activities, clubs, and societies catering to the diverse student interests, coupled with an intense academic workload, took every fresher some time to get used to.

'The first six months are a total pressure cooker!' Dhruv had heard so many seniors say this at parties, where they had gallons of alcohol and a few morsels of barely edible food.

'Pick your battles wisely,' was another common advice. 'There are only twenty-four hours in a day. You can't do everything.'

"Ah thanks! What news." Dhruv mumbled to himself in the corner with a single malt in his hand. Careful to not have his sarcasm be heard by seniors who were getting their ego boost through imparting their year worth of wisdom, by a crowd of blue-eyed juniors scared to venture into this cut-throat world.

It wasn't disrespect as much as disinterest, for Dhruv had been prepared for this (at least mentally), since he was a kid. Every other member of the Malhotra house had forayed into the red-bricked walls of elite B-Schools. So, he was aware of the drill. His choices were pretty clear—academics, football, and finance. Besides, he didn't want to overload his plate with 10,000 activities just to have a fancy resume. He knew what he was good at. 'Do one thing, but do it well' was really his mantra. And given all the mental and emotional overwhelm of last year, he really wanted to take it easy now.

"Why do you have to be a rebel?" Arnav joined him with his drink.

"I am not rebelling. I just don't want to hear the same thing I've been hearing at home for years."

"Well, not everyone had the privilege to come well-prepared."

"I am barely well-prepared, friend. I just happen to know what lies ahead in terms of academics."

"Fair enough. Besides, one truly never knows until it actually unfolds."

"Ah! Words of wisdom by Arnav baba, I've missed this."

"You're welcome," Arnav laughed.

"But then, aren't we all secretly wishing for this place to surprise us?" Dhruv continued.

"Maybe you'll finally find the one."

"That's a tall target," Dhruv gulped his drink and thought about the piece of poetry he had found in the gardens.

"What's the fun in not thinking big?"

"Well then, cheers to thinking big this year!"

They clinked their glasses.

Between classes, assignments, finance club, and football, whatever little time Dhruv had to himself, his mind often drifted to the melody of Vaanya's *jhumkas*. One afternoon in between lectures, he bumped into her in the hallway. She was reading something and he was engrossed in his phone, so they almost crashed into each other.

"Oh hi!" he said, joyful to have a few seconds of her company.

"Hey! Sorry, I wasn't looking."

"That's okay. Looks like you're certainly going to ace the

pop quiz," he said, looking at the comprehensive notes she was carrying.

"Are you jealous?" she arched her eyebrows and smiled lightly.

"Maybe!" he played along.

"Damn! So, they were right when they said there are no friends in this place. Only competitors."

"You're good!" he laughed, which made her crack into a small laugh too.

"I'm barely catching up. Hoping to just pass," she finally admitted.

"I am sure you're downplaying yourself."

"Well, let's talk when we get our grades."

"That's not a good deal. I want to talk to you now," he leaned in and continued to maintain eye contact.

Her deep hazel eyes held his gaze for a few seconds, before she smiled and said, "Too bad. I am late for class."

"Ah! Well, see you around!" he said, watching her walk down the hallway with the late afternoon light casting a shadow behind her. There was something about her energy that calmed him, and also challenged something within him. He wanted to get to know her, take her out on a date, delve into her mind, and read what lay behind that stunning face surrounded by books. But the hectic business school life got the better of him. Always running late for classes, surviving on less than five hours of sleep, preparing for some sudden quiz or class test, he stayed busier than he anticipated. Whenever things slowed down a bit, he hid in his dorm room, clutched his guitar close to himself and play music. Not knowing where life would take him next, he felt a strange void within. And in those moments of quiet anticipation, he opened the paper containing the poem that he found in the campus gardens, and read it to himself. The poem slowly became his gentle reminder that the universe was working for him, not against him. If anything, it was hope wrapped in a paper; a remainder that there were more people who thought, felt, and loved like he did. So, he kept it close, and got on with whatever life had in store for him.

As the word spread about his musical successes in the college band from his engineering days, he became tempted to join the music scene on campus here as well. One time he got invited to an exclusive party, hosted by the music club. He was the only person who was technically not a part of the club, and had still secured an invite. He decided to go because he had just finished an assignment and wanted to blow off some steam.

He reached slightly late. The party had already begun. A bunch of people were singing and dancing. The only difference was that, here people were singing and dancing to classical rock music, some underrated artists, and often gatekept songs, unlike the popular Punjabi or Bollywood music played at other parties. The vibe was eclectic. To his surprise he saw quite a few familiar faces, some from his engineering alma mater.

As he went to get himself a drink, a bubbly, brown-haired girl, about five feet in height walked up to him. "Hey! You're Dhruv, right?"

"Hi! Yes."

"I've seen you perform at college fests last year. I loved your cover of 'Count on me' by Bruno Mars."

"Thanks! That's so kind of you."

"Where's Anisha these days?" she asked, almost casually.

"I'm not sure. We're not together anymore," Dhruv replied after a brief silence.

"Oh, I am sorry. I didn't know."

"That's okay."

"So, you've joined the music club here too?" she asked, changing the subject lightly.

"Umm no. I haven't."

"Oh why?"

She acted more surprised than expected. After a moment of contemplation, he replied, "Umm, I just don't like to do music for people anymore."

"I see."

"What about you? Do you like to sing too? Also, I didn't catch your name."

"My name is Saloni! And no, I don't sing. I like to play the drums sometimes."

"That's pretty cool, Saloni."

"Thanks! I'll show you a video. Or heck, I'll perform live for you sometime."

"Oh. Awesome."

"Yeah sure. In fact, do you wanna grab a cup of coffee sometime?"

Dhruv shuffled on his toes uncomfortably.

"Umm yeah, sure," he said after a brief pause.

"Great. Give me your digits. I'll text you," she said handing out her phone with the dialer screen on.

He looked at her for a second and keyed in his number. But at the back of his mind, he was still thinking about Vaanya.

The next day, he woke up to Saloni's message.

'Hey, it was nice to bump into you last night. Do you want to catch up over coffee this evening?'

He stared at the message for a few seconds, before tossing his phone away and getting into the shower to get ready for the morning class. He knew he would see Vaanya there, and perhaps this time he'd get a chance to ask her out.

At 8:57 a.m. in the morning, as Dhruv rushed to the class just in time before the professor arrived, his eyes found their way to Vaanya who was already seated with her notes and books laid out front. And before he could go and talk to her, the professor entered the class. Dhruv quickly settled down at the seat in front of him.

After an hour and a half of lecture and a surprise quiz, the class finally ended. Unable to find Vaanya anywhere, he walked over to the coffee cart near the main auditorium to get his caffeine before another gruelling class began. Waiting for his coffee, he looked around lazily. And to his surprise, he saw Saloni and another girl from his engineering alma mater walking toward the coffee cart. In no mood for any small talk, and because he hadn't replied to Saloni's message yet, hoping to take some time to frame a proper response, he quickly grabbed his coffee and left. 'I'd rather revise microeconomics formulas than get into this.' He thought to himself and walked back to the classroom.

A few minutes later, Vaanya came to the coffee cart.

"One cappuccino. No cocoa powder on top, please."

As she was looking for change in her purse, Vaanya heard a familiar name that caught her attention. Two girls were discussing something profusely.

"Dhruv Malhotra?" exclaimed the taller of the two girls in a fuchsia pink top that matched the overdone blush on her cheeks.

"Yeah. Him," said the shorter one, in a slightly subdued tone.

"He was just here. You could have asked him in person."

"And what? Be rejected live? He has already ghosted me."

"Aw, you poor thing. Maybe he'll come around."

"I love how he played in our college band. There was something so sexy about his voice and the way he avoided drama, but somehow still got involved in it."

"Classic Dhruv, yes. But it was because of his ex-girlfriend."

"I didn't know he had broken up with her though."

"They broke up almost a year ago. I heard it was quite a scene. But what else can one expect out of Anisha?"

"To be honest, I was always a little jealous of her. But she sang well, so I'll give that to her."

"Yeah, she was talented."

"Correct. But I didn't know Dhruv was single all this time. I would have asked him out long ago."

"Oh no. Good that you didn't. I heard she really broke him. I've heard he and his friends have slept with half of South Delhi since."

"Are you serious?"

"I don't know. I am just telling you what I've heard. But he has changed a lot. Didn't you notice the stark weight loss and that sickly beard? Good thing he has gotten rid of it now. It made him look homeless."

"Oh, come on! That beard was hot. So raw and sexy."

"Look at you crushing over him, Saloni!" the tall girl in pink shrieked.

The short one in blue, blushed, and said, "No. I am just stating facts."

"Well. At yesterday's party even Priyal said that she would ask Dhruv out at the finance club catch ups."

"So, I am right. He is pretty popular."

"He has always been. Although I don't get the hype around him honestly. I like his friend Arnav better. Drama free and mildly cute. My type. He just accepted my follow request on Instagram."

"Yeah. But Dhruv's something else. I've been following him for a long time on all his social media."

"Stalker alert!"

"Shut up. Everyone follows him on Instagram."

"Yeah. I think most girls dig that jawline and the fact that the dude can play a guitar. And of course, the fact that he doesn't seem to give two fucks about most things. I guess that really sweeps girls off their feet."

"It looks like he doesn't give a fuck. But he is the artist type for God's sake. So, he must."

"That I don't know. But I'd just say don't get your hopes too high, girl. Dhruv isn't an easy fish. And the dude probably has some serious baggage."

"That's where the art comes from, babe."

"Whatever. But I am just saying be careful."

"Ahh not like he is replying to me anyway," Saloni said, checking her phone restlessly. "It's been six hours now."

"Well, if he has time to buy coffee, he should have time to reply to you. Get over him already."

Saloni gave her a dejected look before the two of them walked away, drinking their cold coffees.

Ever since she was a kid, Vaanya was the girl hunched over her books. The eldest of the two Sharma daughters, she was the beacon of hope for the upper-middle class Punjabi-Brahmin household of East Delhi. She carried the weight of their dream to have pride and prosperity brought to the family through her accomplishments, a responsibility her parents would've perhaps expected a son to shoulder.

"Study hard, get good grades, go to a premier college, and achieve all your desires through hard-work and sheer grit," was what she heard all her growing up years.

She distinctly remembered how one time in fifth standard, when she got a C grade in her Maths mid-term, her father was so disappointed that he didn't speak to her the entire day. The atmosphere was so uneasy, one could cut the tension with a knife. And when she refused to go to school the next day, her father slapped her in anger. The imprint of his long fingers stayed on her cheek for over a week. Her mother had to conceal the scar with some foundation and loose powder, before she went to school. "He loves you, *beta*! But he is just concerned about your studies," Mrs. Sharma had cajoled her daughter. But the little Vaanya of ten had received the message loud and clear. She always had to keep doing well academically, in order to win her parents' love and approval.

Her sister Mira, on the other hand, was the rule-breaker in the family. Being the younger, more pampered kid, she usually got away with not getting the best grades or killing at extracurriculars without upsetting the parents too much. The pressure on her was not dramatically lesser, but she was usually less uncomfortable displeasing people around her. So, while Vaanya studied Economics followed by an MBA at a premier B-School, Mira chose to go to NIFT and study fashion despite the disapproval from their father.

"Go for what you want. Block all the noise outside," Vaanya had advised her younger sister. "Just listen to what your inner voice is telling you to do. That's your inner Goddess guiding you towards what's meant for you in this lifetime. You only owe her, not everyone else."

Being the elder sibling who was already following the rule-book and doing what she could to please their parents, she felt responsible to protect her younger sister from the same pressure.

So, in her teens, instead of being curious about boys, she surrounded herself with books. And she slowly fell in love with the fictional worlds. Come summer vacations, instead of fancy trips abroad, the Sharmas would travel to the girls' grandparents' house, and Mrs. Sharma would always buy Vaanya a book at the railway station bookstall. Vaanya would spend the entire train journey reading and looking out the window. Books were her tiny portal into any place she wished to enter, without needing a plane ticket or a visa. There were no immigration checks or tight security, she could simply be nestled in the comfort of her bed and explore different universes and ideologies through the minds of prolific writers and thinkers.

It all began with exploring the magical world of Hogwarts and adventuring with Tom Sawyer, all by flipping page after page of a crisp paperback. From *Malgudi Days* to *Huckleberry Finn*, Vaanya soon began exploring stories and finding new friends hidden away in the pages of thick books. As she grew up, her curiosity moved to Khaled Hosseini's intense tales of longing and loss and to Murakami's universe of magical realism, followed by Alain De Boton's romantic philosophy, and then to Elif Shafak's spiritual fiction. Vaanya Sharma began seeing the world with different eyes. She knew there was always more going on in the head of the character than what the dialogue usually captured. And she knew that every story had to have a beginning, middle, and end.

When Dhruv once saw her hunched over books in a state of eternal focus in the library, he kept gazing at her intently, observing her unfailing dedication and attentiveness. It was refreshing to watch her immersed in work like that, for Dhruv himself could never work so dedicatedly.

Her concentration built a strange, alluring aura around her. He felt drawn to her like never before. He wanted to talk to her and get to know what lay behind her quiet demeanour. He knew this was the chance; if he didn't try today, he wouldn't ever be able to ask her. A little uncharacteristic of him, but he felt a weird nervousness wash over him as he made his way to the table where she was sitting.

"Hey," he whispered slowly to not disturb the people reading around them. He waved to catch her attention.

"Hi!" she looked almost startled, shifting in her chair.

While gesturing for her to come out, he started walking towards the door. She took a minute to understand what he was saying, and then silently got up from her chair to follow him out.

"So, what's up?" she asked cooly.

"Umm…" Dhruv paused, trying to read her face. He didn't have his pitch prepared. Usually, though, he'd come up with something witty on the spot and receive a hearty laugh in return. But today wasn't a usual day. He was a little nervous to be funny and spontaneous. After a minute of her staring at him blankly waiting for a response, he managed to speak.

"I think it's time we become friends," he decided to go with honesty.

"Umm, sorry what?" she looked puzzled.

He felt a little rejected, but still went on. "Well, we see each other in hallways, classes, and even the library now, but we are far too absorbed in coping up with the torturous workload here to say anything more than a small 'hi.' And I don't think that's fair. I find you intriguing. And I want to get to know you. Besides, I have a feeling that we could both use a friend."

Vaanya felt a little surprised. With a small half smile, she said, "Well. I like your honesty. But what makes you think we haven't talked just because we're too busy. Maybe I don't want to talk to you. Ever think of that?"

"Wow. That was harsh," Dhruv's face turned a shade of pink with embarrassment.

Vaanya laughed to lighten the moment, and then continued. "Well. Was it? I mean, you do have friends. And many more girls are willing to be your friend. Or perhaps more. But I wouldn't know."

"But nobody I would want to befriend."

"Is that so?"

"Pretty much."

She looked at him. His face showed slight nervousness mixed with a hint of self-assurance that only made his case even more appealing.

As she continued staring at him, weighing all scenarios, he began talking again. His voice, more compelling than before.

"So, are you hungry? I tried the mushroom puff at the canteen last night, it wasn't bad. And the cheese Maggi served by Raju's right across the street is the best cure for hunger pangs."

"You are quite direct," she chuckled.

"Well, it's a short life. Why waste it trying to be anything but direct?"

She almost smiled at his earnestness but deep down she admired his confidence. To be able to directly walk up to someone you don't know that well and strike up a conversation, heck even ask them to accompany you for a meal, it did take guts. At least, enough self-belief and a lack of fear of embarrassment. She knew she couldn't really do it.

"Are you coming?" he asked, nudging her out of her thoughts.

The sunrays fell on his face at an angle that highlighted his sharp jaw and she found herself getting strangely attracted to it. His skin glistened under the sun and somehow looking at it seemed to take away her stress about the ever-increasing academic pressure at campus, and she was tempted to take him up on that offer.

She paused for a second and then smiled under her breath, "The hostel food is pretty inedible and I haven't eaten properly in days. So, I guess, my stomach won't mind something decent to eat," she wondered why she felt the need to justify her going with him.

Dhruv laughed, and they started walking toward Raju's right outside the campus to have cheese Maggi, scrambled eggs, and coffee.

As they reached the small dilapidated shack, the smell of freshly-cooked hot food teased their nostrils.

"Ah… real food after so long," squeaked Vaanya, scooping some scrambled eggs with a fork and popping it in her mouth. She closed her eyes and relished it as if she were eating the most delicious thing ever. Dhruv couldn't help but observe how she would get engrossed in everything she did. She enjoyed the barely decent food as if they were having the most decadent meal in a Michelin star restaurant.

"You owe me now," he said.

She looked up at him, drawing her attention from the food and focusing it on him.

"What? You love the food here, and I told you about it, so you owe me. Simple."

"What do you want?" she said, still stuffing in mouthful of Maggi.

"Let's study together?" he proposed.

"Umm, okay! I wasn't expecting this," she said while taking a sip of the hot café mocha.

"Why not?"

"I don't know. Why do you want to study together?"

"Well, I am an engineer, and I barely know anything about price elasticity, supply and demand."

"I heard you scored an A+ on the quiz though."

"Oh, trust me, I just got lucky."

"Can I?"

"What?"

"Trust you?"

"Your prerogative."

"Hmm. Well, you are in luck. I graduated top of my class in Economics," she announced slurping on her coffee.

"I am lucky, aren't I?" Dhruv said to himself and took a sip of his steaming black coffee before lighting a cigarette.

"You smoke?" she looked confused.

"Yeah. I do, sometimes. Sorry, do you mind?" he asked genuinely.

"No, that's okay," she said politely but her face conveyed the opposite.

He thought she looked very cute with that pinched uptight face.

"You know how harmful it is for you, right?" she said after a pause.

"I mean the packet says 'Smoking Kills' and I can read. So, the answer would be yes."

"Ha Ha. Very Funny," she rolled her eyes and he smiled at her innocence.

"Some things just die hard, Vaanya." He took another puff, looking away.

"Hmm..." she mulled over his last comment.

He stole a glance at her confused face and continued to smoke.

Chapter 3

Rewrite the Stars

I have a thousand suns
Rising red in my body
Burning so bright
They'd make your eyes hurt

And I have a million galaxies
Transcending through me
As I speak to you

My body is a home
To infinite universes
Sauntering in tandem

But here I watch the sunsets with you by my side
Looking at the skies change colour in your eyes

I am not sure if you see
I am counting stars
And crossing light-years
Just to get to you

You are my north pole
My guiding star
In this make-shift constellation

And all I know is to keep looking for
That one alternate reality
In which you'd look at me
Like I was the centre
Of your waking universe

You see, I am your gravitational pull
Holding you back on the ground
Just long enough
To not let you fall flat on your face
While you wander galaxies
For as long as you wantonly wish
Because you see
Gravity doesn't give up
It keeps you tethered
Gently and determinedly
In its safe orbit
For as long as it takes
For you
to find your way.

—Vaanya

The sun shone bright through his slightly cracked window. A sleep-deprived Dhruv closed the blinds in a haste and irritation, still thinking about Vaanya. They had been friends for almost a month now. What started with a plan to study microeconomics together, turned into a genuine bond forged by candid conversations over numerous cups of coffee and multiple rounds of 2 a.m. pizzas between study breaks. One time they were sitting at Raju's, watching the sunset, and sharing a plate of Maggi to blow off some steam. Dhruv was humming a song while Vaanya sipped on her coffee. *'Gravity is working against me.'*

"John Mayer?" Vaanya asked without looking.

"Yes. *Gravity* by John Mayer. It's the top song on my study playlist that I shared with you last night."

"But why is this the top song?" She asked.

"Because I feel like it's all working against me when I study." He said.

She laughed at his silly joke. After a brief silence, Dhruv randomly said, Vaanya?"

"Hmm?" she responded while continuing to look at the sky.

"If alternate realities exist, what do you think you'd be doing in one of those lives?"

"Umm..." she turned her gaze toward him and said after a small pause, "I think I'd be sitting next to a large fireplace in a small cottage in the hills away from everyone, reading and writing."

"That sounds so dreamy and romantic."

"Yeah."

"But it also sounds lonely."

"I think a part of me feels like I was destined to be lonely."

"Why would you say that?"

"No reason," she said, and after a brief moment of silence between them, she asked, "I am sorry. Was that weird?"

"No. Not weird. Just a little sad, I guess."

"Hmm"

"I didn't know you enjoy writing."

"I do. Sometimes."

"How come I've never seen any of your writing?"

"Because I don't post on my social media. But I have a secret anonymous blog."

"That's cryptic and fun."

"It is. It's the one thing I truly do for myself."

"Hmm." Dhruv pondered upon these revelations. After a brief pause, he looked at her and said, "But hey, I don't want you to be sad. Ever."

She could feel his eyes on him as he said that. And for the first time in her life, she really felt seen.

"I am never sad when I am with you," she replied. Meeting his gaze somehow took all the courage in her.

"I'll take that as a compliment."

"It was meant to be one."

"Good," he smiled and ruffled her hair that made her scrunch up her nose and she made a face that immediately made him laugh.

"But do you know what's the worst?" his voice suddenly became deeper, like it was coming from a faraway place.

"What?" she asked, suddenly looking concerned.

"To feel lonely even when you're surrounded by people who are supposed to love you."

"Something tells me you're no stranger to that feeling," she said gazing intently at him, trying to read what made him say something like that.

"Well, you are usually quite on point. That's the one thing about you I really like." He said without meeting her eyes.

"So, I am right?"

"Yes."

"Who was she?"

"What?"

"Who made you feel lonely even when you were with her?"

Dhruv smiled and looked away. Something in him didn't want to taint the beginning of his bond with Vaanya by talking about his past.

She read his face. "It's okay. You don't have to tell me just yet."

"Thanks! Those are not like the best memories that I want to share and relive," he said quite candidly.

"I like your earnestness."

"Do you?"

"Yeah. It's refreshing. Authentic."

"That's nice to hear."

"But hey?" he said, catching her attention once again, "Listen. I want you to know that you deserve to be happy and loved deeply. And I really hope you never have to feel lonely."

She looked at his face and she could see that he really meant what he said.

"At least not in this lifetime," he said after the small pause and they both laughed.

"Thanks Dhruv. I didn't know you were capable of being this sweet," she said with a bright-eyed smile.

"You have to read the man a bit deeper to make that judgement, Ms. Sharma!" he said and got up. "Let's go?"

"Not smoking today?"

"I'll smoke with Arnav. I don't want to make you uncomfortable."

"Look who's being extra-sweet today. What's the matter?"

"Nothing. Let's go! I am late. My study group meets in fifteen minutes."

He started walking ahead and she paced to catch up. As they began crossing the main road to get to the campus, she grabbed his arm, and he felt like something that was dying in him suddenly came alive.

Later that night after his study group meet-up Dhruv went to Arnav's dorm.

"Look who's here!" Arnav commented. "Thanks for remembering your best-friend. That Vaanya girl is keeping you busy, huh?"

"We're just friends."

"Yet," Arnav added and lit a cigarette.

Dhruv smiled and went over to the table to make drinks.

"Please make mine stronger. You mess up the drinks."

"Sorry sir, I need to take bartending lessons from you it seems," he said, handing out the glass to him.

"How did the quiz go?" Arnav asked.

"I got an A+," Dhruv said, taking a puff of the cigarette Arnav had handed him.

"Holy Hell! Woah!" Is it because of her? Are you guys really studying together?"

"Yeah dude. What the hell do you think? I told you we're just friends. And we study together."

"Insane. Who is this new person? Where is Dhruv?" Arnav laughed.

"The new and improved Dhruv Malhotra. Please get used to him," Dhruv held up his glass, as though raising a toast.

"Seems like she has a positive effect on you, dude. All you did with Anisha was bunk classes, smoke, and play music."

"Yeah. She's good for me."

"So does she know you like her?"

"No, not yet. And besides I am not really sure what I feel for her. I mean I do like her. But after last year, I don't want to mess things up again.

"Yeah, you better be careful."

"Yeah."

So, what's the deal here? She thinks she is teaching you while you're really teaching her?"

"Pretty much," Dhruv smirked.

Arnav laughed. "By the way, I spoke to Sneha yesterday. She's good friends with Vaanya I suppose. We're in the marketing club together."

"Oh. That's new."

Before the micro-economics term exam, Dhruv and Vaanya spent the entire day in the library studying. In the evening, they stepped out for a small break. The road adjacent to Raju's in front of campus had multiple street-food shops.

"I want to eat *golgappas*!" Vaanya shrieked.

Vaanya!" Dhruv arched his eyebrows like a parent does disciplining his child. "We still have the last exam tomorrow. Don't risk eating street food, you may fall sick."

"Come on! Live a little!" she said and grabbed his arm dragging him to come along.

"I've clearly been a bad influence on you," he joked.

"Yeah. I think we should stop hanging out," she played along.

"Not in this lifetime!" he said casually and her lips curved into a shy smile. Tucking a loose strand of hair behind her ear, she looked away, trying to escape his gaze. She wondered how in a moment he could say something so significant in such a casual manner, and then just move on to the next moment.

"Let's go?" he asked, pulling her out of her rumination.

At the golgoppa stall, Vaanya asked for extra-spicy chutneys.

"Damn!" he exclaimed, looking at her, stuffing her mouth with the tenth golgappa. He took out his phone and made a small video that he posted on Instagram, with the caption, "Here comes our friendly neighbourhood golgappa champion!"

Later that night Sneha caught hold of Vaanya at the hostel mess.

"How did your golgappa date go?"

"What?"

"Yeah. I saw Dhruv's story. You didn't even tell me. I thought we were friends."

"It wasn't a date!" Vaanya shot back.

"It sure looked like one," Sneha tilted her head, assessing Vaanya's expression as though scavenging for some proof about the real turn of events.

"Sneha! Why will I lie to you? I told you we are just studying together, so we sometimes just grab a bite afterwards. It's purely innocent."

"Why do I feel it's not?"

Vaanya rolled her eyes and put another *gulab jamun* on her plate.

"And you're overeating! That means you're anxious. There's definitely something."

"Yes. It is. The microeconomics exam tomorrow. I am anxious about that."

"You're an Economics topper. You can't be nervous about that."

"Why don't you use these investigative skills to some better use? Help the nation."

"I don't know if the nation needs me. But mark my words, you will," Sneha smirked.

"God! Relax," Vaanya clinked arms with her and took her to eat.

On the last day of the first term, the campus was bustling with activity. A swarm of over-excited college students who had just gotten a taste of freedom after a torturous term, gathered in various groups to organise parties over the next few days to celebrate the short break, before another term began.

"How did it go?" Sneha caught Vaanya near the exam hall.

"It was okay!" Vaanya said with a straight-face.

"Don't believe her, Sneha! She's gonna top," Dhruv appeared from behind them.

"You don't say, okay! You're no less."

"I agree!" Arnav joined the group and casually placed his arm around Sneha's neck, who seemed to look unbothered by his move.

"These two have been studying like insane people, the whole term. And here I am afraid I might flunk. Should have studied well in advance," Sneha said, looking a bit tense.

"You won't, chill! I saw you filling sheet after sheet in the exam hall," Arnav chimed in.

"Didn't you have your own paper to write?" Dhruv asked with a sarcastic smile plastered on his face.

"Yeah, not everyone has studied like a maniac! I do happen to have a chance to look up from my answer sheets during exams," Arnav one-upped him and Dhruv raised his hands in dismissal. "Alright buddy!"

"You guys have no idea the amount of bullshit I've written in the ten-marker questions. I am praying for our poor Professor when he will read it!" Sneha added.

"Chill guys. It's over now!" Dhruv said.

"Yeah. The term is over guys! We need to celebrate. There's a party tonight and then an open mic event tomorrow evening! Let's please forget about microeconomics already!" Arnav announced.

"You guys are coming for the party, right?" Sneha asked.

Vaanya looked a bit puzzled. "Dude, I told you yesterday, don't act confused now!" Sneha said with a deadpan expression, and that coupled with her usually overbearing personality seemed to scare people easily.

"Okay sorry! I am kidding," her attempt at humouring her friend had tanked. "Don't worry! I am coming!" she stepped back.

"Then, I am coming too!" Dhruv said unthinkingly.

"Love-birds!" Arnav whispered, but only Dhruv seemed to catch what he said, and he shot him a nasty look.

"See you guys later, tonight!" Sneha said and scurried off with Arnav.

Dhruv and Vaanya too escaped the chaos for a bit and went to Raju's as per their evening ritual.

"Coffee with no cocoa powder on top?" Dhruv asked.

"Yeah," She smiled to herself thinking how he remembered her preferences like the back of his hand.

She settled on the wooden bench overlooking the street.

He picked up the coffees with his hands and handed them over to her. He then went back to grab a cigarette and took out the lighter from his back-pocket before sitting next to her. Vaanya watched him move effortlessly. Even in such an ordinary setting, everything about him looked extraordinary. With erect shoulders and a broad chest, he had a presence that could not be ignored. He was confident. But it was the kind of confidence that didn't make people around him feel intimidated. If anything, it made people around him feel more at ease when they were with them. When she was with him, she felt like she could hide from everything in his tall and exigent frame, and at the same time she felt like she could face the entire world without blinking an eye. She had never felt this way before.

"Oh, I'm sorry!" he said putting the lighter back in his pocket. "I forgot," he admitted, immediately realising he couldn't smoke with her.

"It's okay. I don't mind," she said instantly.

"Are you sure?" he re-checked.

"Yeah," she assured him, smiling faintly. Nothing about him seemed to bother her lately. Every small and big attribute of his slowly began seeming wondrous to her. He was spontaneous and energetic, but not in a condescending or exhausting way. He could make her laugh but he was also sensitive about things. She could talk to him about anything under the sun and it wouldn't be awkward. He understood some parts of her that she didn't think anybody could ever fathom. When she was with him, she felt like everything in the world was simply right.

He was sitting so close to her. His elbows almost touched hers for a moment and she felt electricity course through her veins. A familiar smell of his metallic-pine cologne mixed with the fumes of the cigarette, acted like an aphrodisiac when it hit her nostrils, and she felt like everything she was worried about was slowly dissolving in that moment.

"What an insane term it has been!" Dhruv said, taking a drag.

"I can't believe I survived it," she replied, taking a sip of her coffee.

"You worked really hard. I am sure you'll get good grades."

"I hope so. But tell me something."

"Hmm?"

"Why did you ask for my help with studying at the beginning of the semester? You clearly didn't need any help."

"No. I did. I need so much help Vaanya!" He looked at her with searching eyes and smiled in a teasing manner.

"I am serious."

"So am I. Always." He kept looking in her eyes intently.

"Okay after a point, I really can't tell if you're kidding or not."

"Ah you still can't figure me out. What a shame. Anyway, you were saying?"

"You didn't need any of my help, you practically taught me before every exam."

"Well, I am pretty useful, what can I say?"

"You're just a fast learner. Or you have a photographic memory. I can't tell. But how you remembered all those scary formulas in just one glance was impressive yet borderline intimidating to be honest."

"Maybe it's you."

"What?"

"Well, you bring out the best in me."

She looked at him for a second, wanting to believe what he said, but she was afraid she might be getting ahead of herself. Just like the presence one couldn't ignore, Dhruv also had a reputation that was hard to overlook. He was flamboyant and probably said these things just for fun. Probably he didn't mean any of it.

"Save your precious material. It ain't working here," she rolled her eyes and sipped on her beverage, scared that it might in fact be working too well. But she couldn't let him know. Not yet. Not when she wasn't sure of what was really happening.

"What's the use of all my material then?" he quipped, bringing her back from her reverie.

"I am sure you have many you could use this on," she gathered the courage to say.

"Nobody I want to use it on," he said with a straight-face.

"I don't know whether to believe you," she said, searching for clues in his eyes.

"It's your decision," he said avoiding her gaze.

Silence followed, as they both looked away, sipping on their coffees, thinking of their failure at deciphering each other's inner thoughts. After a few minutes, Dhruv broke the silence.

"But honestly, Vaanya, thanks for agreeing to study with me. Fuck grades. I am just glad I got a friend out of this."

She focused her gaze at him. It was friendship. That's all it was, she reminded herself and flashed him a vaguely convincing smile.

Later that night, Vaanya got ready for the party. The whole batch was going to be there, and she felt a bit unready to be drinking and talking to people, but she had promised Sneha so she put on a black evening dress and got on with it.

"You look perfect! Don't sweat it!" Sneha said, as Vaanya looked at herself for the third time in the mirror.

"I am just not a fan of big social events," she said, feeling a bit conscious.

"We'll get some tequila in you and all your self-consciousness will go out the window!" she said and dragged along.

As they reached the club, Vaanya's eyes quickly scanned the entire place, looking for Dhruv. But he was nowhere to be found.

She walked over to the bar and got herself some cranberry juice in a wine glass to stay away from the prying eyes of her drunk batchmates who would interrogate her about not having a drink in her hand. She had been using this trick for the past few years to brave social situations involving alcohol, and till date it had worked without fail. The music was too loud for her liking but she tried to have a good time. A few boys from her batch came and tried to talk to her. She received some compliments about her dress too but her eyes were only searching for one person, who finally arrived after almost an hour, dressed in a crisp black blazer looking dapper as always. Vaanya hoped he would find her quickly, but she saw him work the room like a pro, as he talked to half the batch before walking up to her.

"Hi! You look amazing!" he said and ordered his go-to drink, whiskey on the rocks.

"Thanks!" she said in a dry tone.

"What happened? All okay?" he asked, sounding concerned.

"Yeah. Just admiring your social skills," she scoffed.

"Just a few people from finance club and football. It looks rude if you just stand in the corner sulking and ignoring people," he smirked.

"Wow, thanks!" she rolled her eyes, taking the joke on herself rather poorly. But he laughed and put his arm around her, "I am kidding! You're so pretty, you don't even need to go talk to people. They're intimidated by you anyway!" he said, saving the situation with a cocktail of humour and charm.

"Shut it!" she said, trying to maintain character, but secretly blushing.

"Do you want to get out of here for a bit?" he asked.

"Thanks! I was waiting for you to say it. I can't tolerate this stuffy & loud party anymore," she said and followed his lead.

He walked ahead, trying to find spaces between clusters of drunk people dancing and singing to the shrill music. She walked behind him, and he casually extended his hand to her, as he slowly made his way through the crowd towards the exit. She interlocked her fingers in the space between his, and for the first time in the entire duration of the party, she felt like she belonged.

Dhruv left her hand as they reached the open area outside the club and the crowd thinned. A part of her wanted to hold on to his hand forever, but she shushed the voice in her head.

He lit a cigarette and began smoking. "So, what are you planning to do during the term break?" he asked.

"Nothing much. Mira might visit me."

"Your sister, right?"

"Yeah. Sister. Best Friend. Everything. We've never gone this long without seeing each other."

"That's quite nice. I wish I had a sibling. Being a single child sucks, sometimes."

"Does it get lonely?"

"Yeah. Sometimes. It's like you don't have that one human who has been conditioned the same way growing up."

"Hmm…" Vaanya seemed to mull over his words. He sometimes had such insightful observations about such ordinary things.

A few seconds passed and none of them said anything. Dhruv loved how the silences with Vaanya were never awkward. If anything, they were comforting. After a few moments, he finally said what was on his mind for a long time, Vaanya, I sometimes feel a little lost in life."

"As in?"

"Like I don't know what I am really doing."

"You don't always need to know where you're headed in life," she said, after a small pause.

He focused her attention on her as she continued speaking. "Sometimes you just have to take the next step that's in front of you and trust that the universe is leading you exactly where you're meant to be."

"How do you always know the exact thing to say?"

"Well, let's just say I have a way with words," she chuckled.

"Among many other hidden talents, I assume?"

"Ah, you never know. I might surprise you," she said playfully.

"Now see, am I wrong in feeling super lost, when I have peers such as you?

Her cheeks turned pink at the remark.

"But in all seriousness, who doesn't feel lost, Dhruv?"

"Hmmm..."

"Trust me you're doing really well for someone who feels lost," she said frankly.

"That's not the point. Grades have never been the focal point in my life. I am talking about purpose."

"Hmm. What about music? I've heard you were quite the sensation during your undergrad years. Why did you stop?"

"That was a lifetime ago."

"Technically it was just a year ago."

"Yeah, but I am a different person than I was a year ago. For me it feels like a completely different life."

"What changed?"

After a long pause, Dhruv brought himself to say, "I just don't do music publicly anymore. I want it to be just for me."

Vaanya kept gazing at him, trying to read his silences, knowing fully well that there was more to this than what he told her.

"But what about you? How are you so driven? What's the secret?"

"No, I am not."

"You are. You can't take a compliment, can you?"

She smiled, embarrassed.

"There's no secret. It means a lot to my parents that I am at one of the best management institutes doing my Masters. And I know I must get a good job and make them proud."

"I am sure you're already making them proud."

"I hope so."

"But that's about your family. What about you? What drives you?"

"I want to leave an impact on people's lives," she said after reflecting on his question for a while.

"Wow! That sounds impressive."

"No. It's not that ambitious. Wait before you get too impressed."

"What?"

"It doesn't have to be multiple lives."

"As in?"

"I don't care about the width of my impact as much as the depth of it."

"I am not sure if I understand."

"In my opinion, even if one person is truly transformed for the better, by my actions or by my presence, I would have accomplished my purpose in life."

"How do you think that would happen?"

"Through love, I guess?"

"Okay!"

"Love is the only answer. To almost everything in life."

"Yeah, they say everything we do in life is to be loved a little more."

"Yeah. And the true power of love lies in the way it can transform us."

"That's heavy!"

"These are actually Bell Hooks' thoughts from the book *All About Love*. I simply agree," she added, and they both laughed.

He looked at how her eyes gleamed when she laughed. It was the most tranquil thing he had ever seen.

"You inspire me, Vaanya." His eyes gleamed and she felt a flutter in her chest.

Before she could say anything, her phone rang. "Where are you?" Sneha asked.

"I am outside the club with Dhruv," she said but Sneha couldn't hear anything over the music.

"Just text her you'll be inside in five," he said and they walked back in.

Once inside, Vaanya disappeared into the crowd to find Sneha. Bored and alone, Dhruv walked over to the bar to get himself another drink, when he heard a familiar voice call out his name. He turned around to see Saloni and by what he could make out, she looked pretty pissed. Her face was plastered with make-up and an exceptionally bright red-lipstick. She was one of those people who had a permanently gleeful expression, so when she was upset, her face looked like a palette of mixed emotions on a wax statue.

"I knew I'd find you at this party!" she staggered toward him.

"Hey!" he said, trying to hide his guilt of having ghosted her weeks ago.

"I am really drunk and over you now so I don't care and I'm going to confess!" she said with an animated expression.

Dhruv felt confused and a little nervous. "Saloni… Are you okay?"

But before he could complete his sentence she interrupted, "I've had a crush on you for the past three years," she took a deep sigh. "The first time I saw you play in the college band, I was done for. I never said anything because you were with Anisha and I respected that. But when I asked you for coffee the other day, I didn't know you would ghost me. I thought you were better than that."

"Saloni... I... I am sorry," he gathered courage to face her.

"I at least deserved a reply dude," her words blended into each other towards the end, as she tried to balance herself.

Dhruv knew he was at fault. In the beginning, he had not replied while thinking of crafting a proper response to decline her offer in a way that didn't hurt her feelings, but then life got busy and it totally slipped his mind. Later when he remembered, it had been too late. And he was embarrassed to text back after a week. So, he politely let it go.

Her body almost tumbled to one side, trying to find equilibrium.

"Please just sit here first," he said and helped her on the barstool before grabbing some water.

"Here!" you'll feel better, he said, helping her drink from the plastic water bottle.

"They were right," her glassy eyes peered at him. "You're just a playboy, Dhruv. You jump from one person to the next and you still don't know what you really want. In fact, I feel sorry that I ever had feelings for you."

Her words hit him like lightning. Was that his truth?

Just then a shrill noise of shattering glass hit his ears. Two drunk guys had gotten into a bar fight in one corner.

But his eyes sprinted in the other direction, and his heart began sinking.

Vaanya was standing right opposite, and from what it looked like, she had heard every word.

"Vaanya." He licked his dry lips, hoping to come up with the right thing to say but his head began hurting and he felt dizzy.

"Sneha wanted me to check if you could drop us. But you're clearly busy," she said and stormed off.

"Vaanya, wait!" he screamed, and began chasing her down the club. Striding fast, wanting to get away from there as soon as possible, Vaanya sat in a cab before he could catch hold of her. He watched her shut the door of the car behind him with a harsh force.

Later that night he left a few text messages for Vaanya, but received no reply. Saloni's words in the party kept replaying in his mind like a bad dream that one can't forget. He lied in bed and kept watching random videos until he stopped feeling shitty. But even doom-scrolling didn't seem to help tonight. So, he grabbed his journal and scribbled away while questioning all his choices and desires till now. He really liked Vaanya, there was an inexplicable energy between them, he could tell. She was kind, beautiful and smart. But he still didn't feel sure. Scared that he'd mess up something beautiful that hadn't even begun yet. The noise of other's opinions had blocked his inner voice, and he felt torn apart. At that moment, he grabbed his wallet and pulled out the piece of poem he had found in the campus gardens on the very first day. He read it to himself, and like always, those words seemed to have a magically calming effect on him. He slept holding it close to his heart.

The next morning, he woke up to the sound of rain falling on his window. Suddenly, all the anguish from the last night seemed like a distant memory. It was a brand new day. On his way to Raju's to get some coffee and a smoke to start the day, he heard chatter about the open mic, "It's going to be quite a stellar line-up," people were saying.

As he reached the *tapri*, he found Arnav over there. "Are you going to the open mic today?" he asked, sipping on some tea.

"Not planning to," he responded.

"Why? It's supposed to be 'The Art Event' of the term."

"Yeah, but I am not an artist or a musician anymore," he said, lighting a cigarette.

"Do you realise quitting your passion because it was the common thing between you and Anisha has been the dumbest decision of your life?"

"It's not about Anisha."

"Oh really? You're going to say that to me?"

"Yeah. Because that's the truth. Choosing to not perform is about me. I don't like the stage. I don't want that life anymore."

"Okay fine. Don't perform. But just go to the open mic. Experience that vibe again and see how you feel. Maybe you just enjoy being amidst music and poetry again?"

"Let's see. I'll drop by for a bit."

"That's my boy!" he patted his friend's back.

In the evening, with no intentions to perform, he reached the venue almost half-an hour late, just to check out the scene. It was a charming little open-air studio adjacent to the cafe down the road. Decked with multiple little lamps, terracotta pieces, paintings and lots of plants, the whole place had a bohemian vibe. The crowd was a mixed bag. Full-time artists, part-time musicians, poets and writers, drama enthusiasts, and basically anyone with a penchant for literature, music, poetry and performing arts, gathered under one roof to celebrate the spirit of artistic expression.

He met some people from campus, who wanted to try their material in a safe space with like-minded people. Students from other colleges had also come to perform and it seemed like an inter-college art gala. Wishing them luck, he made his way forward.

As he was reluctantly climbing the stairs to the main area where most performances were happening, he heard something familiar. He couldn't not recognise it.

"I'll walk in wearing the cherry red dress you
bought me in August
Carrying cherry blossoms on the tip of my
tongue for you
And there'd be the Lumineers blasting
through the room
When I jump into your arms that feel like a warm
bed of sunflowers
Under the colours you stole for me
From the rainbow
We'll sleep on the floor and make love on
the roof again
I will shed like yellowwood leaves
On crimson sidewalks of estranged
October evenings
I will spill for you like milk
On a cold hard floor at midnight

Drizzle like honey
That dissolves itself
Completely
Trickle by trickle
Again, my love
The November rain will fall too hard
And so will I."

He heard the very same poem that he had been carrying around in his wallet for months. *And what a sweet, majestic voice. But wait, I recognise this voice too.* He began rushing through the stairs to take a peek. He got an inkling that it was her. And he couldn't handle the suspense. Making his way through the crowd of charged college students, he finally got a chance to take a closer look at the stage. And in the biggest surprise of his life, he saw Vaanya. Up there, performing the same poem with absolute finesse.

He couldn't stop gawking at her. She looked almost mystical. Dressed in a white kurta with long open hair, she performed the poignant poem in her sweet voice. Her silver jhumkas jingled everytime she swayed with the poem.

And in that exact moment, he was convinced that it was her whom his soul was aching for. As though, everything in his life was leading him to this point. And it was here, next to her, where he truly belonged.

Chapter 4

Late Night Talking

At the end of a long weary day
When you hit your head
On the soft folds of the pillow
You get to decide who you really want to be
A one-size fit all prototype
Or a tailor-made piece of hurricane.

—Vaanya

At night, Dhruv kept tossing and turning in bed. Vaanya's face kept flashing before his eyes and her poem kept resounding in his ears. *If this wasn't a sign, what was?* He thought to himself. After hours of debating with himself and playing out every scenario in his head, he finally arrived at the conclusion—he'd be an utter fool to let this go. She was perfect and it was time he finally believed in his gut and mustered up the courage. He decided to ask her out on a proper date and confess his feelings once and for all. If he'd reached this far, the universe surely had a plan for the future too, he reminded himself before finally falling asleep at five in the morning. The next day, Dhruv decided to call Vaanya since she had still not replied to his texts from the other night yet.

"Hey!" he said in a low voice.

"Hi!" she sounded a bit slow on the phone, as though she had just woken up.

"Sorry, did I wake you?"

"No. It's fine. Tell me?"

"We never spoke after that night. I wanted to explain myself."

"No explanations necessary."

"Vaanya, listen! That was not okay. Things just blew out of proportion for no reason. Give me a chance to at least explain everything to you."

"Why are you justifying your actions to me? We're just friends, right?"

"Are we?" he finally addressed the elephant in the room.

"Tell me?" he asked again when she didn't say anything. "Tell me you don't feel there's something more than just friendship between us."

"I don't know what you're talking about," she finally said.

"Are you sure you aren't just denying it because you're afraid?" It was as if he had read her mind.

"And I don't blame you," he continued. "I know the gossip and the rumours around campus. And the other night didn't help matters anyway. But give me one chance to change your mind? Come on! Let me take you out tonight?"

"Dhruv, we're good friends, we study together and we make a good team. Let's keep it to that."

"Do you really want to keep it to that?" he finally said only to be met with silence.

"Say yes, and I will never bring up this subject again. You have my word," he said when he received no response from her.

"Dhruv…" she took a deep sigh. Every bone in her body winced at saying no to him. She simply couldn't. Her heart was waiting for this moment for weeks, but her head cautioned against it.

"Vaanya. Do you trust me?"

"I want to."

"I can work with that."

"So? What next?"

"So, let me take you out on a date today! There's this new Italian place in Mehrauli with a gorgeous view of the sunset."

"Why can't we just go to Raju's? Our usual spot."

"Because this is not usual. I want to take you out properly... on a real date."

Vaanya Sharma didn't see this coming. Ever since childhood, her focus was limited to books. Though, one could argue that Vaanya had always been a romantic at heart. As kids around her began gradually exploring the concept of dating, she grew curious too, but no guy ever captured her fancy enough. In the tenth standard, when many girls in school began having real boyfriends, she made do with fictional boyfriends and girlfriends from her books. Up until the eleventh standard, when a boy named Rishabh who was in the same class as her, won a pink bunny for her at the winter carnival and confessed that he liked her. Not sure how to respond, she had simply said a 'Thank you' after accepting the stuffed toy and walking away. Later that night, there was a house party at Sameera—her then best friend.

It was Vaanya's first house party. "Stay away from alcohol and boys. Don't do anything that would bring shame to the family!" her mother had advised, after which Vaanya left home wearing a long tunic dress underneath which she wore a pink crop top and denim shorts.

At the party some kids had even sneaked in bottles of beers and vodka. "It's just fruit punch. Don't worry!" Sameera had said, and forced a glass of a weird vodka-based drink down her throat. It tasted like a funny mix of pomegranate juice and cough syrup.

Vaanya never liked loud music but after just one glass everything seemed better. So, she had another drink, until things began seeming blurry. It was a burst of colours and sounds to her. It was the first time in her life that she stopped thinking and let things just be the way they were, and she enjoyed every minute of it. It was a brief relief from not having to try to be right or perfect, but just be.

Later, everybody began playing truth or dare. Bottles were spinning and people were confessing taciturn secrets, admitting long-standing crushes, and doing all sorts of questionable things in the name of dares.

When the bottle pointed at Vaanya, she chose dare.

"Kiss Sameera!" A lean boy with an annoyingly high-pitched voice had screamed from behind the room, and in a matter of a few minutes everyone began hooting, "Kiss! Kiss! Kiss!"

Vaanya couldn't think straight and for the first time in her life, she didn't want to. So she got up, and suddenly the whole place went dead quiet. Admist the silence she walked over to Sameera and bent over to plant a kiss on her lips. She got a taste of her coconut flavoured lip balm. But surprisingly, she liked kissing Sameera. Her lips were supple and the way she kissed her back felt weird, but good weird.

Soon the taste of her lip-balm mixed with the pomegranate taste of the vodka-infused punch she was drinking made her queasy. She tried to get up and take a walk, but Rishabh followed her out.

"I know you don't love me. But will you please be my girlfriend? I'll make sure you're happy," he said in a single breath.

Vaanya stared at him with droopy eyelids. She felt dizzy. Everything around her was spinning. Bile rose in her throat and suddenly she threw up on his left shoe.

When Vaanya told Sneha about the recent occurrence, she reacted with a stone-cold expression followed by a loud squeal.

Vaanya Sharma, you gotta be kidding me! So, 'The Dhruv Malhotra' has officially asked you out on a date?"

"Apparently yes."

"Dude, every other girl on campus has a crush on him. But how did this happen? I thought you guys were just study buddies."

"I also thought we were just study buddies. I mean he does flirt with me, but I think that's just how he is."

"The word you're looking for, is charming."

"Whatever!"

"You're blushing!"

"No, I am not!"

"Yes, you are! You're such a smitten kitten!"

"No Sneha, I am not even sure if I should go out with him. Haven't you heard the gossip on campus? And especially after I saw him with Saloni the other day!"

"He ghosted her. Maybe because he was always into you. Ever think about that?"

"But he is the ghosting-type, what Saloni said—confused playboy! I mean as long as we were just friends studying statistical analysis and microeconomics together, it was fine.

I didn't care. But it matters if I decide to go out with him. I don't want to get involved in anything messy."

"Babe, you need to learn to chill. It's just a first date. Don't overthink it. Just go out, have fun. Not too much fun though."

"I know. But why start something you can't sustain?"

"Ahh. See Dhruv has a messy past in all probability. But the more important and relevant question for now is, what do you feel about him?"

"Umm I don't know. I mean, he is nice. And he is like my only friend here apart from you. Like he is smart and funny. And really witty. He has an almost photographic memory. Like he doesn't even try and he is just so good at almost everything. And he keeps me on my toes but also makes me feel so safe and seen. It's weird but, when I am with him, is the only time I am really in the moment, otherwise, I am usually in my head overthinking everything under the sun."

Vaanya, are you in love with him or what?"

"Are you crazy? He is just…Dhruv. He has a flock of girls swooning over him and people talking about him around coffee carts. That's just… not my type. I mean I don't believe the stupid little tales floating around. They are all Chinese whispers after all. But then there's no smoke without a fire, is there?"

Vaanya, you've to make up your mind. But not right now. Right now, just go and have a good time. See what he has to say in his defence. And then decide. Now come on! Get your ass off this bed and go look like a snack he can't resist!"

"Thanks for the pep-talk! I love you!"

"I love you too! Now go, get it girl! And give me details after!"

"See you at the main gate in 20?" His text popped up on her phone's screen. She felt a tiny flutter in her heart. Smiling at the screen, she replied and went back to applying kohl on her waterline.

Dhruv had decided to wear a navy-blue shirt with a couple of buttons on the top open that highlighted his broad shoulders and toned chest. The sleeves were rolled a few inches up his muscular arms. He was uncharacteristically excited and slightly nervous. He decided to tell her everything, knowing fully well that she might not feel the same. But that wouldn't stop him from telling his truth. Because now he knew with great certainty that she was his destiny.

At 6:30 p.m., Dhruv picked her up in his car at the campus main gate and they drove down to Mehrauli.

"There's something for you in the back," he said.

"What?" She inquired.

"See for yourself," he said.

She turned around and saw a carry-bag from crosswords. She picked it up and found a book inside.

"Rumi'poetry collection!" she exclaimed. "How did you know I wanted this."

"Don't ruin my gift. Just enjoy it," he chuckled.

She smiled at his gesture.

The cafe was a short walk from the main area where they parked the car. It was a scenic street lined up with multiple boutiques, art galleries and patisseries. A beautiful hedge of magenta bougainvillea covered the stone-wall around the area. It was the first time that the two of them had stepped away from the hustle-bustle of the campus. The new setting felt refreshing. In their short walk to the café, giggles and small talk quickly replaced the unease and nervousness of the previous few hours. They were friends before anything else, and that was here to stay. Vaanya spotted a few kittens hiding in the curb and they stopped to pet them.

Dhruv had already booked the best table overlooking a majestic view of Qutub Minar. The café was quite chic but still had an authentic vibe to it. It seemed well suited to Dhruv's taste.

As they settled on their table, he immediately offered the rather extravagant menu to Vaanya, who ordered a hazelnut latte while Dhruv ordered a classic americano without sugar.

"Why do you always have black coffee?" Vaanya smiled.

"Why? What's wrong with it? It's strong, it gives you a good kick."

"It's pretentious."

"How?"

"I don't know. It's like hardcore 'macho-ness'. No sugar, no milk. Strong, dark, no-nonsense kind."

"What if I *am* all that?"

But you aren't all that, are you?"

"I could be. But then again, we don't know everything about each other."

"That would be a clear no."

"Yeah, because we only spend time sitting in the library or that run-down shack at Raju's, trying to figure out statistical analysis, microeconomics, and managerial accounting, and not really each other."

"Aren't we here to do exactly that for the next two years?"

"Yeah, but also to get to know more people, make lasting bonds, and leave a legacy."

"When you put it that way…"

"Well thinking out loud is your forte, Vaanya. I'm not the poet here."

"You could be one, if you wanted to."

"I can never be in front of you. By the way, I stopped by at the open mic yesterday!"

"Oh, you did? I didn't know you were coming."

"I didn't plan to, but I changed my mind."

"So?"

"I did catch your performance."

"You did?" She buried her face in her hands, blushing, trying to hide from his gaze.

"You were incredible! Your piece was so powerful! And the way you performed it, I literally had goosebumps."

"You really think so?"

"Yes."

"Thanks, Dhruv!"

He thought about telling her how he was already familiar with her poem. That he had found it in the gardens on the first day, and how the universe had been conspiring for so long. This was all meant to be. They were supposed to find each other.

But all he said was, "You're so talented! What are you doing here, really? MBA is for corpses like me."

"Hahaha, now that's a stretch."

"It's the truth."

"Speaking of honesty, I have seen you too hunched over a journal quite a few times. And I didn't really see any microeconomics formulas in it."

"It's nothing!" he tried to brush the topic away.

"Tell me! I know you hide things from me."

"I want to start changing that," he stared into her deep kohl-lined eyes.

"I am glad."

"So am I."

"So, you could start by sharing the contents of the journal."

"I just simply journal sometimes. Helps me process things."

"Things like?"

"Random stuff like thoughts, feelings, and formulas that sometimes sound like song verses. You know, things nobody would want to hear, so I hide them in the pages of my journal."

"Do you write about me?"

"Ahh you!" he paused for a minute and their eyes locked.

"Well, everything about you is worth a song of its own, Vaanya. Those jhumkas and their ringing melody. It feels like they are trying to tell me everything that you won't. And your long black hair, it's as if they carry spring in their soft locks. And that smile. It's therapy for a heart that's beyond repair."

She continued staring at his metallic eyes, as though searching for the verse that followed.

He reached forward and picked up her jhumka that had fallen on her lap. His arm brushed against her shoulder and a sharp current rushed through her body. Her cheeks turned red as a cherry, and she smiled and looked the other way.

"I was kidding by the way. I just made that up," Dhruv said, and regretted immediately.

"Duh! I know," Vaanya shot back. "The last line was an overkill by the way. You could do better."

"Noted."

"Seriously though, you call me the poet, but your on-the-spot solo poetry competition was quite a hit. I'm impressed."

"Ah! Are you now? So, my six hours of practice last night was worth it then," he said inadvertently, and they broke into a loud laughter.

"Laughing at a poor man's misery. Vaanya Sharma, they're reserving a special table for you in hell."

"Only if you follow me to hell too."

"With that smile, how could I not? Also now that we're doing on the spot poetry competitions. Whoever wins has to take the other person on a date. Deal?"

"Okay. Nice proposition."

"Isn't it? We could go to nice cafes, drink amazing coffee. You could write poetry. I could work on my songs. And we could both quit this mad MBA life and live happily ever after in a small cabin by the hills. Sounds like a plan?"

"Well, if only poems paid the bills," she chuckled.

"They could. If we try hard enough, maybe. Why does everything come down to capitalism in the end? It's tragic," Dhruv said, looking away. Slight creases of dismay spread on his forehead. He gulped the remainder of his coffee in one go.

"Yeah. It makes me mad too. But this is the reality of the world we live in."

A few moments of silence elapsed.

"Can I ask you something?" Vaanya said, hesitance dripping down her voice.

"Yeah, of course." Dhruv replied firmly.

"How do you do it?"

"What?"

"Just seem to fit in and belong wherever you choose to?"

"I don't know. Fake it till you make it I guess?" he said, tilting his head to the left.

"So, it's all an act?"

"Not entirely. But on some level, all of us are acting, aren't we?"

"Elaborate, please?"

"I mean, people's true selves are often different from what they allow most others to see. Things aren't how they seem on the surface, Vaanya. You gotta dig a little deeper to unearth the truth."

"I wouldn't know. Not so experienced in digging and unearthing things," she said with a tone of resignation.

"You should then."

"What?"

"Go beyond the surface. That's where the finest ironies and metaphors lie."

"Don't digress from the subject and flatter me with those charming words of yours," she arched her eyebrows and smiled a sarcastic half-smile.

"What's the subject here?" He straightened his back. All eyes on her.

"You!" she took a deep breath, "You. Dhruv Malhotra. This black coffee drinking secretive guy with a complicated past, garnering gossip all around the campus, who compliments me on my poetry but secretly writes songs, who says MBA is for capitalistic corpses and then shocks everyone by being in the top one-percent of the batch and kills it at stupid finance clubs and inter-college football. And then, when this isn't enough, he surprises me all the more by asking me out on a real date. I don't get any of this."

"Easy there!" he said and slid a glass of water toward her. "Breathe!"

"Has anyone told you that you're a little scary when angry?"

"Shut up, Dhruv!"

"No, but seriously, the game face fell? I thought you'd keep up a little while longer," he joked to lighten the air.

"I am a real person, Dhruv. Not this fantasy of a girl you've crafted in your head. And I don't want masks between us," she looked at him, wide-eyed, peering into his eyes.

"That's right. You just answered your own question."

"As in?"

"You're doing exactly what you're holding me accountable for. You've also listened to the noise around you and crafted a version of me that you believe in, instead of really knowing me and my past.

"And as you said, even I don't want masks between us. So today, I want to be absolutely transparent with you Vaanya Sharma.

I know the gossip on campus bothers you. And I understand. I should have probably told you this earlier itself. But I didn't want to taint our bond with the details of my past."

"Hey! I want you to know that you can tell me anything. I want to be your safe space, Dhruv. If anything, we're friends first and I want to be there for you," said Vaanya.

"Last year was quite difficult for me," he said after a small pause.

"I went through a bad break-up. Her name was Anisha. She was my first. And I loved her. Or at least what I thought was love back then.

We had a good few months, but then she started acting out. I knew something was wrong, until I found her cheating on me at a party."

Her stomach dropped as he said that. She didn't know he held so much behind his charm and quiet confidence. But before she could say anything, he continued with his story.

"I didn't handle matters well. I acted stupid and rebellious. Didn't get out of my room for days, skipped classes, missed a few exams, and had to write them again. My family and friends were worried sick.

"I felt like I was in a pit. And to escape that low, I began relying on things like smoking and drinking to feel a temporary high. And hence, the cycle began. Drinking, smoking, and sleeping around. But it only made things worse. I just slowly became numb. Couldn't feel anything. It still makes me nauseous, thinking about that phase of my life," he paused to assess her expression, and then continued, "I think betrayal from someone you trust is the hardest thing to get over. It really questions your beliefs and sense of self. Who you are and what you mean to others around you? It's really your identity.

"I tried therapy for a while. It helped, though not a lot. But what it did was make me realise that in the end you have to find your centre. That's about it. Nobody else will really come and do that for you.

"I don't know why I am telling you all these excruciating details. But I think you deserve to know. Because even if I keep my feelings for you aside, you're still one of my closest friends here, and I don't want you to hear this from someone else."

Vaanya didn't know what to say. She was shocked and caught off guard. She had no clue that behind this tough exterior, he was just a boy, who had been hurt. She wanted to comfort him. She wanted to reach out and hold him. Caress his face and take away those lines of fear and regret formed on his forehead. She wanted to say so much but nothing came out of her mouth except a deep sigh of disbelief.

"You deserve the truth, Vaanya," he said, looking at her.

She held his gaze without blinking her eyes.

"And the truth is that, Vaanya Sharma, I really like you. I know this might sound ridiculous after all that I've just told you. Perhaps timing is not my strongest suit.

"But when I saw you for the first time, in that crowded classroom, lost in your world, unbothered by everything around, I finally felt alive after almost a whole year. I realised

I was no longer numb. And that I was capable of feeling again. And since then, I had a nagging feeling that you and I, we belonged together. And the more I got to know you, the feeling got stronger.

"You're brilliant and beautiful and so kind. And you've got courage. To be who you are. You're comfortable in your own company. Do you know how incredibly attractive that is?"

He paused and took a deep breath.

"I am in awe of you, Vaanya Sharma. And your poems. The things you hide behind metaphors, I wonder what'll happen when they come to life."

She kept staring into his gleaming metallic eyes looking fixedly back at her.

"Nobody has ever seen me the way you do, Dhruv."

He looked at her with rapt attention. After a while, he cleared his throat, "Say something? Anything? What are you feeling right now?"

"I don't know. I can't find the right words."

"Says the queen of words," Dhruv quipped.

Vaanya smiled from behind the coffee cup.

"You're hiding behind that coffee cup now just the way you hide behind metaphors." He laid his eyes on her. She had lowered her eyelashes, as though he would see what she was hiding behind her metaphors and in those deep kohl-lined wells.

Just then, the air in the cafe filled with the music of Dhruv's favourite song.

"*Kahin toh hogi wo, duniya jahaan tu mere paas hai...*" he began humming along.

"*Jahan meri zindagi mujhse itni khafa nahi...*" Vaanya swiftly completed where he left off.

"Dhruv, I...," she almost fumbled, trying to find the right words. "I appreciate your honesty, I really do. And if I am being really honest, I feel something here too. But I'm not quite sure what it is."

He kept looking at her with hope, keenly observing the fluttering of her eyelashes.

"Don't let it get to your head, but you know that you are incredibly attractive," she said tacitly.

Dhruv smirked and she rolled her eyes at him.

"And I love the comfort and the camaraderie we have. But I can't completely ignore all that I've been hearing about you. While I know most of it might be Chinese whispers. But I am unable to turn a blind eye. After all if there's smoke, there must be fire somewhere."

Dhruv's face dropped. Her words hit him hard, though he knew it wasn't her fault. After a few seconds of jaw-dropping silence, Vaanya reached out for his hand and softly murmured, "I want to believe you, Dhruv. But I think I'm not there yet. Where I can simply take a leap of faith."

"I understand, Vaanya. And it's absolutely okay. I just wanted to tell you, my truth. I don't expect anything in return." Words rose from his tightening stomach and made their way out of his bitter dry mouth.

He broke away his gaze from her and took a sip of his black coffee, dissolving the bitterness in a quiet slurp.

Vaanya found it odd for him to be sipping on his coffee in a carefree manner, in the middle of such a serious discussion. Little did she know at the moment, that Dhruv had quite effortlessly mastered the art of hiding his overbearing emotions behind black coffee cups and cold whiskey glasses.

"And in the interest of full disclosure, I've never had a real boyfriend," she was almost embarrassed as she said this, her face turning turnip red.

"Really! How? I mean, why? I'm sure you'd have many guys wanting to be with you."

"Maybe. But never one I felt something for."

"I see!" Dhruv pondered on her revelation. "But tell me something?"

"Hmm?"

"If you've never been in love, how do you even write such powerful love poems?"

"Imagination is a wild thing!"

"Is it?"

"When you don't know how something feels, you can go all out in imagining how it actually might be..."

"I don't even know what to say! I think it'd be a lot of responsibility for me to shoulder."

"Good thing God gave you such strong shoulders!"

He laughed at her word-play. But that evening, his words weighed over hers in the warmly-lit café. The black coffee and the hazelnut latte witnessed a brand-new bond being brewed over the rustic wooden table.

Once they reached the campus, he walked her to her dorm.

"What's the one random fact you really love?" he asked her on their short walk.

"How our fingers have spaces between them so we can hold hands with other humans as an act of love," she said.

He smiled, pondering at the depth of her answer, before reaching for her hand. His fingers brushed against hers and blood rushed to her cheeks. She blushed and their fingers interlocked with each other.

It was a cool windy August evening. The sky was surprisingly clear with no sign of clouds. As they reached closer to her dorm, Vaanya walked ahead after mouthing a small 'Bye!' and gazing up at the stars scattered in the night sky.

"What are you looking at with so much hope?" Dhruv asked sheepishly.

"Maybe I am trying to see where I really belong," Vaanya said without turning back.

"You're looking in the wrong direction. It's here," he said, pointing to himself.

She turned back and laughed at his remark, before looking back at the sky meditatively.

"Vaanya," he called out from behind.

"Hmm?" she replied without turning back.

"For the record, I meant each word I said to you tonight," he said earnestly.

"Write me a love song. Then, we'll talk!" she smiled and went inside.

Dhruv went to his room, still processing what had happened in the last few hours. He picked up his guitar and played the same song that had stayed with him through every confusion, celebration, heartbreak, or failure. The very song that played in the cafe today. Almost like serendipity.

"Kahin toh hogi who duniya jahaan tu mere paas hai…"

He played for well over an hour, after which he began working on the assignment for the next day's class. Before going to bed, he checked his phone and saw Arnav's text.

> "Hey man! We're planning to go out tomorrow night. Rohan is driving down from Noida. I'm also inviting this new girl I met on Tinder last week. Not sure if she'll show up. She's quite hot.

Although, I am checking if Sneha wants to come. Will have to cancel my Tinder date in that case. Check in with Vaanya too? It'll be fun if she also joins."

Dhruv wasn't in the mood for a last-minute plan. He was about to reply with a lousy excuse, but as he began typing, he thought maybe it would be a good idea for him and Vaanya to hang out with the rest of their friends. It would give them both a chance to unwind and bond together in a different setting. With thoughts of her running in his head, he drifted into a sleep.

The next afternoon, he texted Vaanya.

"Arnav told me about tonight's plan. You in?"

Ten minutes later, his phone buzzed with her reply, "Hey Dhruv! Yes, Sneha has been forcing me to come along. But I am not feeling that well. I have really bad period cramps. I can't do loud music and partying tonight. You go and have fun. I'll join you guys some other time."

"Come on, Vaanya! Don't be a spoil-sport. It will be fun. I'll make you a magic brownie that will instantly make you feel better."

"What brownie?"

"It's my specialty. It has a secret ingredient." He added a winking emoji. "And I am dying to see you again., he added the last line with a little apprehension, but pressed 'send' before he could change his mind.

"That's really sweet of you," she replied.

"So, come with us. I assure that you won't regret it."

"I appreciate your effort, Dhruv. But I really don't feel like this time. I just want to stay in bed and read. I am sorry."

"Okay," he texted back.

"Are you mad at me?" she asked earnestly.

"No" was the only answer she got in return for her dismissal.

"Yes, you are," she replied instantly.

"No!"

"Stop replying in monosyllables then."

"No!"

"Dhruv, don't, please!"

"No!"

"Okay stop saying 'No'!"

"No!"

"Okay, I am coming to your room."

She saw typing appearing on the screen below his name. After five minutes, he replied, "Okay."

Vaanya was wearing a black tank top and loose bell bottoms. She threw a shrug over it and rushed to Dhruv's room in flip-flops. With the tank top perfectly hugging her curves and messy hair loosely thrown back, she knocked at his door thrice, while the people in the corridors kept gawking at the unusual sight. After a few more awkward stares by boys in the hallway, he finally opened the door. "What took you so long, Dhruv?" Irritated, she hit his muscular arm playfully.

"I was in the shower. I am sorry," Dhruv said, gesturing to her to come in.

"Guys here stare a lot, I swear," she remarked while walking into his room. It was a small and rather cosy space with some books and laundry littered on the bed. He grabbed the things to set them aside and make room for her. She saw his guitar lying astray in the corner near the window.

"This big boy looks like it hasn't been played in a while."

"What?"

"I am talking about the guitar."

"Oh. Okay. No. Yeah. I mean yes."

She giggled, "It's okay."

He stared at the floor sheepishly.

"Have to start writing that song for you. The guitar will come in handy then," he said looking back at her.

"Ah! Yes," she said impishly, raising her eyebrows while looking at him from top to bottom.

He was wearing a low-waist-blue-jeans that flaunted the lining of his Calvin Klein briefs around the waist. She noticed him closely, in such an intimate setting for the first time. He had a remarkably striking torso and athletic legs. Having just stepped out of the shower, he wasn't wearing a shirt yet and just had a towel thrown around his neck.

Breathing in his naked and fresh, woody, pine-like scent, she was staring at him fixedly, as he pulled her by the wrist and drew her close to him. A few drops of water from his damp hair fell on her face. He slightly brushed his slender fingers on her peach-tinted cheeks to wipe the moisture and then cupped her face in his hands to gently admire her beautiful features. Staring searchingly in his dark electric eyes, which seemed intense at first, but giving away his feelings instantly. She could feel the magnetic energy between them, as their eyes locked, followed by their lips. Soon his tongue was inside her petite mouth, which welcomed it in, with excitingly fresh vigour. Her hands quickly worked their way up as she swung the towel around his neck and threw it on the bed in a swift motion. She gently grazed her soft fingers around his skin. His hands traced the contours of her waist and grabbed her closer. Vaanya felt herself dissolving in an unknown sweet and decadent feeling, a feeling she had never experienced before. From her narrow waist, his hands slowly found their way upward and untangled the waves of her meandering messy hair. The jingling of her earrings created a soft music that filled the space between them as he murmured her name like a divine spell, gasping for breath.

"Please come with us?" he earnestly requested her, still holding her arm.

"Dhruv," she whispered slowly, "I—" she couldn't finish her sentence as she saw the drooping expression on his face.

"It's okay, I understand," he shuffled uncomfortably but tried to put up a straight face while his eyes were still fixed on the floor. All he wanted was for her to have a fun night out and drown her worries in him. But he knew the decision was not his to make.

In the evening Arnav called to check.

"Hey dude, tonight is on, right?" he heard his voice on the other side of the line.

"Hey Arnav! I am not feeling so good. I'm not sure if I should come tonight." Dhruv tried to take a rain-check. But Arnav flipped.

"Come on Dhruv, don't ditch at the last moment."

"I don't want to. But I really don't feel like it."

"Bro Sneha has cancelled too. So, it's just us boys tonight. It'll be damn fun. It's been so long since we hung out. It is anyway going to be the last night out before the term break and the new semester. Don't spoil it."

Dhruv was reluctant to accompany, but then he gave it a thought and decided that maybe he deserved a break too.

"Alright, you better make it worth it then!" he replied, and Arnav instantly sounded happy again. "That's more like the Dhruv I know! See you at the main gate at six."

"See you bro," he hung up.

Before leaving for the night, he texted Vaanya.

"I'll miss you tonight. I wish you'd been here with me."

At the main gate of the campus, Arnav was already waiting for Dhruv and Rohan. By fifteen minutes past seven, the three of them got into Arnav's black SUV, grabbed a few beers from the local wine-shop to begin the party.

"To the boys!!" Arnav screamed and they all drank to it. They went to Hauz Khas, the area closest to the campus that had a decent night scene, as Dhruv whined about having to return at a reasonable hour.

"Man, you're so unlike you tonight!" Arnav reckoned. "You're acting like a little bitch worrying and complaining. *I've to get to bed on time*, Arnav mimicked him.

Dhruv shoved his remarks away in light humour as he downed his third whiskey. Arnav ordered another pitcher of beer while Rohan was already plastered after a few pegs of whiskey and a long island iced tea. At this point, he was near the bar, talking to some girl.

"Oh God! Rohan is at it again," Arnav shrieked. "This man never tires. Despite all the failures. God bless him."

"I'd say God bless the girl he is talking to," Dhruv added.

Arnav rolled on the couch laughing. "Someone stop another disaster."

In a matter of minutes, Rohan was back with them.

"Need a wingman, my boy?" Arnav laughed. "Well, you're in luck tonight. My date is about to be here in a bit and she is bringing along a friend."

"Is she hot?" Rohan got excited.

"Beggars can't be choosers. So, calm down."

Dhruv laughed and tried to enjoy this usual banter, but perhaps for the first time, he felt slightly uncomfortable and out of place. He checked his phone awaiting Vaanya's reply, but his message hadn't even been delivered. He felt somewhat alone and sad in the crowded and loud bar.

"Bro, let's try to talk to those girls over there. They were looking at us before," Rohan tried to shake him out of his zone.

"You go ahead man. I am happy with my drink. It's enough company for me," Dhruv said with no intention of meeting anyone new. Even though Vaanya needed time and they hadn't put any labels yet, in his mind and heart, he felt very much committed to her. And he didn't want to do anything to jeopardise whatever chance he had with her.

Later in the night, Arnav managed to get his date and her friend together with them. For the next two hours, all five of them hopped between bars and drank like fish. Dhruv didn't want to drink more, but Arnav kept forcing beer bottles and whisky glasses down his throat to the point that Dhruv could barely walk straight. He was mercilessly wasted. By around one in the night, they were roaming around virtuously on the streets, celebrating the last night-out before the new semester would begin, when suddenly, Rohan wanted to go to Privee. They knew getting stag entry would be tricky as they were two girls and three guys in total. Dhruv wanted to go back to the campus, but he could barely think or walk straight. Rohan too was utterly wasted and had surprisingly struck a chord with the other girl—Rashmi, the friend of

Arnav's date, Roshni. At the very moment, Arnav saw a familiar face exiting Privee.

"Hey Dhruv, look!" Arnav shouted, trying to bring Dhruv to his senses. Dhruv's ears and head buzzed at Arnav's shrill voice. As he almost focused his inebriated eyes to where Arnav was pointing, he was shocked out of his wits. He thought he was too intoxicated and was probably hallucinating. But he wasn't.

In a silver sequin bodycon dress that hugged her alluring curves perfectly, Anisha Singhania stood right in front of his disbelieving eyes, after one-and-a-half years.

She looked the same, except her hair was shorter than he last saw and she had coloured them a burgandy red shade, which made her look even more bold and sexy.

As bitterly as it ended, his year-long relationship with Anisha ran in his head like a movie in reverse. From the last time he saw her cheating on him in that party to the very moment he first talked to her in the music society auditions where she sang 'Girl on Fire'. As Arnav's diabolically loud voice echoed the empty streets, Anisha looked back to trace the source of the sound. And there Anisha Singhania laid eyes on the shell-shocked and pathetically sloshed Dhruv Malhotra, again.

Chapter 5

Cruel Summer

The polaroids of our consuming intimacy
The post-its of our unkept profound promises
The cut-outs of our wild misadventures
The long letters of our heartfelt longings
The paintings of our ardent desires
The abstract art of our ever so hopeful dreams
I hang them all neatly and symmetrically
On the wall of my memory.

—DHRUV

The next morning, Dhruv woke up with a massive headache. He tried to get up but as the scorching sun entered his eyes, he shut them tight again. He felt as if someone was playing shrill E.D.M. music in his head. He felt an almost instant urge to throw up, but it settled in a few minutes. As he sat up to sit straight, he tried to recollect the events of last night. Nothing came back instantly, but in sparse flashes. Anisha's chestnut hair clogging his vision and her slender body on top of his, taking the lead. Some things never change.

An atrocious nausea laden with guilt settled over him, as he remembered everything. *How could I do this?* He almost cursed himself. *Why did I even go last night? And how did I get so drunk. I should've just stayed back and been with Vaanya.* He silently screamed into the pillow. *Maybe I should just stay away from her. She doesn't deserve all this baggage.* Thoughts ran tirelessly in his head like wild horses, before he passed out again.

At two in the afternoon, he finally got up and checked his phone. There was a message from Anisha that read:

"Last night was amazing. Let's meet for coffee tomorrow? I've missed you so much."

Just when I thought the worst was over. He thought to himself, and a lone tear escaped his eye.

After taking a long shower and gulping down a tumbler of black coffee he thought of replying to Anisha but just then, Vaanya's text popped up on the screen.

"Hey Dhruv! How was last night? Let's meet at the tapri? I want to hear all about it."

Remorse hit him like a crashing plane.

He spent the rest of the day holed up in his room. He tried to sleep it off, wash it down with some more black coffee, play his guitar to seek some respite but nothing helped. Exhausted, he gave in. He stepped out of his room and walked down to the tapri to buy a smoke. The first few drags calmed his brain and he decided to face the storm.

He took out his phone and typed out a text to send to Anisha.

"Last night was a mistake. It didn't mean anything. We were really drunk and things got out of hand. I am really sorry about it. But I don't think us meeting again is a good idea. I wish you well."

As soon as he hit send, it felt like a piece of him got lost forever. He didn't know if it was the remorse from last night, sending this text or the cigarette he just smoked. But a jittery feeling of anxiety took over his body.

Anisha's reply came in a fraction of a second.

"I am not sorry, Dhruv. Not even one bit."

And in less than a minute, another message from her popped up on his screen.

"Dhruv, we never really cleared matters between us. After that night at the party, I tried to reach you for almost a month. But you didn't give me even a single chance to explain myself."

"I saw what I saw, Anisha. Besides, it was a long time ago. It doesn't matter anymore."

"It does, Dhruv. It matters to me."

"But why?"

"Because I still love you."

Confused and hungover, Dhruv didn't know how to respond.

"Say something? I know you too miss what we had. Ever since that night, it's not even been a single day that I didn't remember you. You've been the best thing that ever happened to me. And I know it was all my fault. But God knows we got unfinished business."

"I don't know what to say."

"Meet me once? I am in Delhi this week and I really want to see you again. Give me one chance to explain myself, please?"

"This won't do us any good, Anisha."

"You didn't want to give us another chance, Dhruv. But guess what, the universe does? Why would we bump into each other last night, otherwise? Just meet me once. Please?"

"Okay."

To divert his mind from all the unexpectedness of the past twenty-four hours, Dhruv headed to the library to get some reading done. In the economics section, he spotted Vaanya who was busy with her studying, as usual. Avoiding eye contact, he started walking the other way. But Vaanya jumped up from her seat and caught hold of him.

"Hi!" she exclaimed.

"Oh hi," he said in a small voice.

"Not happy to see me?" she asked with arched eyebrows.

"No. Of course not. What are you saying?"

"I was kidding. Why do you look so messy and surprised?"

"Umm... nothing. Just a hangover from last night."

"Oh yes, you didn't tell me. How was it? What did you guys do? I want to know everything."

"There is nothing to tell."

"What do you mean? Come let's go out and talk. I am really hungry also. Let's get something to eat and you can tell me all about last night in vivid detail," she grabbed him by the arm and dragged him outside.

"I am sorry. I have a ton of work to do. Haven't begun any reading for the new semester. Really lagging and I barely had any sleep last night. Let's do this later, please?"

"You're acting weird, Dhruv. Is everything okay?"

"Yeah yeah. Everything's fine. I just need some time to myself. I hope you understand."

"No worries. Let me know if you need any help," she said politely, feeling confused and dejected within.

Later that day, Dhruv went to meet Anisha. She had picked out the same cafe in Chanakyapuri that they often visited back when they were dating. Dhruv protested and asked to meet at a different place but she argued that it was the most convenient for both based on where they were situated.

With rustic furniture, vintage lamps and pastel walls, the cafe looked exactly the same as it did years ago. It all came back to him. All the time spent with her in this cafe doing nothing, talking for hours, eating everything on the menu, and clicking thousands of photos.

"I am at OUR table," Anisha called him and said in a sleek voice.

He turned around and there she was, dressed in a black skirt and maroon crop top.

"You forgot our table?" she looked up at him as he smiled sheepishly.

"Well. It's been a long time. What can I say?" He settled and ordered himself some coffee.

"No whiskey this time?"

"Haha, got to stay in my senses for this one."

"So, tell me how have you been?"

"I've been good. MBA in India is a little hectic but I am getting by. Have met some nice people who've been a huge help. What about you? You were in Mumbai, right? How come you're back here?"

"I am just here for a short work trip."

"That's nice."

"Dhruv..."

"Hmm?"

"I didn't plan to run into you last night. But it happened. Don't you think it means something?"

"I don't know, Anisha. What do you mean?"

"Don't act like you don't see it. There's still something between us. You can't turn a blind eye to it. This is the universe's second chance. To us. I won't let you mess it up."

"Anisha, please don't do this. Last night was a mistake. A huge one."

"Last night wasn't a mistake. What I did a year ago was one. And I never even got a chance to tell you how sorry I was. I still am. I've spent the entire last year in guilt, Dhruv. But I've repented enough."

Dhruv grew quieter. Her gaze pierced through him.

"I love you, Dhruv. I always have. I really want to give us another chance. Please Dhruv? If you allow me, I'll fix everything."

Dhruv didn't respond. Anisha took it as an affirmation.

"Deep down, I think even you feel the same way," she continued. "You're just not ready to accept it. Because you're afraid. But I can assure you, I've changed. I've repented and suffered enough. I've changed for good. I am ready to be the person you wanted me to be, Dhruv."

"Listen. You messed up. Things got sour. But it's all in the past. I am glad you've done your share of thinking. But it's too late now. I don't want to give us another chance. I have a different life now."

"I broke us. I know I did. And I guess there's no going back. But even if there is a slight possibility, I will keep fighting for it. Because you are worth fighting for, Dhruv." Tears trickled down her cheeks and she stopped to catch a breath.

"Here. Take this," he passed her a napkin and offered her some water. She was almost hyperventilating at this point.

"Deep breaths!" he murmured softly. "It's okay. It's all going to be okay." Those words came out of his mouth in an unthinking reflex.

He placed his hand on hers and ran concentric circles on her skin with his index finger.

"You still remember?" she whispered.

"Hmm," he admitted reluctantly.

"You still know how to take my pain away."

Later in the night Dhruv offered to drop her back to her hotel.

"Stay for a bit?" she asked.

"I have an early day tomorrow," he said.

"It's fate, Dhruv," she said while he was at the door, about to leave.

"And what are we? Mere pawns in the hands of fate?" He smiled and bid her goodbye.

Back at the campus, Dhruv poured himself into classes and assignments. He avoided social gatherings, finance club catch-ups, study group sessions, and anything that required him to talk to people. And most of all, he avoided Vaanya, who grew increasingly confused. Arnav noticed this change in his behaviour and showed up at his room one night with a perfectly rolled joint.

"Ah that's a real beauty you're holding in your hands." Dhruv welcomed his best friend inside.

"I thought you could use one of these and my company of-course." He chuckled and lit the tip.

"Well. It's been a tough few days, I can't deny."

"What happened? Anisha, I assume?" He took a drag and passed it to Dhruv.

"Yeah. You're right, as always." Dhruv inhaled it in, relaxing his tense body and mind.

"What is she up to?"

"She wants to give it another shot."

"What? After all this time?"

"Yeah."

"Insane."

"Hmm"

"What do you want?"

"I don't know."

"What do you mean?"

"I am confused, Arnav. I mean there is something about Anisha, that she keeps showing up in my life. It feels like I am stuck in a loop. This had to happen just when I had almost moved on, found peace in someone who is so much better for me."

"Vaanya?"

"Yeah"

"And the other night, you and Anisha...?"

"Yeah."

Arnav stayed quiet, unable to find the right words to comfort his friend.

"I can't look at myself in the mirror. And I certainly can't look Vaanya in the eye. I am a total fuck-up."

"Dude if you feel strongly for Vaanya, you go tell her. And confess your mistake. A drunken one-night stand doesn't have to mean anything."

"I don't want it to mean anything. But I can't deny that there is something about Anisha that sticks with me all the time. I don't know what, though. It's her passion or free-spiritedness. I am not sure. But last year felt like she was in the driver's seat and she took me wherever she wished. I felt like a piece of cargo attached at the back that just got dragged and bruised. And I hated feeling so powerless."

"It was your first real relationship, buddy. You're meant to feel a lot of things. It's okay. But don't let it define you. Sit with it and then decide what you want to do. In the end we always have a choice."

"Do we?"

"Yeah. Of course."

"Well, I don't think so."

"Why?"

"Well. It's an illusion."

"What is?"

"Choice…" Arnav looked at him, puzzled.

"Who we are, how we think, and how we act is essentially shaped by everything in our lives that we didn't get to choose. Like our family, friends, the people we meet in life and the experiences that change us. All of these things that we don't have much control over shape us into our present selves."

"I am trying to remember if you've always talked like this after smoking pot? Or is this some really good stuff."

"I think both," Dhruv laughed and opened a candy bar.

"Come to think of it. It's almost illusory. Take a relationship, for example. It only exists until both the people continue to believe in it and honor a code. When they stop, it falls apart."

"It's all an illusion!" Arnav said, looking into nothingness before bursting into a loud laughter. "This is some good stuff."

For the next thirty minutes they continued laughing with bloodshot eyes as they finished the entire chocolate bar and then, ordered cheeseburgers.

As the buzz wore off a little, Arnav continued, "But dude, on a serious note, cynicism is not a good look on you…"

"I'd like to call this awareness."

"Stop talking like a yogi now. You are getting the premium business school education. You have a hot ex-girlfriend pining over you. And a potential girlfriend who is so sweet and intelligent. You drive a nice car and you wear branded clothes. You are a picture of materialism, my friend!"

"Yeah, on the outside, sure. But who cares what happens on the inside, right?"

"Well…"

"How long can one run away from what what goes on in here?" He said pointing to his heart and looking blankly at the floor.

For a whole week Dhruv avoided Vaanya. Convinced that he was no good for her, he began cancelling plans and missing her calls.

Once she caught hold of him in the class. "Dhruv Malhotra! What is up with you?" She came rushing to him.

"Hey hi! What's up?"

"You tell me. What the hell is up with you? Why are you ignoring me suddenly? Is it about that kiss? I am really confused."

"No, it's nothing. I am just dealing with some stuff right now. Sorry for being so M.I.A. But I gotta run. Have another elective to get to," he said and dashed off before she could say anything.

"Dhruv has flipped entirely," she whined to Sneha during lunch that day. "I can't believe he has been royally ignoring me since that day."

"But why? Did you say something?"

"No. We just kissed. Once."

"Wow. And you were going to tell me, when?"

"Umm soon. I don't know. It's nothing, really. Besides, everything's been weird since then."

"Well firstly you kissed Dhruv Malhotra. And you're all bothered that he hasn't talked to you properly. You sound like you're madly in love with him."

"Umm what? No! Shut up." With flushed cheeks she looked away to escape Sneha's questioning stare.

"What? Stop looking at me like that," she finally broke. "It's nothing... Or something I don't know. I've never felt like this before. I don't know why it's bothering me so much."

"'Cause you're in love!"

"Sneha!"

"Okay fine, chill."

"I think I miss my friend Dhruv more than anything. Like at least I had him around before. Now he is just pulling a disappearing act."

"But how was the kiss?"

Sneha's question threw her back a week ago, and she could feel his electrifying touch, the taste of his lips on hers.

With red hot cheeks, she smiled. "It was good."

"Well, your face says it was a hell lot more than just good."

"It was."

"Well then now the question is why is he M.I.A.?"

"I don't know, man. What's weird is that just a week ago he confessed his feelings for me."

"Woah woah woah!" Sneha stepped back. "He did?"

"Yeah.."

"Damn."

"Yeah. And suddenly he has been pretending to not care even one bit."

"That is weird. But you know what else it is?"

"The sign of a fuck boy," Sneha said dramatically.

"I don't know." Vaanya seemed lost in thought.

"I am sorry, Vaanya! I know I pushed you to go out with him. But now I don't think he is right for you."

"See this is exactly why I am afraid to go out there and date. This is what happens when you get feelings involved."

"I think you should just remove yourself from this situation. I don't know. Something doesn't feel right."

"I don't know Sneha. Why do I think there is something more to this?"

"Well. Maybe. But I don't think you should waste your time trying to find it out. It's not worth it. It's probably best for you to let it go."

Vaanya waited for another three days but no word came from Dhruv. Having lost all patience, she decided to reach out again.

She picked up the phone and dialled his number. But as usual, no response came through.

Angry and confused, she cried herself to sleep that night.

At five in the morning, she woke up with hot flashes.

"It was just a bad dream," she reminded herself but tears rolled down her face.

"What did I even do? Why are you punishing me, Dhruv? I miss you," she texted him before she put her phone away and tried to go back to bed.

Without him, getting through a single day felt like a death sentence. And with him by her side, she had felt like no mountain was too high. Dhruv had become an integral part of her life at campus. The realisation dawned upon her.

The next day in the middle of the evening rush-hour at the canteen, she spotted him sitting in the corner with his laptop and a cup of coffee.

Something came over her, and she began striding toward him.

"You can't get away from me this easily," she spat out.

He shuffled uncomfortably, seeing her popover from nowhere, hovering over him with a look of determination.

"Vaanya…" he paused to think, but before he could say something, he was already being dragged out.

Holding him by the arm, Vaanya was speeding out, making her way through the crowds of ogling onlookers.

"Vaanya, what are you doing?" he murmured, avoiding eye contact with dozens and dozens of students staring at them.

Embarrassed and shocked, he tried to cut her loose. "Vaanya, you're making a scene."

"Quietly follow me, if you want to avoid a bigger scene."

They walked across the length of the campus, crossing almost all the main buildings, the girls' hostel, the boys' hostel, the lecture halls, cafeteria, and the bookshop. After another five minutes, they reached a strange and quiet spot. Dhruv looked around and realised he had never been there. It was probably the abandoned area at the back of the newly-constructed girls' hostel that nobody had ever stumbled upon. It was dead silent, he could only hear the slight cooing of birds on the tall deodar trees that stood undeterred.

She came closer to him, he could feel her breath tracing question marks on his skin. He could almost hear her anger, as her breathing got heavier. He thought she looked prettier when mad.

Before he said anything, Vaanya grazed her fingers gently along his face. They lightly traced his stubble, and she could feel the coarseness rub off against her skin. She looked in his eyes, and suddenly the anger boiling in her own seemed to vanish in thin air. It was soon replaced with tears, struggling to fall down her deep brown eyes.

"Dhruv," she mumbled and let out a deep sigh.

Dhruv couldn't take it any longer. All the feelings of suppressed angst, fear and confusion melted away. He used his fingertips and dabbed them on her moist, soft upper cheek as tears trickled down his face too.

He pulled her close in a big hug and held her tightly in his warm grip. She buried her face in his broad chest and rested her head against his sturdy shoulders. They didn't let go of each other for another few minutes, after which Vaanya slowly murmured, "Dhruv."

"Hmm?" he replied softly.

"I know something is bothering you. Something is keeping you from me. I can see it in your eyes."

Dhruv didn't know what to say. He gulped down his fear and tried to tell her everything, but words eluded him. The visuals of that drunken night with Anisha hit him like a speeding train. Their intoxicated bodies throbbing against each other, morphed into one unconscious being, flashed before his eyes.

"Dhruv," Vaanya's voice shook him out of his dilemma as her hands held the side of his stubbled chin.

"Tell me, what's the matter? It's going to be okay, I promise."

"Vaanya..." his voice almost quivered.

She kept looking at him in anticipation with dried tears on her sullen cheeks.

"Dhruv, if it is meant to be, we'll find a way."

He cleared his throat, "That night, we went clubbing… when I was asking you to come with us..."

"Yeah! What about that?"

"I messed up."

"What did you do?"

"I didn't even want to party; I just wanted to come back at midnight. But these guys kept making me drink like a fish. I was sloshed and—"

"And what, Dhruv?" Vaanya's voice got deeper and more intimidating.

"Please tell me you won't hate me. Please Vaanya, I don't want to lose you. I am so sorry. I can't."

"Dhruv, tell me what happened. We'll be okay."

"We... we met... Anisha, my ex-girlfriend. And... I messed up."

"Did you sleep with her?"

He hung his head low, unable to meet her eyes.

Her face turned white as a sheet.

He wanted the ground to crack open and engulf him. His tongue felt like a barbed-wire, the words coming out of it could only bleed. But she heard the words that hadn't even made it out of his mouth yet.

She stepped back, and he tried to take a step forward to close the distance that had crept in between them. He was ashamed. But more than that, he was scared of losing her. And in that moment, he knew that only honesty could be his saviour.

"Vaanya, I am really sorry. I know you deserve better. But please hear me out."

"I don't even know how it happened. I don't have any clear memory of the night. It's all in bits and pieces."

"But this is no excuse. I do take full responsibility for my actions. I'm so sorry, Vaanya. I really wanted to make it work with you. But maybe I am not right for you. And I know that I don't deserve you...," he almost broke down and stopped as her name fell out of his mouth, as though it were a holy spell that didn't deserve to roll off his tongue.

"What did she have to say?" Vaanya asked with a deadpan expression. Her eyes were cold as ice and her cheeks looked ashen. Unable to look at him, she didn't move, and kept staring into a corner.

Petrified of the look on her face, he spilled out the truth.

"She wants to make things right. I met her again a few days ago. It's just a lot of water under the bridge. But it has been a long time since we broke up. And I am over her. I didn't expect my past to come to haunt me like this. Especially when I had begun to see a beautiful future with you. Vaanya, I am so sorry. It's just so messed up, and I didn't want to project all this bullshit on you, which is why I was avoiding you. I was so afraid to face you. I am a coward. And a fuck up. I don't deserve you."

Vaanya looked as if she was staring into the abyss.

"Vaanya, I just want you to know that I never meant to hurt you.

"The whole of last year was a bad dream. After I broke up with Anisha, I spent many such nights in unconscious states. But ever since I came here, things have changed.

"In you, I saw hope. I saw a better life. But now it feels as if the shadows of my past are still chasing me. No matter how hard I try to run away.

"But you don't deserve any of this baggage. You deserve better, Vaanya."

"Shhh..." She placed her tender fingers on his lips.

Her soft touch felt relieving and he thought she might forgive him. He thought maybe she had a heart larger and kinder than he could imagine. But before he could make sense of her touch, she slowly removed her fingers. He saw a stream of tears rush down her pale face. She turned around and started walking away. He stood there, frozen in time, watching her fade away into the background.

Thick black clouds hung low in the sky. The yellow shade of the deodar tree suddenly became grey as the sun receded and rain started falling so hard as though the sky was weeping the loss of his love.

Later that evening he received a text from Anisha.

> "My project is extended. I'll be here for about a month. I really want to make this work, Dhruv. Now that I am staying longer, it gives us a chance to reconnect and address all that we've been running away from."

Chapter 6

Ain't No Sunshine

This is not a love poem
This is an apology poem
This is everything I held at the tip of my tongue
But have always been too afraid
To let it roll off the rough edges
Now it catches fire and burns wildly
I carry the charred after-taste in my mouth
And the charcoal ashes in my lungs

You told me you needed space
As if I used your engaged shelves
To store my abandoned fears

You see, I might have accidentally placed my love
In your one empty sock drawer
And suddenly
You became a fan of decluttering

So now I am on the street
With my suitcase of apologies
And a rucksack of extra love

That we couldn't fit
In all the spaces
We created in our hearts

—DHRUV

Anisha was smoking a Marlboro Light. After inhaling two drags, she passed the cigarette to Dhruv who was sitting across from her in an outdoor, airy neighbourhood coffee shop of Saket that they used to frequently visit as a couple.

He politely declined and opened a fresh pack of a different brand of cigarettes.

"You've changed the cigarette. You've changed the woman. Is there anything about you that's still the same?" she asked, looking disappointed.

He smiled weakly, and let out a deep sigh before turning his gaze away.

"Do you remember? You used to drive me to this coffee shop and buy me a mocha latte and marlboro light, every time I was in a bad mood."

When he still didn't say anything, she continued, "I am really trying hard here, Dhruv. If there's any chance in the world that you and I can still work, I want to take it. I'm ready to do all the work. Whatever it takes to win you back, I am ready to do it."

"Now those are big promises, Anisha. And you have a history of breaking promises."

Staring at the coffee cup, she tried to conceal her embarrassment. "People make mistakes, Dhruv! And God knows I've made my fair share of mistakes."

"At least there's something that we both agree on," Dhruv spat out, with a raised chin, taking a long drag from his cigarette. Smoke filled the air between them and she appeared hazy.

"But do you ever think that even though I was never a perfect girlfriend, I might still be the love of your life?" Anisha said in a regretful but definitive voice.

Her words landed on him like a sharp and cold icicle, piercing into the growing confusion clouding his mind, as it wandered off to the night of 31st October in the year they were dating, as they headed to the infamous Halloween Party thrown by Arnav.

Anisha was dressed as Wonder-woman. Pulling off the golden lasso really well, her long legs got accentuated in the blue mini-skirt and stark red, knee-length boots. Dhruv went with his favourite—a classic Sherlock Holmes costume, looking regal in a tan trench coat accessorised with a magnifying glass, pipe and deerstalker hat, which completed the look.

As they arrived, Anisha was down to doing tequila shots with some girls from her class. In just two hours, she was on the pool table, dancing with three junior boys and one of Arnav's neighbourhood friends. At one point, Dhruv heard someone say that Anisha was about to strip. He ran towards the room and carried her out before a lot came off, and she fell unconscious. He carried her to his car and laid her in the backseat. Arnav followed them to the vehicle and patted his back in assurance. Dhruv was about to get into the driver's seat to leave, with Anisha passed out in the backseat, when Arnav said from behind, "Dhruv, be careful. I don't have a good feeling about this whole thing."

Dhruv turned back and stared into emptiness over Arnav's shoulder.

"Do you love her?" Arnav asked.

"More than I thought I was capable of," Dhruv replied in an instant.

"I am sorry man, but I don't think Anisha is the right girl for you."

"Too late man," Dhruv mumbled to himself.

"I don't want to see you heartbroken over her. And I'm afraid…" Arnav stopped mid-sentence and looked at the distant eyes of his friend.

Dhruv looked at him, unsure of how to react. "I'll see you later," he said and let out a deep sigh before getting into the car.

He took her to his place. She was still almost unconscious. He carried her upstairs and put her in his bed. He looked at her striking features as she slept.

He wondered what this strange feeling was. He was incapable of being mad at her for long. His affection and concern for her always exceeded his disappointment in her. And even though he knew this wasn't right, he felt incapable of leaving her alone to protect his peace of mind.

He was lost in thoughts, until he saw Anisha shift in bed uncomfortably. She was regaining consciousness, as she half opened her eyes. He sat next to her and helped her get up.

With a heavy head, she mouthed, "I am sorry," as she tried to recall the events of that evening.

Without saying a word, he went to the kitchen to prepare some lemonade for her.

After a few minutes he came back and handed her the glass.

Anisha looked at him uncomfortably. Her smokey eye makeup had worn off, the dark red lipstick was smudged, and her hair was all messed up. Along with the mascara, a look of guilt and helplessness was smeared all over her face. Like the night of their first kiss on the terrace, she stared blankly into nothingness. He saw the same vulnerable and feeble look on her face and cupped it in his hands. He came close to her. Her breath was laden with the smell of tequila, but he didn't mind. He cradled her face and quietly said, "Anisha, I love you. But why do you keep doing things to push me away?"

Anisha looked at his face that beamed with love for her and the guilt-stricken expression on her own face intensified. She held her tears back. "We're all messed up and miserable in one way or the other."

Dhruv pulled her close in his embrace and hugged her tight. He could feel his shirt get damp as she began sobbing in his warm hold.

"Are you okay?" Anisha placed her hand over his arm, bringing him out of his trance.

"Yeah," he said looking back at her, this time with more clarity.

"I love you, Dhruv," she said in an affirming voice. "Even today, when I touch you, every cell in my body feels like it's on fire."

Dhruv looked at her for a moment. "Love is so much more than that, Anisha."

The last week of September came to a close without any contact between Dhruv and Vaanya. And with October, arrived the dreaded midterm season. The first-week of the month was a small relief before the mind-numbing cramming sessions for exams began. As a mild cold began setting in the weather, Vaanya began staying in bed, and mostly spending time reading. She missed Dhruv, and was tempted to text him, but decided against it. She remembered he had said that he would take her to a cosy mountain theme cafe in Greater Kailash which served amazing hot chocolate, when she had told him that she loved Autumn—the onset of winter, and the soft transition between seasons. Missing him, she scribbled a list-poem about autumn on a piece of napkin and slid it in Dhruv's notebook, which was the only thing she had of him.

Warm lattes
Wistful Weather
Sweet smell of incoming winter
A soft lingering lull
Mixed-tapes
Transitions (of seasons and hearts)

Love notes on Napkins
Fleeting Car Cuddles
Smoky window-panes
Being one-self for Halloween

—Vaanya

"What is my favourite girl doing, hiding in her room like always?" Sneha barged in, at seven, one evening.

"No place like your bed." Vaanya forced a smile and hid under the covers.

"We're going out tonight. Come with us? Last fun night before the mid-term fever began."

"No, you carry on. I am quite cosy with my books and coffee."

"Yeah, I can see. I'd leave you to it if you would have come out of this room in three days. You and this bed have become one."

"So what? It's autumn, officially the season of rest and relaxation."

"Is it? So, you're saying that this seasonal depression has nothing to do with a certain someone with a five-letter name that starts with D for Dick?"

"Sneha!"

"What?"

"Come on. I can be mad at him. At least someone has to be. Because you have apparently shut yourself and your feelings completely under those books and stupid seasonal drinks. Wait, are you reading Sylvia Plath?"

"What do you want me to do? Cry and scream and go grab him by the collar? First of all, I've already done that. And second of all, we were never in a relationship. We went on one date. And we kissed. Once. He doesn't owe me anything."

"Yeah. You're right. As always. I mean, how are you so calm and level-headed?"

"Come read some poetry with me!" Vaanya smirked. Sneha shrugged and made a face.

"He is a mess by the way," Sneha clenched her jaw, awaiting Vaanya's expression.

"Is he?" she asked with arched eyebrows.

"Yes. I talked to Arnav yesterday in class. He told me. Dhruv's skipping classes. His grades are falling. And he has been smoking like a chimney. Apparently, he wouldn't listen to anyone. Arnav told me this always happens whenever something related to Anisha appears in his life. Arnav's trying to be there for him but he's afraid, he's fallen off the hook."

Vaanya's face stiffened.

"Hey! Now don't get worried and all. It's his mess to clean. Don't go all self-reflecting here please. He deserves this for what he did."

"I don't know, Sneha. Nobody deserves pain. But yeah, you're right, I should stay out of it."

"Yeah. Good girl. Now I am asking you for the last time. Do you want to come? It'll be nice for you to blow off some steam and it'll definitely help you take your mind away from all this Dhruv mess."

"No, I swear I am good. You have fun."

"You persistent bitch," Sneha smiled.

"Love you too!" Vaanya blew a flying kiss as Sneha left the room.

Around twelve-thirty in the night, she heard a knock at her door. Wondering who it might be, she got out of the bed and opened the door. And to her shock, she saw Dhruv in an unsteady state, barely able to stand on his feet. He was wearing faded jeans and an old white t-shirt with a small hole on one side, which looked like a burn from cigarette ash. He had grown a thick beard that covered most of his face. A few strands of his unkempt hair fell on his bloodshot eyes, and he looked as if he'd fall if he stopped holding the edge of the door. Seeing him in such a pathetic state, she let him in. He almost tripped at the entrance and held on to her for support.

As she helped him walk toward the bed, he wrapped his arm around her neck and whispered, Vaanya... I...." Slurring mid-sentence, he stopped, almost slipping into unconsciousness as they made it to the bed and he sat down with a loud thump. He held her arm and pulled her close. She landed on his chest. Her hair fell between them and he gently tucked it behind her ears.

"I miss you," he murmured as she kept gaping at his weary red eyes.

"I don't know if I should have..." Dhruv's voice slurred again. He took a deep breath and struggled to complete his sentence, "...said this and I want you to know that I don't want to hurt you, ever. You give me hope, Vaanya. Please stay with me?"

"Is this another one of your empty promises that you don't intend to follow through on?"

"Please don't give up on me, Vaanya. Please." His voice had a feeling of desperation and urgency. "I just need some time. I'll come through. But I need you to not give up on us. Please," he continued.

A lone tear escaped his eye. She couldn't keep up with her icy behaviour anymore. She inched closer and planted a soft kiss on his whiskey-soaked lips. He tightened his grip around her and kissed her long and hard. Soon, she was on top of him, kissing away all the sorrow he was carrying in his heart.

The next morning, sunshine entering through the drapes danced off their bodies, beautifully entangled with each other. Vaanya woke up bitterly as the sunlight pierced her eyes. But as soon as she gained her senses, she smiled seeing Dhruv sleeping innocently on her right arm. Slowly and gently, she tried to pull her arm from underneath him. At the same time, she couldn't help but notice how the beard made him look so much more handsome than usual. It gave him a jagged and dangerously sexy look.

She leaned on his side of the bed, and while admiring the sunlight reflecting on his gorgeous face, she admitted the undeniable truth to herself—she was madly in love with Dhruv Malhotra. Despite all the baggage he came with. She knew it was him. No matter what, she couldn't stop feeling this way about him.

In her heart, she knew that she needed him just as much as he needed her. At that moment, all that bitterness of the past few weeks seemed to evaporate in the warmth between them. She was determined that they'd find a way, come what may.

She bent over him and played with his hair as the cool breeze from the half-open window blew it in his eyes. He woke up to the slight flutter of wind and her soft touch. He felt as though he had woken up in the middle of a dream. His head was almost throbbing but the sweet blissfulness of having Vaanya next to him seemed to numb every other pain. He ran the back of his hand gently on her flushed cheeks. She smiled and kissed him softly.

Later Vaanya thumbed through her phone screen, choosing their first breakfast in bed, when Dhruv suddenly got up and shifted uncomfortably. She could see grim anxiety taking over his face.

"What happened, Dhruv?" she asked, gently running her fingers through his hair to calm him.

Vaanya..." he mumbled and stopped in his tracks as he saw her eyes brimming with love for him. He was scared to see the inevitable, the fact that Vaanya had accepted him for who he was.

"I don't know... I am sorry, I don't think I can offer you the happiness you deserve."

"Why?"

"Because I am capable of hurting you. And you're capable of forgiveness."

"It scares me."

"Shhh!" She pulled him closer and caressed his head with her hands.

"I don't want to hurt you." His eyes welled up.

"It's all going to be okay."

"You're better off without me." He hurriedly started getting dressed and began anxiously pacing around the room.

"Dhruv…" she called out, but he didn't listen. "Dhruv Malhotra," she raised her voice and sat next to him.

"Listen to me!" She almost screamed and held his face in her hands.

"I love you."

The words fell out of her mouth like raindrops from a clear white sky, unexpected, but drenching him with happiness.

He stood there on the cold floor, staring at this beautiful and generous person sitting next to him.

"Vaanya," he inched closer to fill the gap and traced his hands along her skin one last time. "I don't think we should do this," he finally said.

As soon as his words reached her, her eyes turned fiery, and rage filled her voice.

"You, Mr. Dhruv Malhotra, don't get to decide that. I fucking love you. And unlike you, I never let go of the people I love. I hold on to them, and that's what I am going to do. You can do whatever the hell you want."

"Vaanya…"

"Don't, Dhruv!" A sob escaped her mouth. "I can't see you torn apart like this. My body quivers in pain watching you suffer. For all this time, I have tried to run away from the inevitable. I kept convincing myself that I don't love you and that I don't care about you. But I can't lie to myself anymore. I look at you in tears and my insides twist. I love you too much, Dhruv. I wish I didn't. But I do."

He kept gawking at her in quiet disbelief.

"You know, Dhruv? I was taught faith. And I have faith in this. What we have here. And I have faith in us. You and me.

"Love isn't just accepting the best parts of someone. It's about accepting their mess. And loving them despite that. When I say I love you, I mean it. I don't care about the baggage that comes with it." Her words pierced through him.

"I am ready to take the leap. Are you?" she said.

"Vaanya..."

He grabbed her blush face to smother it with the loudest, most fervent kisses.

Her lips tasted like steadfastness of love.

The midterm madness had the students on the leash, as the unfettered aim of every soul on campus was to mug up every single letter in all the notes and presentations, just to get through the soul-crushing five days of back to back exams.

After the hellish week, the term break was a welcome relief, and students began heading back to their hometowns for the next seven days. But instead of driving back home, Dhruv took his backpack and boarded a bus to Manali on the last day of his final midterm exam. Without telling a soul, he left the hostel around midnight, on an excursion to find himself and attempt to look for answers to everything that had been bothering him for quite a while now.

He rolled a joint and smoked more than half of it before reaching the Kashmere Gate to board his bus, which took some time to find. When he finally made it to his seat, he felt a little anxious about going on this trip all by himself in a strange and dilapidated bus that felt even shadier at midnight. But he put on his headphones, clutched his backpack and let the neon lights of the bus, along with its rhythmic swaying and his techno playlist take over the anxiety. After a twelve-hour excruciating journey up the mountains, he woke up with a stiff neck. But as soon as he looked out the window and realised he was in the hills, he didn't mind the soreness anymore. The mountain air felt rejuvenating. The physical distance also helped him distance his mind from the whole mess back in Delhi.

To achieve solitude over the next few days, he muted most of his chats and told his parents he was going on a trip with some friends. He had some texts from Anisha, but he didn't read them. He messaged Arnav that he was going away for a while and would be back in a couple of days. Worried about Vaanya, he decided to leave her a voice note explaining why he needed to get away. A little distance and a new perspective was all he needed. After a five-minute-long voice note, he sent it with a short text that read,

> 'I want to be a better person for you. I see how unshakeable your faith is. And that makes me want to strengthen mine. Bear with me for a few more days. I promise, I'll come through. Better and stronger. For us.
>
> Don't worry too much and use this time to do what lights up your soul. I hope to see some magnificent poems when I am back.'

Vaanya received the text with a heavy heart but chose not to reply. She wanted to disassociate from campus life altogether, so she decided to go home too. She was excited to see Mira and binge watch movies with her all night to get her mind off of things.

"Look who's finally home!" Mira ran to the door as Vaanya arrived, and engulfed her in a big hug. "I've missed you, *didi*," she said and picked her bags up.

"I have the night planned. We start off simple with the sweet and charming *Notting Hill*, then we graduate to the slightly heavy *P.S. I love you* and then we end it with the real tear-jerker, *Eternal Sunshine of the Spotless Mind!*"

"Woah, that's a strong line-up for movie night!"

"It is, right? I have ordered Leo's pizza. The ice-cream tubs are in the fridge. We're sorted."

"Let's go then!"

For two hours they watched Hugh Grant be enamoured by Julia Roberts in Notting Hill while hogging on pizza and ice-cream.

"When will I meet someone in a charming bookstore and have my Notting Hill meet-cute come true?" Mira wailed at the ending scene of them reading on a park bench under the sun.

Vaanya laughed and switched screens to begin playing the next film.

"Wait! Before we start, I need updates!" Mira hit pause at the opening credits.

"What updates?"

"You told me about this guy last time we spoke!"

"Oh! Dhruv!"

"Yes! You've literally had a crush for the first time in your life. What happened there? Come on, spill the tea?"

"There's no tea." Vaanya stared at her finger-nails, avoiding Mira's gaze, unsure of what to say. "I don't understand what's really happening to be honest, Mira," she said, unfiltered.

"What do you mean?"

"He has baggage. A tonne of it."

"Umm... Elaborate?"

"His ex-girlfriend is back in the city and he got drunk and slept with her. He apologised profusely about it. We didn't speak for weeks. But the other day he showed up drunk at my doorstep and I couldn't resist," Vaanya looked up at Mira.

"Okay! I'm listening."

"You know me, Mira. In normal circumstances, I would've been able to think clearly and just handle things practically. But with him, my brain stops working. And I feel this uncontrollable desire for his touch. I keep imagining his tongue in my mouth and when he is in front of me, I can't think of anything else but his body on top of mine. And I give in to the urge," she paused, and said, "I just give in to him. My whole being dissolves in his embrace."

"Woah! Look at you," Mira gasped, taking in Vaanya's revelations. After a brief silence she said, "You know what didi, I do hope this works out, but even if it doesn't, I am just glad you finally experienced this feeling. It's such an essential part of being a human. To experience and exercise desire. To simply love and be loved."

"Yeah," Vaanya said, looking away, as though still processing her thoughts, "It was as if I didn't even know what I was missing."

"Now you do!" Mira gave her a small lopsided smile. "I need more details though. This is not enough."

"Shut up, Mira!" Vaanya laughed.

"What? I've been having a dry spell for a while. Come on, help a girl out!" she said and opened a large bag of potato chips.

Chapter 7

Sign of the Times

With rain, I learnt to fall
Fall fearlessly, and fall with grace
Because that's the only way
And with rain, I learnt to have faith
That even when I hit
The hard, cold ground
There will still be
Soft and warm soil
Somewhere near
To accept and to absorb
My pouring droplets
No matter how long and hard
I fall.

—DHRUV

Dhruv checked into a hostel and decided to sleep off the exhaustion from the trip. Around five in the evening he woke up, took a long shower to wash away the day and put on some fresh clothes.

Having decided to explore the city on foot, he went down the Mall Road, where he passed through rushed crowds consumed by what the hill-town had to offer. He witnessed groups of friends with charged laughter, couples holding hands and sharing ice-cream cones with a love-struck look in their eyes, tourists taking photographs and buying souvenirs from local shops. It looked like a gala of sorts with a long road lined up with shops decked with lights serving the famous pahari momos, *siddu* and other local cuisine. Amid all this merriment, Dhruv walked alone. And he felt nothing but a deep sense of peace coursing through his veins. He decided to have an early supper at one of the cafes in old Manali. The cafe had a vintage vibe and live music. Enjoying the music along with his meal alone, he cherished his own company in this faraway hill-town that made him feel 'at home' in ways he didn't feel back in the city that he called home.

At 6a.m. next morning, Dhruv was up and out in nature to witness the sunrise emerging from the mountains, and he embarked on the excruciatingly long trek. There was an *ashram* at the hill-top, surrounded by dense forests and winding streams. In that ashram resided a mystic, famous for his deep meditative trances, and an unwavering belief that, 'Enlightenment was the true purpose of human life'. His teachings primarily revolved around freeing the soul from karmic ties, which he believed was the only way to achieve true liberation. People from faraway places visited him to seek blessings and be guided through uncertain times in their lives. The mystic had lived in the ashram for over a decade along with a handful of devotees. People came from across the world, leaving behind their old lives and dedicated themselves to a new lifestyle of relentless service and devotion. They meditated for long hours before sunrise, sang hymns, and chanted mantras in the morning. They also did *seva* during the day and had prayer meetings in the evening hours.

Dhruv had heard about this a few months ago through a friend he met at a book club. Ever since then, he was curious to visit the ashram and meet the mystic. And with the current happenings in his life, it felt like the perfect time to seek some divine help and connect with the deeper self within.

He started out alone but met some people on the way who were on the same excursion as him. A common purpose evoked an oddly comforting bond between strangers who supported each other on a journey which was supposed to be as mentally stimulating, as it was physically exhausting. A feeling of brotherhood and divinity washed over the valley as the entire group chanted mantras and shared anecdotes about their healing journeys, throughout the hike up the hill.

As he reached the ashram, Dhruv was mesmerised by the aura of the gigantic establishment. There was something about the air of the place that brought forth a feeling of lasting peace. In the main prayer hall, some devotees chanted hymns. The vibrations of the room made his heart dance in joy.

Dhruv looked around. The whole place was bathed in devotion. One devotee was mopping the floor, another was offering water and refreshments to everyone who had just arrived after the long hike.

As Dhruv accepted the glass of water, he asked, "Can I also help with chores around the ashram?"

"Sure. Everyone who visits is welcome to do seva on and around the premises."

"Seva?" Dhruv asked cluelessly. "Doesn't that mean being of service to others?"

'Yes son. Seva indeed means serving others around us, but it is an act of selfless service that truly counts. One that is performed with a pure heart, without expecting anything in return," one of the devotees calmly explained to Dhruv.

"Hmm..." Dhruv nodded, following along.

"It's when you serve other people with love and humility that you feel a true sense of fulfilment and purpose. It eliminates ego, which is the biggest barrier between us and the divine," the devotee added.

Dhruv tried to assimilate this information in his head.

"Can I meet the mystic sometime today?" he finally asked.

"Guruji, we refer to him as Guruji," his muscles tensed.

"I am sorry. I didn't know," Dhruv was quick to apologise.

"That's okay," replied the devotee. "Guruji is in his meditative trance. He might not come out for another two days. And then, we have other people too who wish to speak with him. So, I think I can set up some time for you only after three days. We have a waiting list. But I can try to squeeze you in."

Dhruv hadn't planned on staying there for this long. But, he didn't want to miss his chance to speak to the mystic.

"Does that work?" asked the devotee.

"Oh yes. Thank you very much," Dhruv responded almost instantly.

"No worries. Meanwhile you can explore the ashram. We have a strict schedule, so it will be nice if you can follow it."

"Sure."

"All the devotees are supposed to start their day by meditating in the prayer hall. Most people break for tea and refreshments post this. Then, we all collectively perform yoga. One of the devotees at the ashram is a yogic expert and he teaches us various poses and *asanas*. The goal is to stay completely healthy and in tune with our *chakras*. You feel truly rejuvenated after doing these activities in the morning. Then we disperse for a meal which is served in the dining hall. We all sit on the ground and eat with our hands."

Dhruv looked slightly dumbfounded.

"What happened?" asked the devotee.

Dhruv tried to form a response.

"Sounds like a lot of work, eh? But trust me, it's worth it."

Dhruv saw a strange resolve in the eyes of the devotee, as if he really talked from experience and not mere hearsay.

"To give up worldly distractions and try living a life without hedonistic pleasure teaches you the true meaning of the human experience. It exposes the stark truth of who you are without the material objects you often draw your identity from. It's a revelation and often leaves a person way more grounded and in touch with his inner values than he was before."

Dhruv decided to stay at the ashram and devote himself to performing seva for the next seven days. The initial days were disorienting, as he found it hard to adhere to the strict routine and order of the ashram life. But from the third day onwards, he felt a deep sense of alignment from within. The resistance that he had faced internally dissipated into a feeling of lasting peace, so much so that he felt like prolonging his stay. He mopped the floors of the prayer hall, washed dishes in the *bhojanalay*, dusted the windows and doors of his room, ate his meals with other devotees on the ground, meditated for long hours during the night, and performed prayers and yoga asanas in the mornings.

Finally, on the sixth day, he got the chance to meet the Guruji. He was an old man with a thick, white mane. His face had a radiant and youthful glow despite the old age.

As Dhruv stepped into Guruji's chambers, he was promptly welcomed. "Come in, my child. Have a seat," Guruji's voice was authoritative yet emanating a sense of altruism, enveloping Dhruv in a feeling of comfort and security.

Perceiving Dhruv's inner turmoil, Guruji spoke in a serene tone, "I can sense something troubling you." Dhruv found himself captivated by Guruji's aura, but struggling to articulate his thoughts. Recognising Dhruv's struggle, Guruji remarked, "Our worries often prove futile, my child. Trust in the divine timing. What is destined for you will inevitably find its way, even when you stray. Now, tell me, what is troubling you today?"

Overwhelmed, Dhruv poured his heart out, "I feel utterly helpless, Guruji. It seems that my past follows me everywhere. I believed that the phase was behind me. But as soon as I feel like I've made progress, I find myself stuck in the same loop, repeating the same patterns."

With an air of composure surrounding him, Guruji replied, "It is the law of *Karma*, my child. You feel trapped in a cycle, unable to forge ahead, due to the karmic ties that bind you to others. As long as there remains unfinished karma, these repetitive patterns shall persist, replaying themselves in your life."

Dhruv looked puzzled, trying to make sense of Guruji's words.

Seeing Dhruv's scepticism, the mystic continued, "Think of it like a cosmic play. You have a unique role in other people's lives—as a son, a friend, a lover. Eventually, you'll become a husband and a father. These individuals, bound to you by karmic ties, are your co-actors in this play. They enter and exit your life accordingly."

Guruji emphasised, "Once the karmic connections conclude, they move on their own paths. Right now, you perceive only the physical realm, but as you raise your awareness and unlock the astral plane, the reasons behind events will become clear. Until then, remember, it's a grand production. As Shakespeare famously said, *'All the world's a stage, and all the men and women are merely players'*. Embrace your role and perform it with excellence while you're here."

Dhruv quietly absorbed Guruji's intricate teachings, before finally breaking the silence, "But how? How can I fulfil my role and make the right choices? I feel paralysed, with no way forward."

Guruji's smile radiated warmth as he replied, "Love is the only way, my child. Love is unavoidable, even if you may not be receptive to it, right now. Love has a way of finding you, always. It serves as the instrument through which you unlock your destiny. So, do not fear opening yourself to love once again."

"I did love once," he responded instantly. "I loved deeply. And I loved sincerely. But all I received for it was betrayal. It shattered my faith. Now, I've met someone who rekindles that hope, yet I struggle to act on it. I find myself trapped in the familiar patterns. And I wonder if I am still incapable of real love and integrity."

"People's actions have nothing to do with you and everything to do with them. You don't doubt your ability to love. It is an integral part of your destiny.

"The one causing you pain shares a past life connection with you— the pain you experience now is merely a reciprocal of that bond. The never-ending cycle of Karma goes on, but fear not, my son, for it too shall pass. Suffering often grows to its zenith and tests your resilience, before finally ending. Life is nothing but moments of joy and sorrow stringed together. While you've experienced pain, happiness awaits you soon. Remember my child, we are all spiritual beings, undergoing the human experience. Embracing this truth shall make this journey of human life easier, with all its beauty and imperfections."

"But I am tired, Guruji. When will this storm end?"

"When you face the storm in its eye."

Guruji's words landed on him with a huge thrust.

"Your soulmate has arrived in your life, but you're unprepared. The cloud of your karma must dissipate before you can embrace her fully. When that moment arrives, it will feel effortless and natural. The resistance and struggle you face now will eventually fade away. Making choices won't burden you like carrying a 1000 bricks on your shoulders."

"But until then, how do I overcome this struggle?" a conflicted Dhruv asked.

"By not trying," Guruji smiled. "Resisting pain causes more pain. You have to give up the need to control. Real peace is in surrendering oneself to the divine design."

"And, how does Karma end?"

"Collect your consciousness and take it within. You'll find all your answers right there. As Rumi said - '*We carry within us, the wonders we seek outside*'. So, remember to use this awareness, and look within, every once in a while. You'll be alright."

After spending another week meditating at the ashram, Dhruv finally headed home.

Back at the hostel, Dhruv switched on his phone only to receive multiple messages from Anisha, asking him to meet him as soon as he could. But despite the uncertainty, Dhruv felt a definitive sense of calm and clarity.

Dhruv arrived in Anisha's hotel room late that evening.

"Where have you been? I've been trying to reach you for days."

"Yeah, I just wanted some peace, away from everything."

"Arnav told me you were at some ashram in the Himalayas. What's going on, Dhruv?"

"Nothing. Just something I wanted to do for myself."

"Hmm…" Anisha inched closer to him and ran her fingers through his hair. "I've missed you," she whispered and planted a soft kiss on his cheek, before beginning to unbutton his shirt. As she thrusted her lips against his, Dhruv quickly pulled away.

"Why did you do that to me?" he asked abruptly, stopping her.

"What?" she asked, puzzled.

"Why did you cheat on me? When I was nothing but loving and honest with you?" he asked.

Anisha looked visibly thrown. "Dhruv. Where is this coming from?"

"It's coming from me. The person in front of you, who never really understood why he got betrayed like that?"

"Dhruv..."

"Come on. Tell me. You've randomly appeared in my life after a whole year, talking about second chances and that I never heard what you had to say. And I thought it didn't matter. But I was wrong. I deserve to know the truth. Where did I go wrong? I've spent countless nights last year thinking about it. But I never had the courage to pick up the phone and ask you. Because I was so scared to hear the truth. But you know what, I am not scared anymore. I trust myself enough to hear the truth and then let you go."

With a horrific expression in her eye, she looked like she had trouble breathing. Her eyes grew wide and it seemed that she would burst into flames.

"So tell me, what was it, Anisha? Was I never enough? Were you bored? Or was it just me in that relationship who felt so strongly? Did you never feel that way for me, the way I felt for you? Was it just lust? What really happened? What were you thinking?"

"I wasn't thinking, Dhruv. That's the problem," she almost yelled to interrupt him. "I wasn't thinking. Ever since my dad's death, I practically stopped thinking about the consequences of my actions." A stream of tears rushed down her sunken cheek and she grew quieter.

After a long pause, wherein, she looked like she began evaluating her entire life, she finally spoke, "I came here because I wanted to make amends. At least that's what I thought. I wanted to offer you the love you gave me. Because you deserve it. But I think I can never do that like you do.

"I think that after my dad, it was only you I could love for real. But in hindsight, I feel like I only used you as a band-aid for my own wounds. Every time I was hurting, I knew you'd be there to take the pain away.

"I don't know what I was really doing, to be honest with you. I went to therapy after we ended things. And my therapist told me that I was just trying really hard to prove to myself that even though my dad chose his bad habits over us and left, there would still be someone who'd love me and wouldn't leave me come what may.

"I wanted that with you. The power to have you whenever I wanted. And in that process, I abused your love.

You see, I am my father's daughter after-all. I screw up every good thing I am given."

She sank on the floor. She didn't sob, she didn't move. She just cried without making a sound.

Dhruv stood in the other corner of the room. Guruji's words flashing in his mind. "People's actions have nothing to do with you and everything to do with them."

"I am sorry," he finally gathered the courage to speak.

"Why are you sorry?" she asked in a feeble voice.

"Because I didn't understand this back when we were together. I didn't see you for all this hurt you were carrying inside. I could have done better to help you navigate these feelings."

"You did everything right, Dhruv. I messed up. Like I always do. I am not sure if I deserve another chance."

"I am sure you deserve another chance, Anisha. All of us do. But not with me. With someone else. And not like this. With so much water under the bridge. But with someone who you can have a fresh start with."

"But I want you, Dhruv. I love you. I do."

"I am not sure what you feel for me is love. It's again your stubbornness to have your way. Besides I can't trust you, Anisha. Love is never enough. Loyalty and integrity matter way more."

The next day Dhruv met Arnav who welcomed his back friend by opening a bottle of whiskey.

Dhruv suddenly felt a slight aversion toward alcohol.

"So how did the soul-searching go?" Arnav asked while pouring him a peg. "On the rocks? Or should I get some healthy ayurvedic concoction?"

Dhruv smirked, "Well, I'd prefer the latter but considering your fine expertise in the former, on the rocks it is."

"Attaboy!" He handed him the glass.

"To ashrams and exes?" Arnav clinked glasses with Dhruv and chuckled at his own joke.

"So how did it go? I can't believe you stayed there for over a week. Apparently, it's the word on campus."

"Wait, why is it the word on campus? I had just told you."

"Well... I told Sneha who ended up discussing it with some of her girlfriends at their girls night after exams," Arnav looked a little embarrassed.

"Dude, this is not fair. Why do you have to tell your girlfriend everything I tell you about my life?"

"She is not my girlfriend."

"Besides the point."

"Yeah. I know. I am sorry. She was really concerned for Vaanya, which is why I told her."

"But you know how these things go. It's all Chinese whispers. Besides, I had informed Vaanya.

"Oh, you did? I am sorry man. I shouldn't have."

"Hmm..."

"Well chuck it. I don't care anymore."

"So, the ashram adventure worked?"

"I am hoping, yes. I mean I do feel more at peace. And more okay with whatever happens."

"Did you talk to Anisha?"

"Yeah. She is apologetic. Explained to me why she did what she did years ago. I think I have more empathy for her now."

"Hmm, I understand. I am glad you got your closure. Besides, I saw you all this time. It was never right for you. I was hoping I was wrong though."

Dhruv nodded along when his phone rang. He was feeling a little light-headed, as he reached across to pick up his phone, his other hand hit the wooden table. With a loud shatter the whiskey glass broke in his hand. Blood oozed out from the crevices of his skin. A small piece of glass was stuck in his palm. Anisha's name flashed on the screen. Dhruv watched it ring as blood kept seeping from his skin.

"I need to talk to you. I am coming over," her text popped on the screen.

"You're only hurting yourself man," Arnav said, looking at his bleeding hand and Anisha's text on his phone screen.

He helped the piece of glass out of his palm and tied a small handkerchief across it to stop the bleeding.

Twenty minutes later, Anisha knocked on the door.

Arnav let her in and showed himself out.

"Don't worry. I am not here to ask you to take me back."

"So, what brings you here?" Dhruv asked.

"I've been up all-night thinking about our conversation from yesterday," she said, and paused to take a deep breath.

"I am leaving tomorrow morning. I've realised my mistake. I just wanted to come and tell you, one last time, how sorry I am, that I didn't appreciate what I had when I had it."

"You're a gem, Dhruv. But you're not mine to keep. I wish you all the happiness in the world," Anisha said, in an affirmative tone.

Chapter 8

Love You Like a Love Song

The night is young and so are we
The music of your voice fills the air around me
I whip up a poem in my head habitually
But I feel the wind change course suddenly

You see I am exhausted of being inspired
So make me your inspiration for once
I have run out of metaphors to dress my love
So let me be your muse tonight

Collect these shattered pieces of me
And weave me into a poem or two
Hold on to me for dear life
And write me down in history
Maybe through a love song or two

—VAANYA

In the microeconomics class Vaanya saw her notebook that Dhruv had borrowed, lying on her usual seat. She opened it to find a note that read,

"I know no apology will be enough. But give me one final chance? I promise to make it up to you. See you at Olive Qutub at 6 p.m. today."

In the evening, as she reached the cafe, a staff member directed her to the backside, where a special table nestled under the glorious shade of the deodar tree, offered a view of the sun setting behind the majestic Qutub Minar. The sky that day was painted in various shades of pink and orange, while the place had a pop of blue and a bohemian decor, coupled with fairy lights, and Vaanya's favourite white lilies. On the other side, a local band was playing live music—instrumental renditions of Frank Sinatra and other traditional pop and jazz tunes.

Feeling confused and angry at his uncertain behaviour, but also mesmerised by what he'd put together, Vaanya tried to centre her mind and soak in the aura of the place, when suddenly Dhruv appeared behind her.

"I know what you're thinking," he smiled and came close to her. She could feel his breath on her neck. "The balls I must have, for pulling a disappearing act like that and then showing up as if nothing happened."

She smiled and rolled her eyes at once. But before she could say anything, he continued, "I am not trying to push anything under the rug, Vaanya. I am aware of what I've put you through. And I am really ashamed of it. I could've handled things better. The past few weeks have been extremely overwhelming. It was a lot for me to deal with. But I know that I should have come to you and talked about it instead of phasing you out. But I simply couldn't gather the courage."

She'd still turned her back on him. He walked over to her in order to close the distance between them. She could feel his hot and moist breath working his way up her neck, toward her earlobe. It prickled her skin and almost sent a shudder down her body. She used all her strength to stay erect, trying to focus on his words, as her entire body ached for his touch.

"Vaanya," he called out. She never liked the sound of her name as much. But coming from his mouth, it sounded like the sacred morning *Azan*.

She turned around to face him.

He was on his knees. Head bowed down in repentance.

"I'm your culprit, Vaanya. I know I've been wrong. And, I've caused you pain. I am here to ask for one last chance. At redemption. A chance to rectify my wrongs."

"Because Vaanya Sharma," he paused and took a deep breath. In one single exhale, like a holy spell, he uttered, "I'm in love with you."

"Dhruv…" she inched closer but something in her resisted.

He accepted her hesitance and took a step back, and continued. "Since the first day I came here. Before I even knew you. I found your poem in the campus gardens. The poem you performed at the open mic that day."

Her eyes widened in disbelief. Her lips parted, trying to form a sentence, but unable to speak anything, she stayed quiet.

"And that poem has seen me through some of the toughest days here. And then, I met you and slowly got to know you. It felt like everything was falling into place. And finally, when I saw you at that open mic, performing the same poem in all your glory, I was convinced, it was you. All that my life was leading up to.

"I love you, Vaanya. You don't even know what you've done for me. You've reshaped my perceptions. Through you, I've been able to explore parts of myself that I didn't even know existed. To put it simply, you've pushed me to be a better person. You're all that my heart was yearning for.

"And I know now, without a doubt that I was meant to find my way to you. In this life and all alternate realities that exist.

"You're my soulmate, my best-friend, my everything."

She knelt on the ground next to him and leaned forward. His lips met with hers, and their tongues conveyed their love in an act of soft rebellion.

As the sky grew darker, they settled in a cosy spot under the willow tree with some wine. Dhruv explained to her everything that had been happening in his life for the past few weeks—the confrontation with Anisha, the closure he didn't know he needed, and his trip to the ashram in the Himalayas. He also told her all about Guruji's teachings, and his meditation experience that brought about an awakening that he was deeply longing for.

"The right things have a way of finding us at the right time," Vaanya said and rested her head on his shoulders.

"I couldn't agree more," he said and squeezed her hand tight, as they sat there late into the night. The sound of his favourite song blasting through the earphones, one cord of which was plugged into his right ear and the other cord in her left ear.

"This song has been my constant companion through so many ups and downs in the past year. I always thought that I'll listen to this with my girl, when I fall in love again," he said.

"Why did you stop singing and song writing, Dhruv?" Vaanya asked suddenly.

"I don't know," he replied instantly.

"Was it because of Anisha?" she added.

"No," he paused and said, "Maybe. But I do miss it."

"What about it do you miss exactly?"

"Everything. But mostly the high of creating."

"It is unparalleled right?"

"Yes. It is."

"I feel the same when I write poetry. And anyone who has felt this knows how precious it is."

"I know where you're coming from. But you know what really makes me wonder?"

"What?"

"How there's a song or a poem for everything! It's as if every human emotion has been captured in songs, poems, or novels etc. "There's all this art in the world to remind our lonely hearts that we're not alone in this journey. There's someone else out there in the world who understands exactly what we're going through."

The next day Vaanya woke up feeling giddy. It had only been ten hours since she saw him, but she still felt the urge to wake up and look at his face and hear her name coming out of his mouth. She caught herself smiling like a fool in the mirror, as she brushed her teeth to get ready for class. To be able to see him was suddenly her only motivation to get to the painstaking morning lectures.

In the class, they stole glances at each other, and as soon as the lecture ended, Dhruv walked up to her and handed her a note.

"Have to get to statistical analysis, sorry! But we're going out tonight. And I've got a surprise for you," he whispered in her ear and she felt a thousand butterflies dance in her stomach as his hand brushed her skin.

Be ready to get serenaded tonight. Turns out, your wish is my command. The note read.

Sneha didn't miss this little exchange between Dhruv and Vaanya, and caught her in the library later in the day.

"So, your boy-toy is back from his ashram adventure?"

"I am trying to study, Sneha!"

"I am not. Come on. Give me some gossip. What's the latest with you two? I saw he handed you a note in class this morning. What are you guys? Twelve?"

Vaanya ignored her remarks, and tried to concentrate on her books.

"Fine. Don't come running to me for help if he pulls off another one of his acts."

"He won't anymore," she replied, without looking away.

"Oh really? Wait, have you guys…?"

"Yeah."

"What? So, is he your boyfriend now? What about the other girl?"

Vaanya rolled her eyes and smiled a shy reluctant smile.

"Oh wow. You've done it. You've landed the whale."

"It's not like that ya, Sneha."

"Then what? He is all whole and healed, is it? After his little soul cleansing in the mountains?" Sneha laughed at her own witty remarks.

"No. We talked and discussed everything that happened over the last few weeks and I understood what he was going through. And like mature adults, we've decided to put it behind us and give this a real chance."

"Damn. Not bad, Vaanya Sharma. Proud of you. No matter what, he is quite the catch. But he better not fuck up this time. I swear I'll burn him to ashes if I see you holed up in your room crying your eyes out over him again. No matter how hot he is."

"Thanks Sneha! I truly appreciate you being there for me during this whole thing. It means so much. I can't thank you enough."

"Shut up! Save this emo drama for him. What are besties for? Besides, if you really want to return the favour, set me up with Arnav? He seems pretty great. Imagine the double dates we could go on!" She chuckled. "No pressure though."

"Ah, someone has the hots for Arnav. Nice. Six-two, much less drama. Good choice."

"I know right. We've been doing case studies together. It's hot."

"Ahh, nerd alert."

"Shut up. You don't say. You and Dhruv are always in the library. We're all nerds here."

"Well, that's true. But let me check with Dhruv, I think Arnav has been single forever."

"Is that a red-flag?"

"Umm less of a red-flag than having his ex-girlfriend appear in the middle of your brand-new relationship. But if I survived that, trust me, you're golden."

"I wonder if he's straight."

"Why?"

"Because I've been dropping hints and they seem to be flying right over his head."

"Hmm..."

"Besides, who can resist this?" She pointed to herself with a voluptuous expression.

"Fair point." Vaanya laughed. "I'll get to the bottom of this. Don't worry. I've got you. Mission 'finding Arnav's sexuality'."

"Ah, finally the best friend I deserved. Thank you, God!" Sneha giggled and hugged Vaanya.

Later in the evening, Vaanya got ready for their date. She wore a fuschia pink dress and silver heels to go along with it. Dhruv picked her up from the hostel gate.

A bouquet of white lilies rested on the passenger seat.

"Aww thankyou," she smiled and picked it up. "Is this the surprise?"

"Umm. No. Have some faith in your boy, I can do better."

"Now I have placed all my faith in you. So, tell me. Where are we going? And what's the surprise?"

"Relax, relax. Let us get there first," he smiled and planted a soft kiss on her hand.

"Okay give me a hint."

"Umm. No."

"Dhruv."

"What? I thought patience was one of your many virtues."

"You're enjoying this, aren't you?"

"I am. I truly am. This is a brand-new Vaanya. Chirpy and bubbling with excitement. Why had you hidden her from me?"

"Maybe she was waiting for you to get your act together."

"Ah. I see, patience has its fruits."

As they reached the place, Dhruv got out and held open the door for her and helped her step out of the car.

"Is this the surprise?"

"Vaanya," he smirked and rolled his eyes. She smiled at his reaction, and felt a strange sense of satisfaction seeing the effect she had on him.

"We're almost there," he grabbed her hand and they walked in the direction of a charming stonework cottage. Vaanya was enthralled by the beauty of the place. Tasteful interiors, plush linens, and soft lightning, it looked like an architect's dream. The master bedroom had a floor to ceiling library with a plethora of books on all subjects. The other wall was converted into a screen with a projector and Vaanya's favourite movie—*Notting Hill*, played on it. On the bed lay a matching set of pyjamas and a custom cushion with their names on it.

"This is like a dream come true! I could live here," she cried in joy and looked for Dhruv.

She heard a guitar strum from the kitchen and hurried to find him.

"Remember. You asked me to write you a song," Dhruv was sitting on the high chair of the kitchen counter with his guitar in hand.

"Oh my God. You did?"

"How could I not?"

He said and started playing his original composition.

Baby, tell me it's not a dream
Tell me I'm yours
And you are mine
I'll love you till this earth keeps spinning'
around the sun
Cuz baby, you are my sun and my moon and
all my stars
You're my gravity, you tether me,
You're the centre of my universe

For you are all I'll ever need
Cause baby, I can't believe
Baby, you're my only relief

You're the air that I breathe
So meet me at our spot tonight
Take my hand and hold me tight
I'll steady you, you'll steady me

On these cold nights my heart aches
Baby, you're the warmth I'll ever need
Baby, you're the sweetness in my life

You take my pain away with your smile
When your fingers slip in mine
I live a little again after all this time

So Baby, tell me it's not a dream
Tell me I'm yours
And you are mine
I'll love you till this earth keeps spinning'
around the sun
Cause baby, you are my sun and my moon and
all my stars
You're my gravity, you tether me
You're the centre of my universe

For you are all I'll ever need
Cause baby, I can't believe
Baby, you're my only relief.

After the date-night at the Airbnb, Dhruv and Vaanya began spending more nights together.

"Being with you feels as easy as breathing," he said to her the night before his birthday, as they lay in bed after making love, tucked under the sheets.

"Isn't that how it's supposed to feel?" she asked, turning to face him.

"Ideally, yeah. I guess. But I didn't know a relationship was supposed to feel this effortless and right."

"Hmm. It wasn't like this with Anisha?"

"No. It was not this effortless. There was too much uncertainty. The energy was confusing. Something always felt off. But this feels right. It feels simple and blissful..."

"Hmm..."

"You're very monosyllabic. What's up?" he asked, looking at her, as she turned away.

"Nothing," she replied looking at the ceiling.

"Tell me. What's going on in that beautiful mind of yours? I don't want to decipher it in another poem," he chuckled.

She smiled and said, "It's funny how you have something to compare this with. And I don't."

"Is that a bad thing?" He thought out loud.

"Not really. I don't know. But I sometimes feel like I am out of depth here."

"Hmm. Can I do something to make it better?" he asked, genuinely.

"No. You're already doing so much. Even though you're my first, I know for a fact I lucked out."

"Not more than me."

She laughed, "Is it a competition?"

"I don't know," he smiled.

"Well, if it is one. We're both winning," her eyes gleamed.

"That we are!"

"Okay tell me something."

"Hmm?"

"What's the deal with Arnav?"

"What?"

"Is he dating? Does he like someone? Is he even into girls or he swings the other way?"

"What kind of pillow talk is this?"

"The real kind. Sneha likes him, but he is not picking on any of her hints. And I remember you had said that he's been single forever."

"Yeah, he has been single forever because he is not the relationship kind of guy. He does sleep around quite a bit. Although I don't support all that."

"Hmm…"

"You're judging him, right?"

"No. Why do you say that? Who am I to judge? I am just looking out for my friend."

"I can tell it from your face. It's written all over it. His promiscuous choices do not meet the standards of Vaanya Sharma."

"Well, you said it. Besides, I can have an opinion on the guy my best friend is interested in?"

"Well."

"Sneha has been there for me when you were absconding. She is really important to me. So please don't make that face."

"I am not making any face. I am glad you and Sneha are tight. I also need some time away from you," he cracked.

"Shut up. Get out of my room. Enjoy your time away from me," she laughed and threw a pillow on his head. He scooched in and pulled her closer to steal a kiss.

Weeks turned into months, and the placement season was knocking on the door. The pressure was surmounting. After classes all morning, they spent most of the day solving case studies and preparing for interviews, taking only a few breaks to go grab some food and tea at the *tapri*.

"This coffee is reviving my soul right now. I so needed a break," Vaanya said, holding the hot paper-cup in her hands.

"You work too hard. You need to learn to relax," he said, taking out the lighter from his back pocket. Just when he began lighting the cigarette, he noticed her staring down at him with a straight face.

"What?" He grunted.

She looked at him with an expression of dismay like a mother who is disappointed in her son for disobeying the rules of the house again.

"I haven't smoked in two months. I deserve one smoke break now," he pleaded, while lighting the cigarette.

She grew quiet and turned her gaze away.

"Okay fine," he gave in. "You win!" He dropped the cigarette and crushed it with the tip of his shoe.

"You look so sweet on the outside. Nobody can tell how sinister you really are," he said. She smiled at his remark and held his hand, interlocking her fingers in the space between his.

They sat on the side-walk, sipping turn by turn from a single paper cup while watching the sun set behind the horizon.

"This gorgeous sunset is definitely better than nicotine. Trust me."

"Hmm..."

"What?"

"Thankyou."

"Why?"

"For just being there. And keeping me together. You tame me."

She held his hand and squeezed it tight.

"I can't believe two years at campus are almost ending. It feels like I met you yesterday."

"It's surreal how time flies," she said, stroking his hand. "I am worried about placements."

"You'll do great. I have faith in you."

"What if I don't get a good job?"

"Well, in that case, you can be a stay-at-home wife, while I rock at my terrific job," he laughed and pulled her closer in a hug as her mouth turned into an angry pout and she began hitting him friskily.

Dhruv's birthday fell between the last exam and the placement season. They had been studying together the night before, and he had slipped into a nap before midnight.

"Happy birthday, Dhruv," Vaanya whispered in his ears to nudge him out of sleep, at sharp twelve. He woke up and rubbed his eyes in astonishment to see the whole room decorated in fairy lights and helium balloons.

"Oh my god, when did you do this?" He stared in disbelief.

"While you were asleep."

"I can't believe this!" He flashed her a teary smile.

And immediately, the loud sound of 'Happy Birthday' by Stevie Wonder filled the room. He laughed, and said, "You're amazing!"

She pulled out a bottle of tequila and screamed, "Birthday shots!"

He grimaced at her shrill voice and smiled at how excited she was for his birthday.

"We don't have shot glasses," he pointed out.

"Oops, I forgot." She made a puppy face.

They drank straight out of the bottle.

"Come on, get up, we're dancing it out!"

"What?"

"Get up, you sloth!" she wailed, half-drunk and pulled him out of bed.

He grabbed her close to him as they danced wildly. They made a silly drunk dancing video in which Dhruv picked her up, and she sat on his shoulders, throwing her hands up in the air and singing loudly.

She gifted him a photo-book with tiny cut-outs of their photographs together, and some poems that she had written for him.

She read out one of those poems for him,

"You made my body your temple
You slowly lit the candles of love
In the dim corners
Of my calloused consciousness
And fragnated the pathways of my prosaic past

You worshiped at the altar of my heart
Chanting our memories like offering prayers
At the break of dawn
And singing lullabies at the fall of night
Like a hymn echoing
In the empty hallways of my bones

And now your name is etched
On the walls of my soul
Like the holy spell
Scripted over the shrine
You made my birthmarks your prayer-bed
And whispered hallelujah in my ears

Hallelujah to this body
Hallelujah to the pain
Hallelujah to this grace
Hallelujah to you

You made my body your temple
I made you my religion."

"I love you so much," Dhruv said with moist eyes, and pulled her close in a bone-crushing hug.

"You have to stop being so nice. I'm not used to it," he laughed a teary half-laugh.

"Shush, make a wish," she said, bringing out a delicious blueberry cheesecake from the fridge, with a tiny candle on top of it. Dhruv blew the candle and kissed her on the lips.

"Thank you. I don't deserve this."

"Ah, stop talking and feed me the cake, Dhruv! Pay me for my hard work."

He laughed and fed her a slice.

"Although I have better ideas to pay you back," he smirked and whisked off some frosting with his finger and applied it on Vaanya's bare neck.

"What are you doing?" she rolled her eyes and flashed a shy smile. Knowing fully well what he was up to, she curled her arm around his neck and drew him closer. He bent over, and his tongue swirled around on the tender skin of her neck to lick away the frosting. She put some of it on his face and began eating it off his jaw. "The cake never tasted better," she sighed, as he continued to kiss her.

"Happy birthday baby," she moaned, unbuttoning him.

Chapter 9

Can't Take My Eyes Off You

Had we known
That the last time we pulled away
From each other's arms
Would turn out to be like the parting
Of a dried leaf from the willow tree
On a dreary autumn afternoon
Would we have tried and wrapped
Our dangling arms around each other
A little while longer?

—VAANYA

The exam season came and went by like a speeding train, and placements were starting in a day's time.

"Dhruv," she said, clutching onto his arm.

"Hmm?"

"What if we end up in different cities?"

"I don't know. We'll cross that bridge when it comes."

"It's almost here, Dhruv. Why don't you want to talk about it?"

"Because talking about it makes it real."

She said nothing and held his arm tighter.

The next day, Dhruv got placed at the topmost investment bank that visited campus. Vaanya, on the other hand, was waiting to hear from a few companies. On the final day of placements, a leading FMCG company was visiting to hire for a few brand marketing and operations roles. After rigorous rounds of tests, group discussion, and case studies, it was time for the final interview round.

Dressed in a coral blue blouse and a black pencil skirt, hair neatly tied in a slick ponytail, Vaanya looked absolutely interview ready.

"Go get 'em, love!" Dhruv held her hand and looked her in the eye, as her name was announced.

He hid his nervousness behind his carefree smile, but Vaanya could see the worry in his eyes. At that moment, she knew that irrespective of the interview result, she was already a winner, and she walked into the interview room gracefully.

Dhruv paced nervously down the hall, waiting for her. Half an hour later, she emerged from the room looking more poised than ever.

"How did it go?" He rushed toward her.

"It was good."

"Was it? Thank God. Come, let's get you out of here!"

From the placement cell, they went to the cafeteria to pick some coffee and Maggi and headed towards the campus gardens, where they sat on a bench, quietly sipping coffee and sharing spoonfuls of Maggi. The cooing of the birds kept them company.

This silence was soon interrupted by Sneha's voice, Vaanya, the selected candidates' list is out," she yelled from a distance. Her voice echoed in the lawns.

Vaanya froze. Dhruv squeezed her hand, and opened the portal on his phone to check the list which read the names of the selected candidates:

Ishan Maheshwari
Rohit Sen
Anadi Mehta
Vaanya Sharma

"I told you, you'd make it!' Dhruv pulled her in a tight hug.

Vaanya was still muddled.

"I am so proud of you," he whispered softly in her ears. "These lawns are definitely lucky for us."

She closed her eyes, trying to process what had just happened. She was placed in the company of her choice in a role she aspired for. But was the struggle finally over?

"They've not revealed the location yet," Vaanya murmured, pulling away from the hug.

Arnav and Sneha both got placed in product roles of Bangalore-based tech startups.

"Bangalore it is?" Arnav came up to Sneha who was sitting by herself, eating a burger and scrolling something on her phone.

"Yes! You too?"

"Yeah. Apparently!"

"Bangalore is nice. The tech scene is better. And it will be a good relief from Delhi's weather."

"Yeah. I think so. But, I am going to miss Delhi! You can take a Delhi-ite out of Delhi, but not the other way round."

She laughed at his remark, and looked at his facial expression suddenly change into a slightly nervous smile.

"What happened? The placements are over. Why do you look so tense now?"

"Umm... Do you want to take a walk?" he suggested, hands tucked in his pockets.

"Okay" she said and got up.

"What's up?" she said after a while of silence, as they began crossing main areas of the campus to reach secluded corners with no people around.

"Look! I don't know how to do this! So, let me just get it out. Today in the placement cell, when I thought about where we'd all end up, the thought of being in a different city from you, not having you and your stupid jokes, and your self-amusing drama around, made me really sad."

Sneha looked at him, he was barely able to meet her gaze.

"Are you embarrassed to admit that you like me?" She smiled.

"Don't make this harder than it already is, okay?"

"I will. As I please."

"You're evil!" He smirked.

She laughed.

"Look I am not the relationship kinda guy. And I don't know what kind of a boyfriend I will be. But with you, I want to try."

"Did Dhruv say something to you?"

"No this is all me. This is not Dhruv talking!"

"Tell me!"

"Okay he might have nudged me into realising what I should have, long ago."

"And that is?"

"That I like you."

"How hard is it for you to say that!"

"Excruciatingly hard. Now spare me? Say that you like me back?"

She looked at him for a brief moment, and then said, "When was the last you said to a girl that you liked her?"

"Ugh, I don't know in ninth standard?" he said with a furrowed brow, looking visibly irritated. "But why?"

"How did that turn out?"

"Horribly. She laughed at me in the school corridors for a month. And my friends made fun of me for the entire year. Okay? Are you happy now?"

"Very!"

"God! You're a handful!"

"I am! So, are you ready to put up with this?"

"I am. I have a feeling it'll be fun!"

She smiled and elevated on her toes to kiss him. He grabbed her waist and kissed her back fiercely.

While the air of uncertainty caused them a bellyache, Dhruv and Vaanya decided to postpone the worrying for a little while.

"We can't just keep thinking of the next course of action. We need to celebrate now," Dhruv said. "It's the end of an era. And the beginning of another one."

In the evening, the entire batch got ready to party the night away. Vaanya was wearing a sleek, white sequin dress. She paired it up with a pair of silver pumps, minimal make-up, and left her hair open. But the thing that immediately caught Dhruv's attention was the silver-gold Swarovski pendant around her neck.

"The pendant never looked better," he smiled and kissed her on the cheek. "I gifted it to you months ago. How come you never wore it before?"

"I don't know. I think I was never ready for it."

"So now you are?"

"You bet," she leaned and kissed him on the lips.

As they reached the club, Arnav pulled them in for shots. All the gentlemen looked suave in their blazers and girls looked stunning in low-cut dresses and high-heels. A couple of drinks later, Vaanya was slightly tipsy.

The whole batch was drinking and dancing like maniacs, celebrating their freedom and achievements. Sneha dragged Vaanya on the dance floor, who was shy in the beginning but soon after Sneha forced a tequila shot down her throat, Vaanya became unhinged. Dhruv watched her from over the bar, as she shut her eyes close, stretched her arms above and swayed freely with the beat.

As the music played, Dhruv watched Vaanya lose herself in the rhythm, moving with a fluid grace that he had never seen before. He couldn't help but admire the way her body moved, her dress clinging to her curves with each motion. Slowly, he made his way over to her and wrapped his arms around her waist, drawing her close. Vaanya, startled at first, quickly recognised Dhruv and relaxed into his embrace. As he kissed her forehead, she felt a sense of warmth and safety wash over her, and she clung to him like a child. Together, they danced the night away, with Frankie Valli's 'Can't Take My Eyes Off You' playing softly in the background. Dhruv felt a surge of happiness seeing Vaanya so carefree, that he held her tightly, feeling even more protective of her when she was drunk. Vaanya rested her head on Dhruv's chest, feeling secure in his sturdy arms, and they slow-danced, humming along with the song.

"I love your voice," Dhruv whispered closely, tingling her ears with his hot breath.

She smiled and lifted her face from his chest to look at him directly. She pouted her lips and said, "Just my voice?"

He spun her around and picked her up in his arms. "Let me show you what else."

They left the dance floor and slipped into the parking lot.

In the backseat of Dhruv's car, Vaanya sat in his lap and played with his beard, as he kissed her supple lips with invigorating passion. He slid the strap of her dress down her shoulder with one hand and unhooked her bra with the other, all in one clean, swift move. The tingling sensation of his breath on her warm skin kept growing, as he moved effortlessly from her soft lips to the steep valley of her chest. Her body was feeling warmer and nimble with every minute. Their tongues played with each other, as he continued kissing and feeling her, before gently sliding his fingers inside of her and making her writhe over him in pleasure, as though playing a fingerstyle tune on his favourite electric guitar. She moaned his name like a divine spell. Breasts pressed against his chest, legs wrapped around his torso, her entire body shuddered with desire. Hands wrapped around his neck, she sucked on his ear lobe to not scream in the dark and quiet parking lot.

The final days at campus slipped away quickly. Vaanya was anxiously waiting for a response from her company, unsure of where her career would take her. Meanwhile, Dhruv was starting his stint at his company's Mumbai office next month and secretly hoped that fate would bring Vaanya there too.

On the last day at campus, Vaanya was busy packing to leave for home. Dhruv had already shifted his stuff yesterday, so he was helping her sort her things out when her phone suddenly chimed. She picked it up and announced that it was an email from her company.

Dhruv held her hand, "We've got this."

She licked her lips and clicked on the notification bar. The email popped open:

'Dear Vaanya Sharma,

Hope this email finds you well. We are thrilled to welcome you to our team at the Gurgaon office from the 10th of June...'

She looked at him with a blank stare and handed him the phone. Dhruv stood there, staring at the screen.

Chapter 10

Love In the Dark

Love is so much more powerful than fear
But most of us are helpless lost souls
In search of love
A pair of arms we can call home
And maybe that's why we hide
Behind the veil of fear
Until we finally become capable of love

Will these words be my redemption?
Or will I keep writing a hundred something songs
Until I finally smell liberation
In the draining ink of my pen."

—Dhruv

"I'll talk to you later. I have a headache."

"Let me order you your favourite ice cream? You'll feel better."

"No. I'll just go to sleep. I had a long day."

"Okay. But stay with me for five more minutes?"

"Okay"

Silence followed for a few minutes before Dhruv finally said, "Vaanya..."

"Hmm?" she replied in a muddled voice.

"I love you."

"I know," she hung up and sank into the soft folds of her bed, squeezing her eyes shut. Her mind wandered off to the last time she had seen him. Six months ago, at the Delhi airport. They got off at Terminal two. He collected his luggage and dumped it into the trolley.

"Here, take this! It'll protect you from all evil and take care of you when I am not around," she said, pulling out a small idol of *Ganpati Bappa* as a parting gift.

Dhruv took it with a heavy heart and planted a gentle kiss on her forehead. She couldn't hold it any longer and broke into tears. He pulled her in a big hug and gently caressed her hair. He could feel his tee-shirt getting moist from her tears, and his heart began racing.

Her body trembled as he pulled away, getting ready to leave. She realised how much she had begun to love him. He saw it in her eyes, and kissed her hands profusely, as the moments of their togetherness slipped away like fine sand.

She stood at the gate with tears in her eyes, waving at him as he slowly disappeared into the crowd of endless people. And just like that, her love flew away to a different city.

It had been six months since then, and life had changed dramatically for both Dhruv and Vaanya. Starting a new job and settling in a new city and new routine was hard as it is, and not having each other by their side made matters even worse.

Mumbai was completely new to Dhruv. Most of his friends were either in Delhi or Bangalore. But while he was staying at the company accommodation during the first month of his stint, he got a call from Rohan who had just moved to Mumbai on a new job, so they decided to rent a 2BHK flat together.

Vaanya, on the other hand, took up a studio apartment, a ten-minute drive from her office. She didn't have many friends in Gurgaon, but she didn't mind living alone. Besides, her family lived a two-hour drive away in Delhi and she visited them often. But coming home to an empty apartment night after night left her feeling lonely.

For the first couple of months, they had a nice routine going. Vaanya called Dhruv every morning to wake him up. They started their day with each other's sweet morning voice and had breakfast together over video call. After which they continued to share updates of their day over text through messages and photos.

One time, Vaanya was having a bad day at work. She had spilled coffee over her brand-new top, then lost some crucial work as she missed saving some files, and in the end, she had an argument with her boss.

"Can it get any worse?" She texted Dhruv with a washroom selfie of her annoyed expression that also captured the big coffee stain on her white satin top.

"Well, the good news is, it can only get better from here," he replied to her.

As soon as she came home, she received a surprise delivery of her favourite white lilies.

The card on the bouquet read:

It's just a bad day. Not a bad life.

Love,

Dhruv.

"As long as I have you," she replied to him along with a photo of her smiling tooth to tooth, holding the bouquet. Half an hour later arrived her favourite pizza, some coffee, and a cheesecake. And a text from him that read:

> "Your comfort food to make up for the absence of your comfort person. The pizza is a big hug from me. The coffee, a pat on the back for getting through a crappy day like a boss. And the cheesecake is a sweet indulgence. Imagine all of me, devouring all of you."

"Could I love you anymore? I must have done something right in my past lives, to have you in this one," she replied.

Their night-time ritual included spending hours on phone calls and video chats, coping with the distance by trying to be with each other virtually as much as possible. But after a few months, seeing each other over a screen became less exciting as they settled into their new lives. As work piled up and responsibilities took over, physical distance soon crept into emotional intimacy.

With clashing schedules and hectic days, video calls became fewer in number. In a rush to get to work in time, Vaanya missed calling him in the morning. At night, Dhruv got busy with deadlines and social engagements, forgetting to check on her before she'd already be in bed.

In the mornings she'd wake up to his texts that read:

> 'Hi babe! Sorry I couldn't call you today. Was neck deep in work and then Rohan called some people over so we were playing snooker and drinking beer. Will call you tonight for sure. Love you.'

And when his call didn't come the following night either, she stuffed her mouth and feelings with spoonfuls of chocolate chip ice cream while binging on another rom-com before passing out on her couch.

With October slowly approaching, the days grew shorter and the leaves began to turn brown. Vaanya began spending more time with herself, going on long walks, practicing yoga and meditation and visiting coffee shops on her own with her journal and a book to read. She loved the transformative power of the fall season. The subtle signs of winter's arrival covered everything in a bittersweet nostalgia and she felt a strange hope fill her veins. As the dried leaves fell from old trees adorned the sidewalks, it looked like a wistful golden-brown festival celebrating the gradual process of change. The month also marked their two-year anniversary and Vaanya thought this would be the perfect opportunity to rekindle the spark.

But for Dhruv, October posed unforeseen challenges. A small project that he performed pretty well at, transpired into critical staffing at Hyderabad for a month. His days were filled with meetings, and nights with crunching numbers. Downing numerous cups of black coffee a day, he stayed glued to his laptop forgetting to eat or sleep.

'Made Bhindi and rajma chawal today. Missed you so much. Did you eat dinner? Please don't skip meals, Dhruv. Call me back when you see this.'

He opened his phone to Vaanya's text and a picture of bhindi and rajma chawal that she had cooked.

When he called her back at one in the night, she was already asleep. So, he left her a text.

'Looks great. But not better than my cute lil' rajma chawal chef. I'd skipped dinner today, I wasn't feeling up to it. But this scrumptious looking meal has made me hungry now. Will probably order some room service before going to bed. Sorry to have missed your calls. This project is crazy. The entire team has been pulling all-nighters for a week. Besides, year-end reviews are around the corner and I am in the race for a fast-track. So gotta put in the work for now. But I'll call you in the morning, for sure. So sorry babe. Love you so much. Thanks for putting up with me. I swear I'll make it up to you soon.'

The next day, Vaanya kept checking her phone every ten minutes hoping for a call or text from Dhruv. Every time her phone rang, her heart skipped a beat, and she reached immediately to pick it up in case she missed a call from him. But every time it was a work call, or a call from her mother. In the evening she tried reaching him but his number seemed busy. Fighting the urge to keep trying his number until it would be reachable again, a teardrop trickled down her cheek. She stuffed her phone in the bedside drawer and went into the kitchen to chop, dice, and fry things.

Recently, Vaanya had found joy in cooking. Spending time alone in the kitchen, listening to a nice playlist or a podcast, while preparing a whole meal felt therapeutic. Playing around with different ingredients to create a complete meal from scratch. And the best thing about it was, that it took her mind away from everything worrying her as she was able to focus on the present moment, losing herself in aromas and textures of different spices and condiments.

Hoping to make a nice pasta dish tonight, she started chopping some onions and peppers when she suddenly heard the doorbell ring. Wiping her hands with a washcloth, she walked briskly toward the door.

"Surprise!" Mira exclaimed and threw her arms around Vaanya.

"What are you doing here?" Vaanya asked wide-eyed, looking at her suitcase trolley which she dragged inside the house.

Mira shuffled for something in her hand-bag for a second as Vaanya continued to look at her cluelessly.

"We're going on a trip!" She announced retrieving two tickets from Delhi to Goa from her tan Lavie handbag.

"What?" Vaanya's mouth fell. "You didn't even tell me."

"Then it wouldn't have been a surprise, would it?"

"Mira!" Vaanya's lips parted.

"Come on Didi! It's just for the weekend, so you can't even bring up the excuse about taking leaves from work. You know you need this. We get that you've always been a homebody but you've stopped stepping out of the house recently. This is getting unhealthy! Now come on pack your bags, we have to be at the airport in two hours. Quick!"

"Damn, when did you become so bossy?" Vaanya smiled as Mira went to her bedroom and started ripping apart her closet to pack her bags for their girls' trip.

Later that night they flew to Goa and checked into a stunning boutique property with a remarkable sea view. Mira had made all the reservations and planned their itineraries rigorously.

"So, what's the order of business?" Vaanya asked, buttering her toast at breakfast the next morning.

"Just trust me!" Mira winked, and whisked Vaanya off to a charming art gallery in a hidden lane.

"This is exquisite!" Vaanya said, admiring the paintings. After which they visited the Se Cathedral church before stopping for a late lunch at a chic cafe overlooking the sea.

She posted a photo of their delicious lunch spread containing mimosas, a fat burger, some fries, and a large bowl of spaghetti, against the background of the ocean, on Instagram. In about half an hour, Dhruv viewed her story and immediately replied, "You're in Goa?"

"Apparently, I am." She picked her phone and typed out the text.

"When? With who?" His reply arrived instantaneously.

"With my new boyfriend," she wrote back.

"Bad Joke," his reply felt oddly satisfying to her.

"Just like the one you're pulling on me since the past few days!" she continued their banter.

"I've not had time to breathe, babe. I am really sorry. I'll try to call as soon as I can," he wrote.

Vaanya stared at the screen for a moment before typing a huge text, only to erase it and hit send with, "Cool."

"Did I mention the no phones policy!" Mira said, snatching Vaanya's phone and shoving it in her purse.

"Fine, but you don't dare post your holiday spam on Instagram now!" Vaanya muttered.

"Deal!" Mira grinned.

In the evening, they caught the sunset at the infamous Agonda beach, as they walked leisurely across the shore. The sea breeze blew against the ocean, messing up their hair that they had spent forty minutes straightening in the morning. But the feeling of wind in their hair and sand in their toes was worth it. The sound of waves hitting the rocks and made it feel like time had slowed down a little was exactly the feeling they missed amid their fast-paced lives back in the city. Vaanya was a little light-headed after a few pints of bcer.

"I don't remember feeling this relaxed in a long time," Vaanya said, looking at the vastness of the ocean in front of them.

"There's something about being near water. It always helps," Mira replied.

"Yeah.

"Remember when we last came to Goa with Mom and Dad?" Mira said.

"Yeah. One of our worst fights ever, right?"

"Yeah. I mean you were not wrong to be mad at me. I had sneaked off to a stupid party in the middle of the night and then I came back completely wasted."

"And I had to sneak you back in our BnB without Mom and Dad knowing. I was so angry, I gave you such an earful about being responsible."

"'*I am sick of covering for you and always being the responsible daughter because you won't stop acting like a selfish, irresponsible, rebellious teenager!*' These were your exact words," Mira chuckled.

Vaanya looked embarrassed. "I am sorry. I didn't mean all that."

"It's okay if you did. I think I needed that to get my act together. Anyway, I know Mum would always put it on you, to try and parent me."

"But hey you turned out fine, so I can take some credit."

"All yours!" Mira smiled. "But you know what I really properly remember from that night?"

"What?"

"That despite our terrible fight, you still held my hair above the toilet when I threw up for hours."

"Yeah. I was mad at you. I didn't stop loving you," Vaanya said without thinking.

"But Didi?"

"Hmm?"

"I take back what I said to you the next day."

Vaanya kept looking at the large waves crashing at their feet, as Mira said, "That you blame the people around you for your own unhappiness."

"It might be somewhat true," Vaanya said after a small pause, without meeting her sister's gaze. "I think I sometimes feel so exhausted trying to be perfect and pleasing everyone around me."

"No matter what you do, you can't make everyone around you happy. You need to choose your happiness first."

"Yeah."

"Besides, perfection is overrated. People who love you will love you in all your imperfect glory. And if they can't, they don't deserve your love."

"Yeah. I know you're right. And I think I do know this in theory. But applying this in real life is sometimes so tricky. It feels as if we're all running this race that has no rules and no finish line."

"And in this mindless race, running around like headless chickens, we forget to just live."

"Yeah. You know, I read this somewhere. We're called human beings and not 'human doings', for a reason. We forget that we're simply allowed to just be, instead of continuously do things and derive our self-worth from the amount of work we can get done in a given amount of time."

"Yeah. I sometimes think how we don't even realise when this starts. It's all so unconscious. We just wake up one day and we're a part of this race, right?"

"It starts when you enter school and you're told to get good grades so you get into a good college, and then you'll be happy. But once you enter college you realise you need to continue working your ass off so you get a good job, and then you'll finally be done. Happy, loved, accepted in society. But then when you enter your first job, all those illusions also come crashing down and you realise you were always fed lies for breakfast. This was never meant to end. It's like being on a carousel that never stops turning."

"Which is exactly why we need to stop thinking about what's next and just live in the moment. They say the past and the future are only versions of the present moment, which is the only absolute truth."

"Come to think of it. It's actually true."

"Yeah. All we really have is the now."

"Yeah," Vaanya said, staring into the red sun merging with the boundless sea.

"When did you become so wise?" She smiled and looked at her little sister who was suddenly not so little anymore.

At night, post dinner, despite Vaanya's reluctance, Mira dragged her to a few nightclubs to check out the party scene where she surprisingly met an old friend.

"Mira!" They heard a familiar voice coming from a distance. As she turned around, a short girl in an electric blue bodycon dress was walking toward her.

"Shikha!" Mira went to her and they exchanged a small side hug.

"I haven't seen you since school! How are you?" Shikha looked genuinely happy to see her.

"I've been good! How've you been?" Mira replied.

"Pretty good! So, what are you doing here?" Shikha asked.

"Oh, I am here on a weekend trip with my sister," she pointed at Vaanya. "What about you?"

"I am here to celebrate a friend's birthday. You want to come say hi?" She asked with a bright smile plastered over her face and wide eyes waiting for a response.

Mira looked at Vaanya uncomfortably hoping for an answer. Both Shikha and Mira were looking at Vaanya at this point, who tried to muster the courage to say NO, but somehow the corner of her mouth turned into a polite half-repressed smile and she said, "Sure! Let's go!"

"Meet Mayank, Mahek, and Priya!" Shikha made the introductions.

Vaanya missed Dhruv and kept looking at her phone, hoping for a text or call from him. After some forced small talk across the table, a round of tequila shots was ordered and Vaanya downed three of them, assuming that being drunk will perhaps help her get through this unexpected social situation. But in half an hour, the awkward conversations were replaced with endless laughter and promises to meet each other back in their own cities. At some point they exchanged Instagram IDs. Mayank tagged Vaanya and Mira in an Instagram story which was a very cosy and slightly blurry picture of the entire group. He had captioned it, *'To blurry nights and gaining friends for life'* and added three heart emojis after it. Everyone looked pretty drunk, smiling obliviously from tooth to tooth. Mayank's hand was carelessly but quite comfortably wrapped around Vaanya's shoulder and he was looking at her in a rather adoring manner. Mira happened to re-share the story in a state of sheer drunkenness, failing to note the minute details.

After some dancing and another round of shots, Vaanya excused herself and went to the restroom. As she came out after a few minutes, she saw Mayank waiting for her with a bottle of water.

"You okay?" he asked, offering her the water.

"Yeah. I am good," she said and refused it. But he kept standing in her way.

For the first time in the night, she noticed Mayank properly. He had a strong jaw and a light but neatly trimmed stubble. He was quite muscular. He had the kind of body that one could tell had been sculpted by excessive gymming and supplements. But nonetheless, he was quite easy on the eyes.

"I didn't mention the entire night, but I think there's some connection between you and me," he finally said.

Vaanya felt a little sweaty. She didn't know whether it was his sharp beard or that muscular frame, but she felt a strange pang of attraction for him. She found herself imagining what he'd look like beneath the salmon pink linen shirt whose top three buttons were teasingly left open.

"What happened?" he asked, tapping her out of her daydream. "So, I am staying at the Taj. Have an entire suite to myself. Great view. Great room-service. But no company. Do you care to join?"

Vaanya's lips parted.

"Don't worry. No one will tell your boyfriend," he finally added.

She scanned him from top to bottom, wondering what made him ask such a question when he knew she had a boyfriend.

"How do you know I have a boyfriend?"

"Come on! You've been checking your phone more than you've been checking out the boys in this club. It was easy."

"Hmm, was it?" she smiled and walked away.

The next morning at 8 a.m., Vaanya woke up to the sound of her phone ringing.

"My head is throbbing. Please shut your phone," Mira who was sleeping next to her, groaned in a languid voice, almost kicking Vaanya out of the bed.

Vaanya picked up her phone and went to the balcony. "Hey!" she answered.

"Hi! How's the trip going?" Dhruv said from over the phone.

"Quite eventful. Although we're flying home tonight."

"Yeah. You two have been quite the social butterflies in Goa. Who was that entire group you hung out with last night?"

"Oh! Those were some friends of Mira's school friend Shikha whom we accidentally ran into at the nigh-club. But wait, how do you know?"

"I saw Mira's story."

"Oh!"

"That muscular guy looked like he was into you."

"Are you jealous?" Vaanya smiled.

"I am not jealous!" Dhruv muttered.

"Now you're suddenly not busy?" she grimaced.

"I had a few minutes before my morning meeting, so thought I'd check on you. I miss you, *jaan*."

"Hmm. I miss you too."

"Yeah. And I am sorry for not taking enough time out for you."

"It's okay. Let's talk about this later. I have to wake Mira before we miss breakfast."

"Yeah. Sure. Have fun."

"Okay! Bye."

"Vaanya…" he said, just before she was about to cut the call.

"Is there anything I should be worried about?"

"What do you mean?"

"About that guy?"

"Dhruv! No. What are you saying?"

"I am sorry. I didn't mean it like that. I think it's my guilt talking. Of not being very available lately."

"Dhruv, no matter how difficult things get, I need you to know that this is one thing you never have to worry about."

Chapter 11

I've Got You Under My Skin

The letters of my name
Form a delicate one-word verse in your mouth
Resembling the faint sound
Of the sacred morning Azaan
Echoing through the walls of my house
As you call my name and say,
That it was your favourite word in the
whole wide world

When the syllables of my name slip
from your tongue
And reach my ears, I wonder why is it that
In your voice my name carries a lost identity
And I discover a brand-new sense of self
As you call out for me
I show up as the person I always wanted to be

I had particularly never loved the sound of my name
That was until the syllables of the very same word
Lingered on your tongue slowly and tenderly
Comforting like the sweet taste of cinnamon rolls

And cold coffee after a lazy Sunday nap
Precious like the five extra minutes of sleep
On mind-numbing Monday mornings

The letters of my name
Form a delicate one-word verse in your mouth
Resembling the faint sound
Of the sacred morning Azaan
Echoing through the walls of my house
As you call my name and say,
That it was your favourite word in the
whole wide world.

—Vaanya

Their anniversary fell on the sixth of October and this year, the very day marked two years of togetherness for Dhruv and Vaanya. She planned to order his favourite cake and surprise him, and had baked the same for herself at home. She hoped that way, they could video call and cut the cakes together.

At midnight, when she tried to call him, to her utter dread, he didn't pick up again. She tried a couple of times more, but still no answer. At 12:20 a.m., she picked up the cake she had baked for herself and threw it into the trash-can.

At 5:30 a.m. Dhruv woke up from a broken sleep. Eyes puffy and red, he checked his phone to find ten missed calls from Vaanya. As he saw the date 10/06 flash on top of his screen, he collapsed back into the couch with regret. He didn't realise when he fell asleep last night while his phone was on silent. He checked the voice-mail in his room and there was a message from the hotel reception informing him about a cake that had arrived last night. He hurried downstairs to fetch the cake.

He was filled with deep remorse to find a small blueberry cheesecake on top of which was written, *'Two Years Stronger'* with cream cheese frosting. He took the cake upstairs and cursed himself for being such an ignorant jerk. He sank into the couch, threw away the tie still hanging around his neck like a noose and checked the time again. One more hour before Vaanya would be up. He decided to take a shower and get some coffee into his system to look alive before he apologised to her.

At 6:30 sharp, he called her. After fifteen rings, she picked up.

Her groggy morning voice made him feel at home.

"I'm sorry, jaan. I completely lost track of time last night. My phone was on airplane mode. And I passed out while working. This project is so consuming. I wasn't prepared for it. But this is no excuse for being MIA last night. And I loved the cake. I am feeling like such a loser. But I am your loser. Please forgive me. I promise to make it up to you soon."

"Dhruv," she interrupted his monologue.

He waited for her to say something, but the only response he received was silence.

"Vaanya," he broke her quiet rebellion. "I love you. Please bear with me for now? We'll get through this. I promise. You mean the whole world to me. I just need some time and mental bandwidth to remind you of that. My actions will speak louder than words. Just put up with me for a little while longer."

"It's not about that, Dhruv. I understand that you're going through a tough time at work. And I am not an inconsiderate bitch who expects attention from her man when he himself is struggling with his stuff. So, stop talking to me like that.

"I want to be there for you, baby. I want to support you. I want to love you. And I want to love you right. And all I ask is for you to let me," she paused to catch a breath.

"Just a small text message or phone call telling me you're doing okay, whether you've eaten or not. That's all I am expecting. But when I don't even get that, it makes me question everything about us."

"It's scary to love someone and not know whether they are doing okay," she let out a deep sigh.

"Love between a man and woman takes various shapes and forms. On some days my love for you is like the love a mother has for her child. A mother who is worried if her child has eaten or not, has reached home safely or not. On other days I feel for you what a wife does for her husband, who is terrified when her husband doesn't come home at night. Just because we don't have those labels yet, doesn't mean I feel any different or worry any less.

"Loving you is like my meditation. You're always in my remembrance. Your thoughts, they never leave me."

He stood on the other side of the phone tongue-tied and regretful, wondering what he'd done to deserve a woman like her.

"You can't forget to call someone who is on your mind twenty-four-hours-seven-days-a-week."

"I am sorry, Vaanya. But please remember that you are, and always will be my number one priority," he finally managed to say.

"No. I am not your number one priority. This project and your work are. And honestly, I am okay to let your work take twenty-three hours and fifty-five minutes of your day. But even if I would have gotten those uninterrupted five minutes, I would have believed you."

"I am sorry, Vaanya."

"I think I want to take a break."

"Please don't say that, Vaanya."

"Dhruv, try to understand. Being in this relationship is giving me more pain than happiness. It's coming at the cost of my peace of mind. You take care of yourself and please don't skip your meals. I am late for work. Bye."

"Vaanya,"

"Hmm?"

"I am deeply sorry for everything. I've heard you. Loud and clear. And I promise to be a better man for you. Just give me some time."

"Hence, the break."

"I am sorry."

"So am I."

"Come on, Vaanya! I swear I'll make it all okay. Please don't do this! Nothing has changed."

"Everything has changed, Dhruv. Everything. We spent all our waking hours together back at campus and look at us now. I don't get to talk to you for days. I don't know if you're okay or whether you were hit by a bus on your way back from the office and are hooked to IVs and in need of a blood transfusion, for God's sake," she screamed from over the phone.

"Vaanya, stop being so dramatic," he blurted out. "Okay I am sorry. I am really sorry jaan. It's just the stress talking. I am literally working like fifteen to seventeen hours a day. I don't know what's happening around me. Goddammit, I don't know what the hell is happening with me. I barely sleep for three-four hours and get back to work. I am surviving on five cups of black coffee and five minutes of stress-guitar-playing every day. Please try and understand."

"I do Dhruv. I do understand. That's all I've been doing for the last two months. I know it's hard for you there, but as hard as it is, if something or someone matters to you, you take out a minute for them. I am not asking you to talk to me for hours every day, because I *understand*. But you need to understand that if I don't get a text message or a call back from you for over twenty-four hours, my mind makes up the worst possible scenarios and I imagine all the bad things in the world happening to you. And I get so scared."

"Vaanya… I just wish I was there. I would have held you so tight. All your fears would've gone away."

"But you're not here, Dhruv. This thing between us, for the past few weeks, it's torturing me now. And I can't go on like this. Which is why I am saying let's take a break. You don't have the bandwidth for me. And I can't keep hurting myself worrying about you and waiting for you to call me."

"Vaanya, baby, please don't say that. I know I've been terrible. You don't deserve any of this. But I promise to fix this."

"I don't want to give you the remote control of my life anymore. Because trust me it feels like I am tied to you with a rope. And for the past few days, I've been feeling strangled."

"Vaanya…"

A lump formed in his throat.

"I am sorry Dhruv. Take care of yourself and do well at this project. I've to get to work. Bye."

Ten days passed without any contact from Vaanya. He tried to check in on her by leaving her text messages every now and then but not hearing from her day after day left him worried-sick. One time he sent her a video singing the same song he wrote for her back in college. Hoping for a reaction, he waited an entire week. But when the last week of October drew closer without any word from her, he knew he had to do something to turn this around.

As a final attempt to get in touch with her from a different city, he wrote her an email pouring his honest self:

'Dearest Vaanya,

I hope you are doing okay.

I don't know what to say and where to start. I have so much to tell you. I can't believe this is the longest we've gone without speaking to each other in the entire year... I am convincing myself that it's just a phase. Because I cannot imagine the possibility of this being anything more than that.

This is the hardest yet the simplest thing I've ever had to write.

I am not trying to apologise anymore, because I know, no amount of apologies can reverse the damage.

I've been thinking about how can I make this better. And I realised how our relationship is based on honesty more than anything else. And you're my only truth, Vaanya. I love you. I love you with every fibre of my being. And I know our love is resilient. This storm won't break the home we've built in each other's hearts.

I've been having these visions lately, as soon as I wake up in the morning. I feel you are next to me, sleeping peacefully. I move over to hug you, but all I find is empty space. I wake up to reality and pray for us. It's all so fleeting. But I know our love is not. It will stand the test of time. I am sure of it.

Love,

Dhruv'

Another week went by, but no word came from her. On the seventeenth of October, at 12:30 p.m., he left work mid-day and booked himself on an evening flight to Delhi. At 10:30 p.m., he peeked outside his window to find himself above the shimmering and smoky Delhi skyline.

Half an hour later, at Terminal two, standing at the same spot where he had last seen her, he was overcome by an unsettling wave of nostalgia. But the excitement to see her again triumphed. With flushed cheeks, he headed over to the cab pickup zone to hail a ride to her place.

On his way he stopped by the florist and picked up a few stems of fresh white lilies. Nothing says sorry better than your girlfriend's favourite flowers! He also visited Vaanya's favourite patisserie to pick up his order of four custom-made cupcakes, each with a small hand-written note.

At 11:15 p.m., he rang the bell of Vaanya's house and waited at her doorstep with a nervous smile. Oblivious to all this, Vaanya, who had just finished having her dinner, came rushing toward the door in her yellow SpongeBob SquarePants flip-flops and brown horn-rimmed glasses, wondering who could come visit her at this hour. She grabbed an off-white throw lying on the couch before opening the door to cover her see-through, beige tank top.

As she clanked open the lock, her mouth fell open. In the most unexpected surprise of her life, Dhruv stood at her door-step, geekily smiling at her, with a bouquet of fresh white lilies and a takeaway from her favourite bakery in one hand, and his tan grey American Tourister suitcase in the other.

Vaanya kept gawking at him in sheer surprise.

"Can I please come in, ma'am?" He chuckled, sensing her disbelief and letting himself in.

Vaanya still stood at the door. Dhruv kept his stuff on the coffee table, turned back and went down on one knee. "Please forgive me?"

"Get up, Dhruv! What are you doing?" Vaanya fidgeted.

"Trying to apologise to my girlfriend for being such a bad boyfriend this past month."

"Dhruv…" she moaned while tugging at his shoulders and gesturing to him to get up.

"How did you come… what…when did you?" she tried to form full sentences, but words failed her.

"You weren't answering my calls or messages, and even emails. You didn't leave me much of a choice there," he said sheepishly.

"That doesn't mean you get on the next plane and fly fourteen hundred kilometres!"

"People cross oceans for love; I just flew a few hundred kilometers, love," he said, closing the distance between them and brushing his finger on her lower lip.

Her gaze lowered as it traced the course of his fingers but his hands stopped as she said, "I was giving you a taste of your own medicine," she looked up. "How does it feel, not hearing from someone you love so deeply? Not knowing whether they are okay or not?"

"Aah, feisty and petty. Nobody better than my Vaanya can pull this off," he said with a smirk that almost made her crack up but she didn't budge.

"Ah, there it was. Almost there," he said pointing at her face.

"What?" she asked with a puzzled expression.

"That trillion-dollar smile. Haven't seen it in a while."

A shy smile appeared at the corner of her mouth. "Okay stop trying to charm your way out of every difficult situation. It won't work this time," she rolled her eyes.

"It almost did," he said gently, holding her from her waist. "Tell me you don't love it." He came closer. She could feel his breath on her neck and her knees giving in. Not able to stand any longer, she leaned forward to place her lips on his.

"I want to say something first." He shrugged his shoulders and took a step back.

"I want you to know that you're my home, Vaanya. And I need you to remember, that no matter what happens, this is it. We're always coming back to each other. And I'll do anything it takes to piece us back together, each time we fall apart. Because loving you is the only thing I am really good at. And I'll never stop doing it."

Vaanya inched closer to him. She raised her hands and brought them closer to his face in an attempt to hold him, but stopped mid-way. Her mouth opened and then closed.

"Vaanya…" he sighed but she shushed him with her fingers now tracing his lower lip.

"Dhruv…" she moaned and bent forward to press her lips hard against his. All the anger in her body melted as his warm tongue entered her soft mouth. She threw her hands up in the air and the shawl covering her body fell on the floor. Squeezing her waist, he pulled her tank top over her arms and picked her up in a swift motion. She wrapped her legs around his torso and began planting violent kisses all over his face. His grip tightened around her buttocks. She removed his coat and unbuttoned his shirt, as he continued to kiss her, his tongue leaving no part of her body untouched. Her skin burnt with desire, as she shut her eyes close and let the world around her melt into nothingness, giving into the sweet heavenly pleasure. He pinned her against the living- room wall in front of the kitchen, and freed one hand to hold her neck, as he continued to kiss, squeeze, bite, and caress every part of her body, until she was shaking underneath him.

"Dhruv!" she moaned his name in a high-pitched voice, and it sounded like music to his ears after months of separation. He quickly carried her and placed her on the kitchen table. She unbuttoned his pants. He entered her right there. And she felt full after months. As though she was missing a piece of herself that just got returned to her. His hot and moist breath was tingling the skin between her neck and her shoulders, as he pulsated inside of her. The world as she knew it, seemed to dissolve in that moment. She could feel the energy of the entire cosmos course through her body. Her eyes squeezed shut so tight that she saw circular streams of bright milky white light. Her toes curled and she dug her nails on his back.

After a few seconds, still heavily breathing, with a pounding heart and a shaky voice, she said, "Promise me... you'll never leave me again."

"I promise," he gasped for air as she grabbed his face again and started kissing him with feral intensity, leaving no spot un-caressed, before he felt sudden moisture from her cheek rub on his face.

"Hey hey? Vaanya!" He held her face, and wiped off the tears on her face, only to have another stream of tears rush down her supple cheeks.

"What happened, jaan?" he asked, feeling a well of moisture form in his own eyes.

"I am here now. And I am not going anywhere," he said, as she stayed quiet.

"Vaanya? Say something," he nudged her slightly, but nothing came out of her mouth. Only tears escaped her deep brown eyes. Months of unspent love and yearning spilling out of her like a leaking orifice. Her skin had goosebumps, as she curled in his lap and wept like a baby. He tightened his grip around her body and gently rocked her, while rubbing her back, trying to soothe her.

In the morning, Dhruv woke up first and saw Vaanya sleeping next to him. Her arms still wrapped around him from last night, like a traumatised child refusing to let go of their parent who had left her home for hours to go to work. He kissed her on the forehead, and silently thanked God for the biggest gift he had been given in this lifetime, and went back to the best, most blissful sleep he had in months.

When he woke up again, a few hours later, he found the bed next to him empty, and immediately missed her. She was probably in the shower, he thought.

"Vaanya!" he screamed as high as he could in his early morning low-pitched voice.

With a white towel wrapped around her, she peeped from the bathroom door. "Why are you shouting?"

Hair still wet from her bath, she quickly put on a bathrobe and came out staring at him lying comfortably under the covers, "What happened?"

"Why are you so far?" he said with widened eyes, and an inverted smile.

She came closer and nestled in his lap. Opening the knot of her white knee-length bathrobe, she coiled her arms around his shoulders. "Better Now?"

"Best!" he said, before starting to kiss her neck gently.

He threw back a few damp strands of hair on her neck. A few water droplets landed on his face. She slowly kissed the moisture away. He rolled her over on the bed and climbed on top of her to plant a trail of kisses starting from her neck, down to her chest and stomach. She arched her back as he reached her navel. A thousand butterflies raced in her stomach with his every touch.

But she interrupted him in the middle, "Dhruv!"

"Hmm?" he replied, still nuzzling up against her.

"Listen. No, Dhruv," she groaned, pulling away.

"What? I'm doing some of my best work here," he smirked with a wink and tenderly bit her lower lip.

"I have some good news," she announced.

"So soon? I am not even done yet," he grimaced.

"Shut up, Dhruv! I am serious. Stop joking."

He almost snorted as she hit him playfully on the chest.

"Okay, sorry tell me?"

"Brace yourself!"

"What, have we won a lottery?"

She rolled her eyes. "Better"

"Okay, what? End the suspense," he said, holding on to the edge of the bed.

"I got transferred to the Mumbai office," she finally announced.

"W-H-A-T!" Dhruv looked at her in disbelief.

"Vaanya Sharma, you better be serious before I actually decide to jump in joy."

"I am serious. I am shifting next month. Look at this!" she held out her phone and showed him the email confirming the news.

He kept looking at her in silence, too afraid to believe.

"It's finally happening," she beamed at him.

He picked her up and danced around the room in excitement.

"Holy shit! I can't believe this," he squealed.

"We need to celebrate!"

She popped open a bottle of sparkling white wine lying in her pantry.

"To us!" They clinked their glasses.

Chapter 12

Say Yes to Heaven

The sun moves over
Like a heavenly act
Each time my lips
Curve in your name
Like a solemn hymn
Echoing in the temple
Of my body
We were nothing short
Of a religion.

—Vaanya

Dhruv and Vaanya's togetherness was a kaleidoscope of love's many hues. It often came wrapped in generous friendship, sometimes it mirrored a sweet intimacy, other times a wild passion and fleeting vulnerability, but beneath it all was an unwavering belief in each other. They discovered the tiny nuances and joys of sharing a life together in the bustling streets of Mumbai, a city they began calling home.

They moved into a 2BHK apartment to save up on exorbitant rents. Being a morning person, Dhruv would be up at 5 a.m. to read, after which he'd head for a run. By 8 a.m., he'd have taken a shower, meditated for thirty minutes, and cooked Vaanya some breakfast.

"How do you end up having an entire day before I even wake up?" Vaanya would ask sluggishly when he woke her up with coffee and breakfast in bed.

"Mornings are pious," he'd casually say and go back to reading *The Economic Times* while sipping on his black coffee.

"Mornings are bad. You've to wake up."

"Come on. They aren't as bad. The peace and focus when the rest of the world is asleep, the endorphin rush of a good workout, watching the sunrise after a long run. It's priceless."

"Did I mention you've to wake up?" She'd rub her eyes and slurp on her large mug of coffee.

"Let your caffeine jolt kick in." He'd laugh and settle in the rocking chair opposite the bed. The sun from the half-open window reflected on his face.

How did I end up getting so lucky, she bemused, and clicked a picture of the breakfast plate with him in the background reading his paper and sipping his coffee.

Engrossed in his reading, Dhruv didn't realise a thing until his phone chimed. He tapped open the notification on his screen to find a photo of Vaanya's breakfast against the backdrop of him reading posted on her Instagram, the photo especially focusing on his bicep glistening through his running vest. The picture was cleverly captioned,

"Breakfast with a view! #bestchefintown."

He sniggered and reposted it with the caption, *"Always a party, cooking snacks for my snack."*

"Good game," Vaanya looked at the caption and said, stuffing her face with food.

While Dhruv conquered his mornings, Vaanya took her night time ritual very seriously. From work she'd directly go to her yoga class and after a long bath, she'd cook a healthy dinner. Steamed rice, tofu, and stirred vegetables or a nourishing curry with a coconut or tofu base and lots of hidden vegetables that Dhruv wouldn't otherwise eat. After dinner she'd nestle into bed with a nice book, some scented candles, and a warm cup of chamomile tea.

"You got new candles, again?" he groaned the other day.

"Pumpkin spice flavour. Yes." Her eyes lit up as she sniffed the thick jar of the soy-wax candle.

"What? Is that even a thing?" he asked, jerking his head back in surprise.

"It's almost October. Autumn's here. It's pumpkin spice season."

"Only you can say something like that and make it sound so cute."

"One of my many talents." She threw her arms around him and began kissing his neck.

"Okay love. I am not complaining anymore," he nuzzled and wrapped his arms around her waist.

"Good. Because night time is holy," she stepped away and continued speaking, "No deadlines and responsibilities until the sun is up in the sky again. You can just be yourself until then."

"Okay. And this is me being myself." He pulled her closer and started kissing her neck.

"Stop it. I am serious," she shrugged away. "I don't disturb your mornings. Why do you make fun of my night-time routine then?"

"Okay fine. I am not making fun. Hands off. I am all ears." He folded his arms and got ready to pay attention.

"It's important to me. Coming home and unwinding properly, washing away the day."

"With the most expensive bath salts and candles. Noted ma'am."

"Dhruv!" she grimaced.

"What?"

"You're making fun of me again."

"No, I am just agreeing with you."

"Yeah, right!"

"Okay. I am sorry, jaan. Why are you so adorable?" He pulled her closer and started kissing her irritation away.

"Dhruv!" she moaned and wrapped her arms around him.

After working hard and hurrying through the week, the weekends were all about slowing down. On Saturdays, they often ended up staying in bed doing movie-marathons and eating margherita pizzas out of cardboard boxes. On Sundays, Dhruv would prepare an elaborate spread with Vaanya's favourite Nutella pancakes, nicely diced fruits, and freshly squeezed juice along with a few stems of white lilies that he'd pick on his morning run.

"Oh my god these are delicious! Perfect temperature, perfect texture, gooey!" she exclaimed digging into her plate, as Nutella oozed out of the fluffy pancakes.

"Is it?" He sniggered and took a bite from her hand. "But not as yummy as you!"

"Oh, definitely not!" She gave him a teasing smile and licked the chocolate off her finger in a titillating manner.

"Are you enticing me?"

"Your prerogative."

"Alright," he sat at the opposite end of the bed and gently massaged her foot.

"How does it feel?"

"Like I am in heaven."

"Wait for it," he smirked and slowly began licking her toes. Before she knew it, he was gently nibbling on her thumb. His hands quickly moved forward reaching her calves, gently stroking her muscles.

"Dhruv!" she moaned, and pulled him closer. His mouth made his way up. One hand continued to massage her inner-thigh and the other held her neck with a gentle but possessing force. She tugged at his hair and drew his mouth closer between her wide-open legs. She threw her head back, giving into the sweet ache as her entire body yearned for him. They stayed between the sheets for the rest of the morning.

Late into the afternoon, they'd hop in the car and drive around the city aimlessly, exploring new cafes, book shops, and art galleries. Often, they'd just spend their Sunday evenings reading together in silence.

Fortnightly, they would pack their bags and go on a weekend getaway. Vaanya hated trekking and Dhruv loved long hikes in the hills. So, they would settle somewhere in the middle and often end up discovering new experiences and things to do around the city. One time while driving somewhere in the outskirts of the city, Vaanya spotted a vineyard.

They tagged along a tourist group and joined an exclusive wine tasting event.

"First smell, then gently swirl and finally take a sip," said the wine-tasting expert, but Vaanya grabbed the wine bottle next to her after accidentally breaking the wine glass in a drunken state.

"Swirl and then sip," she said cheekily, shaking the wine bottle before bringing it to her lips and drinking straight from the orifice of the bottle.

"Okay, enough! *'Little miss, I want to go to a wine tasting event'* while already drunk!" Dhruv grabbed the bottle from her hand and dragged her out to avoid more stares.

Skipping the wine tasting, they went to the property's lavish restaurant and had a big lunch overlooking the vineyard, after which they spent the rest of the day lying on the cool grass and watching the thick white clouds drift in the sky.

"Dhruv"

"Hmm?"

"I sometimes think…"

"I am listening."

"What if we wouldn't have made it work?"

"Why this? Suddenly."

"I don't know. I think about it sometimes."

"I think it was destiny. We were meant to be together, so we found our way back to each other."

"It's also your own choice. It's not all destiny."

"Well. Yeah. But we do have limited choice. It's called conditioned free will."

"Hmm. Meaning? Choices to a certain extent? Under pre-decided conditions?"

"Exactly. Get this. How we think and the larger reasons behind our actions are often a mystery to our own selves. It's because most of our life is predestined."

"Is this what that mystic told you? When you ditched everyone and went to that Ashram."

"Yeah. I'd been thinking about those things for a while. Guruji reinstated my faith in a few things."

"Hmm. You never told me much about that experience."

"There's not much to tell."

"I am sure that's not true."

"I mean it was a very humbling and profound experience. Meeting many other devotees. Listening to other people's life stories. Their struggles and inner work. Meditating for days and finally experiencing your racing monkey-like-mind quiet down. And slowly feel a tinge of calm and clarity wash over you. It's life-changing. It was pretty tough in the beginning but then you get in the rhythm. And then you don't feel like going back to normal life."

"Is that where you picked up your morning meditation?"

"Kind of. I mean I was trying to meditate on and off before that. But I think after meditating at a stretch in the Ashram I just realised its importance for my mental, emotional and spiritual health."

"It improves your intuition, right?"

"Absolutely."

"So, after meditating you realised I am the one for you?" she enquired with a bright shine in her eyes.

He didn't say anything. But she noticed his lips crack in a faint smile, as he avoided her gaze and looked away at the lush grass. She leaned closer and cupped his face in her hands to kiss him softly on the cheek.

About a month after the vineyard escapade, they found themselves at a strange yogic campus near Pune. An impromptu trip to what they thought would be a wellness retreat, had turned into a celibacy weekend as they found themselves at a cult's campus which did not allow men and women to stay in the same room. So, they wore large white gowns, drank ash gourd juice, ate millet porridges, did breathing exercises and yogic meditation the whole weekend. Dhruv eased into the routine pretty quickly as it reminded him of his days spent at the Ashram. Vaanya was irritated in the beginning, as she expected healing massages, spa therapies, and bird watching. But, she eventually ended up relishing the much-needed mind-cleansing break, from screens and the chaotic city life.

Just like that, before they even knew, it had already been six months since they first started living together in Mumbai. And as an unexpected surprise to sweeten the celebration of their six-month move-in anniversary, Dhruv got promoted at work. The team leader of his last project had to move out unexpectedly, and the management asked Dhruv to fill in temporarily. But since his team loved him, they vouched for him. That coupled with his excellent performance at the Hyderabad project, the company promoted him and gave him the project lead position permanently. He knew things would get tougher professionally, but with Vaanya and him under the same roof, he felt much more confident going into this new phase. Vaanya threw a cosy dinner and drinks party at their place, inviting their closest friends and some colleagues to celebrate Dhruv's promotion.

Arnav and Sneha also planned to fly down to Mumbai and have a mini reunion with their friends, but Arnav's leave requests at his office didn't get approved. So, the congratulations were in order over video call and via the delivery of Dhruv's favourite scotch.

"Neat!" Dhruv opened the bottle and thanked his best-friend.

"Long distance friendships suck!" Sneha wailed from the glassy phone screen.

"But we love you! Thanks for the gift!" Vaanya smiled.

"Take a trip to Bangalore with all the extra money you're getting now, buddy" Arnav joked.

"Let the money first hit the bank!" Dhruv chuckled.

"Gotta go, now! Have fun! We love you guys!" Sneha blew kisses before hanging up.

With a decent hike in salary, Dhruv knew exactly what he had to do next. It took more than a week's worth of planning to get everything right, but he hadn't been surer of anything ever.

"What's the occasion?" Vaanya texted Dhruv after receiving the delivery of a bouquet of white lilies and a huge white box which she unwrapped to find a slick A-line satin, salmon-pink dress.

"I've wanted this dress for over a month. How did you know?"

"I have my ways," he replied instantly.

"Stop being cryptic," she texted back with a rolling eyes emoji.

"Pick you up at seven!" he responded with a kissing emoji and went offline.

He had the entire evening planned. He had made reservations at her favourite rooftop restaurant with a stunning view of the sea. Despite all the preparation, he felt oddly nervous before driving down to pick her up. A sudden urge to smoke rose within him, but he took a deep breath and gulped down a glass of water to calm the jitters. But as soon as he saw her walking towards the car, all his anxiety vanished in thin air. He could see the rest of his life walk toward him.

"Are you okay?" Vaanya stroked his arm to nudge him out of his trance.

"Now I am," he said and leaned forward to kiss her. "You look breath-taking."

"Thank you. I love how this dress fits me. Like it was made especially for me".

"I am glad you liked it.".

"But what's the surprise?" she asked sounding excited and restless all at the same time.

"Patience. My love, he smiled and accelerated to move past the traffic.

The plush roof-top restaurant was decked with warm lights and regal architecture. The sound of waves crashing at the beachfront mixed with the soulful tunes of an Indie band that tried out their fresh singles in the central spot right next to the bar. Dhruv had reserved the best table in the restaurant. And before they could order, the waiter served them some artisanal cocktails along with some exotic finger-food.

"Okay someone's really well-prepared today. I am curious. What's in store for me?"

"Maybe something life-changing," he said casually and took a sip of the cocktail.

She arched her eyebrows and smiled. "Cheers!" She played along, as they clinked their glasses and drank while holding each other's gaze. Dhruv was grateful for the generous amount of gin in his drink whose every sip calmed his nerves and helped him continue his charade of appearing cool as a cucumber. He finally got up. "I'll be back," he murmured in her ear and left.

"Okay," Vaanya said calmly, although feeling a little perplexed inside.

Waiting distractedly for the next few minutes, she looked around to absorb the energy of the place but her eyes immediately fell on Dhruv, who all of a sudden was perched upon a bar stool with a guitar in his hand, right where the band was just a few minutes ago. Wide-eyed, she opened and closed her mouth, trying to figure out what he was up to. But before she could put two and two together, Dhruv's fingers tugged at the strings of his guitar, and his husky voice reverberated in the cool air.

"Hi everyone! Hope you're all having a wonderful evening. First of all, a big shout out to this amazing band who was kind enough to give me a few minutes in their gig. But coming straight to the point, this one's for my beautiful girlfriend, Vaanya, who is sitting right there, looking more stunning than ever. I love you," he said and then went on to sing one of '*The Train*'s' major hits perfectly suited to the occasion.

'Forever can never be long enough for me
To feel like I've had long enough with you...
Forget the world now we won't let them see
But there's one thing left to do
Now that the weight has lifted
Love has surely shifted my way
Marry me,
Today and every day...

Marry me
If I ever get the nerve to say
Hello in this cafe
Say you will
Mm-hmm
Say you will
Mm-hmm
Marry me'

As he finished, he was met with a loud cheer from the exhilarated crowd in the restaurant. But in split seconds, the whole place fell dead silent, waiting in apprehension.

And before Vaanya could process any of this, Dhruv was on one knee, pulling out a tiny blue velvet box from his pocket. He held it open and a giant solitaire glared at her. But the sparkle in Dhruv's eyes overshadowed the solitaire's, red as tomato with a twitching left cheekbone, a sweet reminder of his nervousness similar to when he had asked her out for the first time.

"Vaanya, I have been planning this in my head for almost a month now, but here I am and I still have goosebumps," he stopped and cleared his throat while searching for reassurance in her expression. Her fluttering eyelashes gave him the confidence he needed to keep going and he continued.

"Vaanya, I have been in love with you since… a forever now.

"You're magic, Vaanya. You take every ordinary thing and make it extraordinary. You're the wind beneath my wings, but you also keep me grounded.

"With you by my side, I feel like being a better person. Because you believed in me when I couldn't. And you've stood by me since then, like a rock through thick and thin.

"You're my home, Vaanya. And I can't thank God enough to have given me my soulmate, my best-friend and lover, all in one person.

I honestly have no idea what I would have done, had you not walked into my life on that sweet summer morning in that classroom. You've made me the happiest man ever. And if you give me a chance, I'll spend forever trying to make you exactly as happy as you make me."

Vaanya broke into tears. She couldn't believe that this was happening for real. She turned beet red and cried, "Yes! A thousand times, yes."

He slid the stunning solitaire on her finger, and she kissed him hard on his dry lips. She thrust her face in his chest as he caressed her hair. She whispered in his ear, "I love you so much Dhruv Malhotra."

He softly murmured, "I love you more, soon-to-be Mrs. Dhruv Malhotra."

"I can't believe you're getting married!" Mira jumped out of bed when Vaanya broke the news to her the next day.

"I can't either. I just feel like I have been in a state of daze since last night. I still haven't processed anything," she beamed from over the phone.

"I am so happy for you!" she cried in joy, but deep down, her heart began sinking. *Her elder sister, best-friend and secret-keeper would suddenly be someone's wife.*

Vaanya and Mira were more than just sisters; they were a close-knit circle within themselves. Growing up, they had shared their whole lives with each other. The room, wardrobe, clothes, books, shoes, food, nail-paints, tic-tacs, family drama, and boy troubles. Basically, everything under the sun. And even when life took them to different cities, their sisterhood continued to thrive over daily hour-long phone calls and weekly video-chats. Nevertheless, she'd always have the first rights over her sister. But things would change now, and the realization deeply moved Mira. She swallowed her insecurity and booked herself on the first flight to Mumbai.

Dhruv and Vaanya both went to receive her at the airport. Dhruv picked up her bags as the two sisters reduced to a giant ball of hugs and tears.

"Congratulations to you two! I am so happy!" Mira cried.

"Thanks for coming. I was dying to see you!" Vaanya continued holding her as the two of them bawled.

"She has been my sister long before she was your girlfriend or your to-be wife. You better remember that," she joked with Dhruv, with tears still forming in her eyes.

"I am very well aware of that, ma'am," he said sarcastically and made some tea to calm them both after their intense crying session that started at the airport, continued in the car and finally ended on the couch in their apartment.

"I am not going to be sold in a cup of tea, okay?"

"Okay. Let's look at it this way. Now along with your sister, even you get free access to all the awesomeness of Dhruv Malhotra, which comes in really nice cups of tea, delivery of white lilies on bad days, impromptu unplanned trips, long drives at night to go eat the best desserts in town, and many other perks that you shall come to know of later."

"Is that how you smooth-talked your way into my sister's life?"

"Well, my secret is out."

"I am not going to be this easy to impress."

"Oh, the younger Sharma has higher standards?"

"Wait till you meet our mother! She is the OG!"

"Oh, aunty will love me"

"No, she won't."

"Yes, she will. I'll get her some white lilies and a Jhumpa Lahiri book." He arched his eyebrows, waiting for her reaction.

She rolled her eyes, accepting her defeat.

"Well, your dearest sister gets her love of white lilies and books from aunty, I know that," he shrugged his shoulders.

"So how was it, doing your PhD on the Sharma women?" She chuckled.

"Intensely gratifying, I must say," he squinted his eyes and continued the playful banter.

"Okay fine. Who am I kidding? She will obviously love you. And so do I. Just for the record. But I am not ready to share her with you. And honestly, I just can't believe all this is happening so fast."

"It is happening. But it isn't so fast. Is it? I mean it was about time. Don't you think so? We've been together for so long. This was the right next step," he said while sipping on his tea, nestled on the couch between the Sharma sisters.

"I know. Honestly, I did think about it. But I wasn't very well prepared."

"It's okay. You'll live," he smirked.

She rolled her eyes and threw a cushion at him. All three of them laughed.

"Okay so tell me how do you like this house?" He pulled out his phone and shuffled through the photos of a plush apartment near Carter Road.

"Oh, it's lovely. I really like this third room. It looks so sunny and ventilated from the photos."

"Well, that's your room in our new house," he said casually.

"What? Oh my god. You're the best!" Mira jumped and wrapped Dhruv in a hug.

A wide grin of satisfaction spread on Vaanya's face watching the two most important people in her life getting along so well.

Convincing the parents, though assumed to come with its own set of challenges, happened without any major hiccups. Sure, the common Punjabi angle, since Dhruv was a Kshatriya-Punjabi who came from a family of refugees, and Vaanya from a Punjabi-Brahmin household, did play a significant role in getting both sets of parents onboard, but despite that both the Sharmas and the Malhotras were thrilled with the match.

After months of preparations and exhausting shopping sprees, the D-day arrived. It was all happening, for real. They had zeroed in on a beautiful sea-side venue in Goa for a gorgeous beach-themed destination wedding.

Day one of the three-day-long grand affair, Vaanya woke up in the morning and felt a little jittery. Staring at herself in the mirror, she realised it was her last day as Vaanya Sharma. She'd soon be Mrs. Vaanya Malhotra. The thought itself gave her chills. And right at that moment, her phone rang. The screen flashed Dhruv's image.

"Hey you," she blushed at his perfect timing.

"Hi, babe! How's my prettiest doing this morning? All set for the big day?" Dhruv was cheerful over the phone.

"I don't know. It's really happening, Dhruv. It's hitting me. Let's just run away, no? No big ceremonies, no one staring at us on that huge-ass stage. No pretentious smiling in hundred kilograms of clothes and jewellery. Phew!" she exclaimed.

"Okay, let's escape this drama and get married, naked in the fields," he smirked.

"You are imagining this already, aren't you?" she scoffed.

He could imagine her rolling her eyes from over the phone.

"Well, you know how to read my mind, love. One of the many reasons I'm marrying you."

"You bet, Mr. Malhotra. And this isn't going to be all fun and flirtatious forever. You know that, right?"

"I know exactly what I need to know, and that is, I love you. And I can't wait to see you in that wedding lehenga, looking like the dream that you already are. And more than that, I can't wait to live the rest of my life with you."

"I love you."

"I know. Now go get ready so I can see my beautiful bride soon."

"Ugh… Dhruv! I'm going to trip over that never-ending lehenga in front of the entire clan of both our relatives ogling me."

"And I'll be the first one to laugh," Dhruv giggled.

"I hate you," Vaanya shrieked.

"And I love you. And I am going to hold your hand so tight, I won't ever let you fall. And certainly not over one lousy lehenga on our wedding day."

"Promise me we'll be alright?"

"We're going to be just fine. I promise. Now cheer up and go get ready. Okay? Can't wait to see you tonight."

"Neither can I. I love you. Bye."

"Bye. I love you."

"Come on, it's your wedding! Go take a shower, then we'll give you a turmeric bath," Mira stormed into the room. She had inherited the high-spirited gene of the Sharma family. Hopping around the place, taking care of all the arrangements while dancing around and making sure everyone had a good time, making them laugh with her goofy antics, she breathed life into all the ceremonies.

The outdoor venue had a Persian décor with yellow marigolds at the entrance, peach and mint green drapes, and popping colours everywhere. Friends and relatives dressed up in vibrant clothes adorned the whole place. Some holy scriptures and a large pot containing the turmeric paste sat on the carpet next to which a few neem leaves were scattered around. Some cheery cousins were waiting to apply the turmeric paste on Vaanya's skin. Her friends from college had also come over, and the entire place was full of life and enthusiasm.

The moment Vaanya walked through the door, everyone stopped and stared. Dressed in a simple yellow saree with no make-up, she glowed naturally even before the Haldi ceremony was performed. Long dark hair braided intricately, a shy smile that gave away her slight nervousness, she looked like the perfect bride.

The ceremony began, and Mrs. Sharma started to apply the holy paste on her cheeks. Then Sneha smeared a small portion of the thick paste on her feet, and slowly everybody moved on to cover the remaining parts of her bare skin. Smiling, laughing, chatting, singing and dancing, they were all overjoyed to see her get ready to embark upon a new journey of her life.

Mira stood at a distance with moist eyes, seeing the lively group of uncles, aunts, cousins and friends gathered around her sister, who sat in the middle with a strange peace and contentment on her face, smiling away at everyone, cherishing the last few hours before she'd be wed-locked. The area was bustling with people, still Mira felt as if time had stopped right there in her sister's innocent smile. And in that exact moment, Vaanya's eyes began searching for her little sister. She saw her, crying silently in a corner. When their eyes locked, Mira wiped her tears immediately, and hopped towards Vaanya, hurrying through the crowd. She dipped her hands in the turmeric paste and rubbed it gently on Vaanya's cheeks and arms. A single tear escaped Vaanya's kohl-lined eyes.

On the wedding day, Mrs. Sharma was busy obsessing over all the tiny details from the décor to the food, ensuring that nothing could possibly go wrong on the pious occasion of her elder daughter's wedding. So Mira, like the perfect maid of honour, was handed the responsibility to be at Vaanya's beck and call the entire time, as she started getting ready for her big day. The stylist asked her to wear her outfit first, and then the make-up would begin. She went into the changing room to slip on her lehenga and fasten the stunning pastel-pink embellished blouse, but to her utmost shock, the blouse got stuck at her chest and didn't slip further down to her waist.

"Try to push it down. Bring the seams closer before zipping it," Vaanya pleaded for help to Mira who tried to shove the petite blouse down Vaanya's body, but looked like she was wrestling with the zipper. "Come on! This can't be happening. Hold your breath. Let me try again," Mira groaned.

"Wait, let me stretch it from here. Scoot over," Vaanya trembled.

"Oh, come on! How can you put on so much weight overnight!" exclaimed Mira. "Wait are you pregnant?" Mira looked at her flabbergasted.

"No. Shut up!" Vaanya shunned her.

"Okay, I'll tell you something, but promise me you won't tell mom. She has been running around like a mad person planning this wedding. She'll torture me for a decade for missing this," Vaanya shot Mira a ghastly look.

"What?" Mira looked pale.

"Promise me first."

"Goddamn it, Didi! Tell me already. We are running late."

Baffled, Vaanya finally broke, "I didn't try the blouse earlier. I did try it like a month back. Mom was nagging me to try it for two weeks, but it slipped my mind amidst everything else. And now I hate myself for this," Vaanya pursed her lips.

"What!? Are you kidding me! What a dumbass you are! It's *your* wedding. Do you even realise it? What are we going to do now? The *barat* will be here in two hours."

"What do we do now?" She looked sorry, and Mira decided to cut back on the scolding.

"This is insane. Okay, wait! You get your make-up started. I'll get it altered from somewhere." Mira bit her lip.

"Are you sure?" asked a terrified Vaanya.

"Do we have any other choice?"

"Okay, don't stress out. You can't look stressed on your wedding day. I'll fix it. Relax! I got you."

Mira hurried out of the bridal suite towards the main entrance of the resort. But unfortunately, she couldn't find a ride. The resort was on the outskirts of Goa, so finding a cab was impossible, and most of the in-house cars were occupied. She couldn't tell mom. She couldn't tell anyone. On top of it, she had no clue where she would find a tailor's shop? And how would she get there?

As she was anxiously wandering around the main gate, trying to look for a cab or an in-house car, she spotted someone in a blue kurta getting off a bike. He seemed about Six feet three inches tall and had a solid build. As he took off the helmet and got off his bike, Mira got a glimpse of his face. He looked robust with a square jaw and long hair nearing his shoulders. He took off his shades and began walking toward Mira who was standing in the middle of the compound with a perturbed look pasted all over her face.

"Hey, is everything okay? You look tense," he came over and asked her.

"Umm," she noticed his small eyes that looked too sincere for his broad-built and smouldering personality. "Yeah, I'm trying to find a ride. It's an emergency."

"What happened? Where do you have to go?" he asked, looking at the turquoise-pink embellished blouse she was carrying in her hands. She realised she had even forgotten to put it in a bag.

"Long story short, I need to find a tailor's shop. Like, really urgently."

"Well, if it's that urgent, I could give you a ride."

She hesitated at first and stood there for a minute, assessing him from top to bottom, evaluating her options.

But she knew she had no other choice. She had to do this for her sister.

He looked at her staring at him in apprehension, and gathered that it was on him to break the ice and make her comfortable.

"Abhay. Abhay Khanna," he said and watched her expression change as she figured that he had sensed her hesitation.

"I am one of Dhruv's friends from work. I have known him and Vaanya for like a year now. I have a beach-house fifteen kilometres from here, which I visit every few months. So, it's safe to say I know my way around this beach-town. I know where you could find the nearest tailor's shop because from the looks of it, if you are carrying a bridal blouse, you must be Vaanya's sister or friend. You probably have to fix this piece of clothing ASAP, so my friend Dhruv does not have to wait any longer to see his bride on his wedding day," he paused for a minute and then said. "Am I right, or am I right?"

She rolled her eyes. He seemed cocky but trustworthy.

"I'm Mira, Vaanya's sister. And I think we better hurry," she said before wasting any further time.

Abhay chuckled. "This way, please."

She hopped on to the bike and settled cross-legged behind him. One hand holding the blouse, the other tightly holding the seat. The roads connecting the resort to the main city were filled with potholes, and the bike jerked every few minutes. Her soft curls wildly blew against the direction of the wind and covered her face. She held on to Abhay to steady herself each time he had to apply the brakes to get through the broken roads. She was scared, uncomfortable and awkward. Her heart raced in her chest. But all she knew was that it was her sister's big day and she'd do anything it takes to fix this situation. After half an hour of searching for a tailor's shop, they finally came across one. She jumped off the bike and scurried away to plead to an old Goan tailor.

"I got you. Take this and try it out. It'll fit you now," screamed Mira, rushing towards Vaanya.

Vaanya ran toward her and hugged her affectionately.

"You're such a saviour. Nobody else could have done this for me today."

"I am your sister. I signed up for this. And now you owe me big time, dumbass."

The Sharma sisters giggled and hurried to get ready. Mrs. Sharma came in after another hour, unaware of all the debacles her daughters had endured.

Vaanya emerged from the room and Mrs. Sharma's eyes welled up, seeing her little girl turn into a breathtakingly beautiful bride. She wiped a tinge of kohl from her eyelid, and applied a speck of it behind Vaanya's left ear, to save her from all evil.

The beach-side venue was decked up with a charming décor of white-hydrangeas, pink spray roses, and vintage gold lanterns. The magnificent crimson sun setting into the deep white and blue waves of the sea created a dream-like setting. The flock of bridesmaids, dressed in light pink and mint green, ran around merrily. It seemed as though the entire place was dancing in joy, celebrating the union of two lovers.

After a long wait by Dhruv who stood patiently, looking sharp and dignified in an ivory-gold sherwani, Vaanya emerged on the scene. It was finally happening. He brushed away a tear escaping his eye, as she walked down the aisle toward him, in a stunning pastel-pink lehenga and *kundan* jewellery, looking like a dream come true.

For a moment, it felt all too unreal. He couldn't believe his eyes as she walked gracefully beneath an extravagant floral sheath, a spectacular sun setting in the ocean behind her. This is what heaven must look like. He couldn't fathom that his dream-like bride, his Vaanya, his girlfriend from the last three years and the one true love of his life was finally going to be his solemnly wedded wife.

Chapter 13

Nothing's Gonna Hurt You Baby

There is a strange and odd calm
That settles silently like dust
On dilapidated window-panes
Of deserted houses

I cherish it like an ephemeral thought
In the moments stolen
From the crevices of memory

Transient, it used to rush out the half-open door
Like a cool breeze on balmy summer afternoons
But lately, it has begun to settle
Like an estranged winter-time visitor
In a postcard like a snow-covered inn.

—DHRUV

"Dhruv, what are you doing? Stop, I'm ticklish," Vaanya laughed hysterically, as Dhruv continued to plant a trail of breathy kisses on the smooth valley of her back.

"I don't want to go back!"

"Neither do I. But let's wake up and smell the coffee. We've been holed up on this continent for a month. It's time to go back to real life."

"Only twenty-eight days. Not a month!"

"Okay, two days short of a month. But you get the point."

"No, I refuse to get the point. Let's just hide out here in this spacious sun-lit room and look at the beautiful ocean at our feet, while kissing the daylight out of each other."

"Very tempting. And I hate to break it to you, my love, but we're flying out tonight," he smirked and kissed her forehead before drinking his coffee that had gone cold, in one erratic shot and pacing through the room packing their scattered things.

"The best twenty-eight days of my life!" Vaanya sighed and recounted the past month.

Meandering hand in hand through the captivating canal-clad city of Venice; riding the gorgeous London Eye at Sunset; skinny dipping in Amalfi Coast surrounded by the magnificent sky-high coastal cliffs; visiting archaic museums and cathedral churches of Santorini, spending a weekend in a plush white Airbnb encircled by deep blue coral seas; enjoying a romantic wine and cheesecake dinner at Paris's Eiffel Tower—their dreamy honeymoon had taken them on many beautiful adventures.

"Time to wake up and smell the coffee, love!" He broke her daydreaming, and her face dropped.

"Hey, I promise to try my best to make the rest of our lives feel like a honeymoon. Okay? Here, one and a half teaspoons of sugar. Just how you like it," he said, handing her a cup of black coffee. A faint smile appeared on her face.

"Now cheer up. I am not taking home a sad and grumpy wife with me."

She rolled her eyes and took a deep breath. "Okay Mumbai, here we come again!"

"That's my girl."

She smiled and climbed on top of him to make love to her perfect husband, one last time on international lands.

Savouring the sweet afterglow of their wedding, they embarked on the journey of married life. They settled into a spacious 3 BHK apartment in a posh neighbourhood, complete with a breath-taking view of the sea. Vaanya thoughtfully decorated every corner of the house, turning it into their own little sanctuary that spoke volumes about their story. From an artisanal lamp that Dhruv had gifted her years ago, to a wall hanging of their journey captured in polaroids, every object in the house held a special memory. The kitchen was adorned with fridge magnets from all their trips and their recent European honeymoon, and a ceramic coffee mug painted with their college pictures. On the gallery wall leading to the bedroom hung a stunning star-map of the night of their first kiss. In the bedroom, the earthy scent of Dhruv's metallic-pine cologne mixed with Vaanya's love for natural *ittars* and scented candles. These aromas blended perfectly with the smell of white lilies perched upon the apothecary table and a fresh pot of coffee always brewing in the kitchen, creating a unique fragrance, characteristic of their home. Time flew by, and they soon realised that their first wedding anniversary was just ten days away.

Vaanya woke up feeling a little dizzy and nauseous. Before she could wake Dhruv up, bile rose in her throat and she ran to the bathroom.

Dhruv woke up to the sound of her retching and rushed inside. Hunched over the toilet seat, covered in a layer of sweat, Vaanya looked pale. He held her hair, stroked her back until she was done throwing up, after which he helped her sit back up again and dabbed a dry towel on her moist face.

"What is happening to me?" she panted, squeezing his hand hard.

"You might have eaten something bad last night. Should I call the doctor?" he asked, rubbing her back and fetching her some cold water to gargle.

"No. I am better," she gasped.

"Are you sure?"

"Yeah!"

He helped her out of the bathroom.

She sat on the bed, and he adjusted her pillow to help her relax. Tiny droplets of sweat had accumulated on her face, and it looked like she was trying too hard to think of something. Suddenly, she jolted out of bed. "I might be pregnant," she blurted out instantly.

"What?" he shook his head in surprise.

"I missed my period too. I was supposed to get it last week."

"Why didn't you tell me?"

"I thought it just got delayed because I was stressed at work."

"I should take the test. Get the kit from the back of my closet, please," she said, clutching the sheets in nervousness.

Dhruv hurried to fetch the test kit and handed it to her hastily. Some fifteen odd minutes later, Vaanya returned with a blank face and a pink stick. Dhruv looked at her in anticipation, but she didn't say a word and sank on the bed silently. He took the stick from her hand anxiously, and she announced with a voice reduced to an almost inaudible sigh, "I was right. I am pregnant."

His eyes gleamed, and he wiped the sweat from his forehead to pull her in a large hug.

And before he could say anything to express his excitement, Vaanya pulled away, "Are you sure we want to do this?" She looked at Dhruv hesitantly.

"Umm...what?" He looked visibly confused.

"This is huge, Dhruv. It's a big responsibility. And we're not prepared. This has come as an unexpected surprise."

"I know we hadn't planned. But we have always wanted to be parents. And I think we're ready. Even though this is unexpected, I think the timing is right. And anyhow, this is great news. I am so happy," he exclaimed and kissed her on the lips.

She stood there with a growing pallor on her face.

"I know what you mean, Dhruv. I have wanted a baby too. And I am happy, but not sure if I am ready for this yet."

"Jaan, it's okay. It's normal to feel overwhelmed and scared. It's a part of the process. But don't worry, we're in this together. It will be fine." He caressed her hair and kissed her forehead while she sat there, pale-faced, unable to process this any further.

"I am not sure if I am ready for a baby yet," she mouthed again, this time, her voice louder and clearer than before.

Not a single word was exchanged between the two as they holed themselves up in separate rooms. Dhruv skipped the office to work from home and stayed in the study the entire day, only stepping out to make himself some black coffee. Vaanya called in sick at work.

In the afternoon, he peeped in the bedroom to check on her. She was still sitting cross-legged, with her thousand-yard stare. He didn't say anything and headed over to the kitchen. He cooked a simple *daal khichdi* and poured the cooked stew in a bowl to take to her. She looked at him with the tray of food in his hands but couldn't find the strength to acknowledge or react. He sat next to her and without uttering a word, fed her the entire bowl. She looked at his metallic eyes that refused to meet hers.

After he left, she sat on the floor, pulling her legs close to her and cried profusely. She hated the distance between them, but was scared to deal with the sudden change that her body and life would undergo. She placed her hand on her stomach and for a single heartbeat, felt something other than fear. For a split second, as she realised that a life was growing inside of her, the anxiety gave way to a sense of satisfying calm. It lasted for a fleeting moment.

It was as if she couldn't think clearly. Nothing made sense, nothing felt real. Her heart felt torn apart. She pressed her head onto her clammy hands and a river of tears flowed down her eyes.

After an hour of uncontrollable heavy sobs that hurt her ribs, she eventually stood up and started pacing around the room. Gasping for air, she finally picked up her phone to call Mira who had moved to Mumbai a few months ago and stayed a short drive away.

"Hi, Didi! What's up?" Mira picked up her call after a few rings.

"Mira, I need you here. Please come as soon as you can," Vaanya let out a whisper.

"Are you okay, Didi? What happened?" Mira's voice grew worried.

"I'll tell you once you're here."

"Okay. I'll be there in ten."

Vaanya splashed some water on her face and got out of the room to look for Dhruv, and found him sitting on the stairs to the terrace, resting his head on his hands. She took a step forward to try to talk to him, but he pulled back immediately, unable to find the strength or the right words.

Dhruv didn't notice her standing nearby until the noise of the ringing doorbell nudged him out of his ruminations. Vaanya opened the door and broke down, engulfing her sister in a tight hug.

"What happened?" Mira asked anxiously.

"I am pregnant," she exhaled, tears trickling down her face.

Mira's eyes welled up in happiness. "Congratulations!" she mumbled and hugged her sister again, but she scowled in confusion to see Dhruv walk away carelessly.

Perplexed, Mira looked at Vaanya, "What is going on? Why did he walk away like that?"

"I don't know. It's just all so strange since this morning. Since we found out."

"What? Why? Tell me what's going on?"

"I am scared, Mira. I am not ready for this. This is a life-altering thing!"

"Yes, it is. But it's also beautiful, and it's okay to feel confused and unsettled. Why did *jeeju* walk away like that?"

"I don't know. He is mad that I am not over the moon about this, I guess. I just said that I'm not sure if I'm ready for this. This is absolutely unplanned, Mira. It's so sudden. We're just not on the same page about how we feel about this, I guess. We haven't spoken since this morning. And I can't take this cold indifference," she said dejectedly, sitting at the terrace steps herself, as Mira stuttered to sit next to her.

"My whole life will turn upside down. And my career, what about that? I've just started. I am not ready to take a maternity break. And I want to do motherhood right. I don't want to have a baby, abandon it, and go to work in three weeks. I want to experience motherhood. It's such an exciting and challenging time in a woman's life. And I want to be prepared. It's not like I don't want to start a family. I just want to be ready. I want to prepare my body, my mind. I want to read all parenting books under the sun. Create a perfect nursery in the house. Interview baby-sitters. Plan our life and finances accordingly. I want to be a little more settled in my head and my body. Besides, we've been married only a year."

Mira looked at her sister's eyes, agony reflecting through them.

"Do you remember what you said to me a few years ago when I was confused about going against dad's wish and studying fashion instead of medicine?"

Vaanya paused and smiled. "Just listen to what your inner voice is telling you to do," she said.

"That's your inner Goddess guiding you toward your true destiny. You only owe her, not everyone else," Mira added.

"Yeah," Vaanya looked like she was staring into oblivion. Mira noticed her sister's dilemma, but knew that she needed to let her figure out what she wants, on her own. So she stayed quiet, and held her hand.

"I am going to keep the baby," Vaanya said after a brief pause.

Mira nodded, looking for definitiveness in her eyes.

"I want this baby. I cannot not want it. It's a part of me. It's a part of Dhruv. It's Us. It's everything we are," she beamed.

Mira smiled, hearing the surety in her sister's voice.

"That's all jeeju needs to know," she said. "Instead of saying that you're unsure and leaving it at that, you should have tried and explained to him what scares you. Of course, it's different for you. Your body is going to go through changes. But walk him through your feelings. He'll understand. He is just a man who was so happy that he was going to become a father. You being shocked and dismissive initially might have hurt him. We both know he can be really sensitive. And that's because he loves too hard."

"Yeah, you're right." Vaanya took a deep breath and looked at her. "Thanks Mira! You're like my mirror. When I can't see things clearly, I look for you to be able to look into myself."

"You guys are a power couple, and you will make kick-ass parents, I can guarantee that. But just don't be the overly controlling and neurotic parents. Because then, I'll have to steal my nephew or niece and take on the role of the fun cool aunt."

Vaanya laughed and hugged her sister.

Just then, they heard Dhruv.

"I'm sorry. I've been eavesdropping," he said standing near the kitchen. He began walking toward them.

"It's okay jeeju, we forgive you. We Sharma women, are just too kind," Mira tried to lighten the atmosphere, but Dhruv and Vaanya still looked shaken.

"I am sorry, Vaanya," Dhruv stepped closer. "I should have been more understanding. I know this is very new and unexpected."

Vaanya looked at her husband's eyes. They looked different today. There was a glint of maturity and kindness in them. She felt relieved just looking at them.

"It's alright, take your time to process it," he said. "And I know as much as I say that I am in this with you, it won't change the fact that you will have to carry the baby for the next nine months. Your body will go through changes, and yes, it will be hard. But what I am trying to say is that it will be worth it. And that I'm here to make the transition easier. That's my biggest job from now on. To try my best to not let you feel that it's so hard."

Her lips curved in a bright smile of satisfaction hearing the earnestness in his voice.

"You are not pregnant Vaanya. *We* are pregnant," he finally said.

A tear escaped her eyes and she threw her arms around her beautiful husband. Burying her face in his neck, she wept. All the anxiety and confusion of the past few hours melting in his safe embrace. "I am sorry too. I love you so much Dhruv," she whispered in his ear.

He wiped her tears with his forefinger.

Mira shot them a nostalgic half-smile, standing at a distance. "And you know what, one's never ready for something as big as this. You'll always feel like you're unprepared, and that the time is not right. But I think this baby coming unexpected is just life's way of telling you that you guys are ready," she said.

"And apparently, this one is so much more mature and sensible than the two of us. Isn't she?" Dhruv exclaimed pointing towards Mira, and both Mira and Vaanya broke into a repressed laughter.

Dhruv gestured for Mira to join them, and she ran to wrap her arms around her sister and brother-in-law, joining in the family hug.

After such an eventful day, at night, Vaanya settled in bed with a cup of hot chocolate and a nice book. For Vaanya, reading had always been a coping mechanism. The quiet calm of holding a thick book, and listening to the crunch of its tossing pages, losing herself in imaginative other worlds, escaping the chaos of real life—it always helped her unwind and centre herself. Dhruv walked into the room to see her engrossed in reading and quietly lay beside her.

He finally broke the silence an hour later. "Nine months from now, we'll be parents," he said, staring at the clock on the wall opposite the bed.

Vaanya noticed him not looking at her. Her heart broke a little, but she gulped her feelings.

"We're going to have a baby," she smiled at him.

Dhruv still stared into the empty space, looking lost in thought. Vaanya thought of saying something but couldn't bring herself to speak.

"You know, before I met you, I had just dated Anisha. But after I had my heart broken, I was convinced that the idea of true love was an illusion. One could write poems and songs about it, watch it in movies, read it in books. But it's fictional.

"And infact, I used to think we glorify love in art, because we're probably trying to make up for its absence in real life.

"The point being, for a whole year, I was pretty convinced about the inexistence of love in real life. But suddenly, one summer day, I saw you, and all my prior misconceptions changed. I didn't have the slightest clue that it was so easy to have something fundamental within you that you've believed for so long, change in a split second.

"I believe there are certain defining moments in one's life. You don't see them coming, but when they happen, you know your life won't be the same again.

Seeing you was one defining moment of my life. And this feels like another."

Vaanya looked at her husband who seemed like he was in a state of trance. Sometimes she loved how her husband's mind worked. He was one of the most objective and analytical man she knew, but unlike most others with a strong left-brain, he was also capable of being highly intuitive, and he understood nuanced, deep, and complex emotions of the human experience.

"You know, when the first time you meet someone, you see how they look, because that catches your eye at first," he continued, "But in some time, it starts fading. You see other more invisible things. Like their value systems. How they think? What excites their soul? And later on, when you sleep with them, you explore the shape of their muscles, the touch of their bare skin against yours. But at the end of it all what matters and governs the relationship you're going to have with them, is the fact whether you can have a proper conversation with your partner," he paused for a moment.

"To understand and be understood. To see and be seen. That's what we all crave for deep down. To feel a deep sense of bliss when you're with someone. That's love. The feeling of comfort and safety, of having a home in another person and knowing with undeterred surety that come what may, you'll always have that home in someone's arms. That's love with commitment. And I consider myself so lucky to have found all of those things in you."

Vaanya was equal parts overwhelmed as touched with his words.

"You know when I first saw you, I found you to be very attractive. But what caught my attention was the way you'd lose yourself in whatever you did. Like you were really in the moment. Always, giving it your all. They say, how you do something is how you do everything. I knew, you were an all or nothing kind of girl. I had a nagging feeling that you were the one who'd bring the change my soul had been waiting for."

Vaanya could see the honesty in his eyes. He was finally looking at her.

"And right now, it feels like another defining moment. It feels that this baby growing inside of you, is what all of my life is probably going to be about. Again, I never thought how something inside of me could change entirely, in a shooting second. I already can't imagine what lengths I'd go to protect this little life breathing inside of you."

"You know there is no heartbeat of the baby yet," she raised her eyebrows and made a face.

He laughed weakly at his wife's failed attempt at humour, "You know what I meant."

"I know," she smiled. He rolled over to her side of the bed and placed his head in her lap.

It dawned upon her suddenly, that in that very moment, she had everything that she had ever wanted in her life.

"The baby looks perfectly healthy," Dr Kashyap, their gynaecologist, assured.

They held hands and looked at the growing foetus on the screen linked to the ultrasound machine.

"It's okay to be a little nervous. It's very common with first-time parents. What you're looking at is a healthy, growing baby. So, drop all your worries and enjoy this phase. I know it feels like it's too hard right now, but when you hold your baby for the first time in your arms, it will all feel worth it," Dr Kashyap smiled.

Although finding about the pregnancy had overwhelmed them, as the realisation sank in, they gradually discovered little joys on the road to parenthood. The excitement and happiness increased with every small milestone in the journey—the bi-monthly doctor visits, seeing their baby grow from a tiny blip to the size of a pea, then a pear and finally a watermelon, testing new formulas to help with Vaanya's morning sickness, dragging their lazy asses to the Lamaze classes, filling the house with pregnancy handbooks and tool kits that they seldom read. Everything made them a little more prepared to take on parenthood as it came.

One evening, back home from the visit to the gynaecologist, Vaanya spotted Dhruv putting up the sonogram on the soft-board above their bed.

"What are you doing?" she looked confused.

"Putting up a picture of our baby so we can look at it whenever we feel like," he explained sincerely.

"Are you serious?" she scoffed.

"Yeah. Why is it so funny?" he asked with a naive smile.

"You're so cute," she laughed. "I guess I am going to have two babies at home now," she said, ruffling his hair.

"Yes, I am always going to be your first baby. Our baby better not take my place," he said laughingly and held her from the back, wrapping her hands around the seven-month-old baby bump.

She interlocked her fingers with his, "I feel so warm and secure. You won't ever leave us, no? You'll stand by us forever?"

"No. I am taking the first flight out and never returning."

She laughed and hit him on his arm playfully.

Sometime during the eight months, Vaanya started her maternity leave. Staying home, away from work, doing nothing made her cranky and added to the already soaring hormonal mood swings. She spent half of her day reading, though now, her go-to books on psychoanalysis, philosophy and poetry had been replaced with books on parenting and baby-care. She spent the remainder of the day sleeping and snacking on home-made pregnancy treats sent in by her mother and mother-in-law, *besan laddoos*, dry fruit cakes, coconut *barfis* made with cashews and jaggery. The pantry was stocked with love from soon to be grandmothers.

"Thank god you are home, Dhruv. I've been so bored. I'll rust away within these walls," Vaanya started wailing like a toddler as Dhruv came home.

"Babe, I had so much work today. It's getting crazy these days with the recent merger." He sank into the couch next to her and rested his head on her shoulder.

"Hmm..." She massaged his temples gently.

"Dinner is in the kitchen," she murmured, nudging him, as he almost began drifting into a quiet sleep, burrowed between her chest and right arm.

"Don't sleep on an empty stomach. I'll lay the table, you go freshen up," she said, struggling to get up from the couch, placing one hand under her bulging belly and the other on her back for support.

"No, you don't have to get up. I'm doing it," he assured her while sampling the food.

"Listen, I'm not hungry anyway. Just serve yourself," she said, walking toward the kitchen with swollen feet.

"What happened?"

"Just don't feel like it. I'm sick of eating healthy home-cooked bland food," she whined.

"Okay then, I am your chef tonight. Tell me, what do you feel like having? This delightful man is at your service, ma'am!" He bowed and tied the apron around his office trousers. She laughed, admiring his whimsical ways.

"Listen, you are exhausted. So, stop! I'll eat whatever the maid cooked, it's okay. And you don't have to suffer because of me. Order in for yourself if you want to. It's ridiculous that you too have given up on your favourite foods."

"It's the bare minimum that I can do," he shot her a convincing smile. "So tell me, what would Madame prefer tonight? A lip-smacking lasagna, fresh from the oven with a side of delicious tomato and basil bruschetta? Or creamy mushroom pasta and stuffed garlic bread along with a scrumptious apple pie for dessert?" He wandered around her lyrically reciting his authentic menu.

"Umm, *Dum Biryani*," she chuckled and licked her lips.

"Such desi choices," he teased her. "But we aim to please."

For the next half-an-hour, she settled on the kitchen table, reading out the instructions from the cookbook, and he followed them like a doting husband and a gourmet chef in training.

Mouth-watering Hyderabadi Dum Biriyani was served for dinner along with vegetable *raita* and *mirchi ka salan*.

"And here we present, chef's kiss!" He surprised her by pulling out her favourite Lindt Sea Salt dark chocolate from his pocket and planted a tiny kiss on her lips.

"Chef's kiss, quite literally," she smiled and broke off a large cube. He bit into the chocolate bar placed between her soft lips.

"Dhruv, do you wonder what kind of parents we'll be?" Vaanya asked one night while Dhruv was reading *What to Expect When You're Expecting*.

"I think we'll be great parents."

"But what if we stink as parents?"

He laughed and stroked her hair, "What makes you think that?"

"Just wondering, it doesn't come with a warning sign. You never know."

"I think as long as we're together, we'll ace whatever we do, even parenting. This baby is damn lucky to join Team Dhruv and Vaanya, you know. We make a solid team and we'll raise a kickass baby."

"Well yeah, our baby is going to be pretty kickass. My good-looks and well… my brains," she laughed, and he smothered her with breathy kisses.

Half an hour later they fell asleep in each other's arms.

At one-thirty in the night, a peacefully sleeping Dhruv woke up abruptly to Vaanya's voice, whispering something softly in his ears.

Half asleep and panicked, he pulled her closer, "What happened!? Are you okay?"

"I am craving hot chocolate fudge so bad," she bit her lower lip, clearly embarrassed to have woken him up.

"Babe, you scared me," he took a deep breath and plunged back into the covers.

"I am sorry," she licked her lip and sat upright.

"It's one-thirty in the night, Vaanya," he growled, checking his phone. "Go back to sleep, we'll get you your hot chocolate fudge tomorrow."

"But I am craving it right now."

"We are not going right now. I am exhausted, jaan. And I have work tomorrow."

"Of course you do! And what about me? I am just a hormonal, crazy, unemployed, pregnant woman."

"Vaanya..." he moaned, pressing his temples with his fingers. "I am really tired, jaan. Please try and understand. Besides, where will we find hot chocolate fudge at this hour?"

"Yeah, of course, you're tired. I am the one carrying our child. I am the one who's eight months pregnant and miserable. Do you have any idea how it feels?" Her face was beet red by now.

"Do you know I can't get up when I am sitting without supporting my huge inflated belly, and this nagging backache keeps me in constant pain. I pee like... I don't even know how many times a day, as if my bladder is some squeeze-ball. And these food cravings and aversions drive me nauseous all the time. And the worst of all, I get these strange urges to cry and scream. I feel so helpless, I can't," she burst into tears mid-rant.

"Holy F—What's there to cry in it, jaan!" Dhruv exclaimed.

"Nothing! Go back to sleep," she crawled out of bed, pouting and sighing.

"Jaan, wait, listen! I love you no, come back to bed, Vaanya..."

"Ugh, why didn't I use better protection," Dhruv muttered to himself and dragged his sleep-deprived, exhausted shell of a body out into the living room to find Vaanya sobbing on the couch.

"Dhruv, go to sleep. I am sorry, I shouldn't have woken you up. I don't know what's happening to me. You have to work tomorrow, and I am being so inconsiderate and stupid. The normal, unpregnant, sane Vaanya would never have done this. You know that, right? I am really sorry, baby," she spoke softly, letting out deep sighs and then hyperventilating, slipping into a hormone-induced panic attack.

"Shh..." he pulled her into his arms, tucked her hair behind her ears and stroked her back gently. "When I married you, I promised to love you at your best as well as your worst. I signed up for hysterics too."

"Right, I am hysterical?" she said, arching her eyebrows and snuffing out her nose.

"No, no, no! By hysterical, I meant upset! I don't even know the meaning of hysterical. What makes you think I have got such a rich vocabulary! No!"

She peered at him with large eyes and a pinched uptight expression. He stood there looking pale-faced.

"What?" he asked unnerved. And she burst into a loud laughter.

"You look so cute when you are confused and scared," she ruffled his hair and cupped his face in her hands to kiss him loudly on the cheek.

"I love you!" he mouthed and pulled her closer to kiss her neck.

"Ah, I love it when you kiss my neck. It calms me," she closed her eyes, losing herself in the sweet touch of his lips.

"Why do you think I am doing it?" he whispered softly.

She smiled at his reply. She loved how he was always a step ahead of her. Even in the middle of the night, when he was dragged out of bed mid-sleep.

Watching her smile, he began kissing her more passionately. She moaned in response. Enjoying his touch, she drew him closer and coiled her arms around his neck. But he pulled away and got up to grab the car keys from the cabinet.

"What! Come back," she squealed, throwing out her arms in the air.

"Come on, let's go!" he smirked.

Her mouth fell open. “Finish what you started first!” she said, gesturing to him to come back.

“Ya. Let’s finish satisfying our cravings.” He walked back to her and brought his lips near hers, almost kissing her. “Of hot chocolate fudge, my love. What did you think?” he smirked and pulled away before their lips could meet.

“Are you teasing me?” she rolled her eyes.

“You bet I am!”

“Okay jokes apart. I know I was ridiculously unreasonable. We don’t have to go anywhere.”

“Well, now we do,” he pulled her arm, helping her get off the couch.

“But where are we going?” She blankly followed. “You have to be up early for work. Let’s not, please.”

“Well, guess I’m going to be very sick soon. My team will have to make do with me being on a leave for the day,” Dhruv said with a poker face.

“What lie are you going to come up with when they ask you what made you sick?”

“My pregnant wife. I don’t lie.”

“Ha Ha Ha”

“Besides, if my pregnant wife wants hot chocolate fudge, she’ll get it. No matter what time of the night it is. And if I have to call in sick tomorrow. I don’t care. What matters right now is this. You...this baby. If it wants hot chocolate fudge. It is going to get it.”

“We’re going to have one spoiled baby,” she laughed.

“Two!” he joked. “It’s going to take after the mother.”

Vaanya laughed and hit him in the arm mischievously, before thrusting her lips on his and kissing him profusely, “I don’t know what I did to deserve you.”

As they reached the parking lot and walked toward the car, he swung open the door for her. She hopped in, and they began wandering the streets of Mumbai in pyjamas.

"Thanks, baby!" Vaanya said suddenly.

"Why?"

"For putting up with me. Every time I lose my mind."

"Hmm…"

"Everytime I get 'hysterical'," she flinched and looked at him with playful eyes waiting for him to laugh at her choice of words. But to her surprise, he said something completely different.

"You didn't leave my side when I was at my worst; this is nothing. Besides, I am doing this for us. I meant it when I said I am going to do anything that it takes to make this easier for you."

"I know, I love you so much. It's just that I get these stupid rushes, weird urges from time to time. I don't know, it's partly pregnancy, and partly because sitting at home is a little frustrating, you know."

"I know. I wish I could do something to make it better."

"Hmm, I was talking to Mira. She has a few important projects running at work right now, which is why she is pretty busy. But she said she was trying to clear her plate to be able to be with me more often."

"That's good. Although where do you want the hot chocolate fudge from? Look up *na*, see what place might be open right now."

"Listen, let's go to that place near Marine Drive, 'Cakes N Bakes.' They are open most of the night, I think."

"Wait, let me take a detour."

In fifteen minutes, they reached the place, only to find a big "CLOSED" sign hanging on the door.

She bit her lip in nervousness, feeling guilty to have dragged him out on the street in the middle of the night.

"I am sorry," she murmured, pouting her lips.

Dhruv looked dejected.

"I really wanted you to get the hot chocolate fudge," he said, hitting the steering wheel with his fists before reversing the car to drive back.

"Dhruv…"

"Yes, jaan."

"These empty streets, the street-lights reflecting on the rain-soaked pavement, sitting next to you in the car, driving aimlessly listening to our playlists, this was exactly the therapy I needed tonight," she looked at him for a response, but continued when he didn't look at her.

"It's okay if we didn't get the hot-chocolate fudge. I just wanted us to do something together. Get out and spend some time doing something fun, something different."

She looked at him nostalgically, "like the good old days."

"Hmm…" He forced a smile.

"It's been weeks. You stay stressed at work, and I remain indoors with nothing to do. We both needed a change. And you need to blow off some steam anyhow. To get ready and prepare yourself mentally and emotionally for the baby to come. I am so glad you took tomorrow off."

She leaned in and cupped his face in his hands to kiss him on his cheeks. He smiled shyly and looked straight ahead on the road.

"Look, here we are, on the streets of Mumbai, wandering together at night, with me being eight months pregnant. It's crazy how life turns out. Border-line magical."

And suddenly, rain began to pour. The headlights reflected brightly on the soaked highway… And the same song that had been their constant companion since college, began playing on the radio. She held her head out of the window and hummed along with the tunes.

"*Kahin toh hogi wo …*
Duniya jahaan tu mere paas hai…"

"Remember this song?" She ran her fingers through his hair and the back of his neck, making small concentric circles on his skin with her fingertips.

"How can I ever forget this song?"

"And how this song started playing in the café on our first date," she chuckled.

"Yeah, that was my first big sign from the universe, that this is meant to be." He smiled.

"You know, sometimes I feel we have come such a long way, no? Did we imagine back in the day that we'd be together like this? So many years down the lane, I'd be pregnant, and we'd be hunting for a lousy hot chocolate fudge in the dead of the night."

"I did," Dhruv said instantly.

"You did?"

"Yes," he said, his gaze still fixed on the road.

"Were you this sure of us even back then?"

"I was, Vaanya. From the day I saw you. Remember when we had that huge fight? When I had to travel to Hyderabad for that critical project, around our anniversary and we didn't speak for so many days?"

"Yeah." She nodded.

"I was damn sure after that. I hadn't been as sure of anything in my life. When you weren't with me, I realised I was incapable of living without you."

"Dhruv, don't."

"No Vaanya, I am just telling you the truth. We're soon going to be parents. It's a big chapter in our lives. Let me be honest. A lot of things will change when the baby comes. I know our lives will revolve around the baby. I can already imagine myself doing anything and everything in my power to ensure that this baby is safe and loved. But I also need you to know how vital you are to me. And I am selfish, you know. I need you for me. So, if I worry for you, I am actually looking out for myself."

"You know, the pregnancy has been tough for me. The doctor did warn us that my uterus isn't so strong. I am scared, Dhruv. Everything will be fine, no?"

"Of course it will be… the doctor said that we've taken all necessary precaution and there's nothing to worry about. You've grown stronger; it will all be just fine. Don't worry about a single thing..." He squeezed her hand tight.

After a while of chilling silence, Vaanya said, "You know something about loss?"

He stayed silent.

"We always think we cannot go through it. But we are usually more resilient than we think. And God only gives us what we can handle."

Once they got back home, Vaanya settled in bed, flipping through the pages of the latest Jhumpa Lahiri novel, when Dhruv walked in with two mugs. One of which had 'The world's best boyfriend' written on it with Dhruv's caricature.

'World's best boyfriend!" Vaanya laughed. "Where did you find this mug?"

"Doesn't matter. As long as I still have the tag. And the prize," he sneered and handed out one mug to her.

"What's the prize?"

"This!" He leaned forward to kiss her and settled in the bed beside her. "If we couldn't get hot chocolate fudge tonight, let's make do with some steaming hot chocolate?"

"You're still the world's best boyfriend." She snuggled up to him, sipping on the hot beverage under the blanket.

Chapter 14

Somewhere Only We Know

Do you think even the twinkling of stars
Is nothing but tears of shock-waves
To mourn
How light leaves
To travel galaxies
Millions of light-years away?

—DHRUV

On the cold but sunny afternoon of the 10th of December, Vaanya suddenly experienced a searing pain that pierced through her. She felt as though lightning had struck her in a soundless instant. Her due date wasn't until another month, and there she was, unable to move, soaked in her own water, glued on the warm and sticky couch that suddenly felt like a sharp bed of needles.

The pain came in waves, hitting her incessantly in intervals of a few minutes. As another wave of pain receded her body, she shuddered and somehow grabbed the phone.

"Dhruv," she winced, unable to put her pain into words.

Vaanya, what happened?" Dhruv jerked, sensing her discomfort from her quivering voice.

"I think... my...," she sighed and mumbled, "water just broke."

"What!?" his voice was as loud as the pounding of his heart.

"I am scared, Dhruv. I don't feel okay..."

"Don't worry, jaan. We'll take care of everything. Stay strong, you can do this..."

At eleven-thirty in the night, after enduring seven tormenting hours of labour, Vaanya was lying exhausted and heaving on the cold hospital bed. With multiple Ivs attached to her body, she looked pallid.

"Push one more time, Vaanya. Come on!" Dr Kashyap encouraged her.

Vaanya struggled, but followed.

"Take a deep breath and push one more time," Dr Kashyap murmured while monitoring the heart rate of the baby on the ECG.

Vaanya was sweating profusely. With one hand, she squeezed Dhruv's hand, and the other grabbed the sheets beneath her in a tight fist. Whimpering in pain, legs pulled apart, she mustered the last ounce of strength in her withering body to push her baby out into the world. Her husband stood next to her, scared, helpless, and anxious. He pulled her hair back and wiped the increasing beads of sweat off her soaked forehead. He couldn't see Vaanya in such terrible pain, and flinched at the sight, but stood beside her, nonetheless, praying...

"You're going to be alright. I won't let anything happen to you," he cried as the doctor bent over between her stretched legs, as though looking for a missing piece of belonging in a deep rucksack.

"Shh, close your eyes. Imagine us and the baby at home. In our bed. The baby is beautiful. Exactly like you," he whispered in her ear, holding her hand tight.

She cried, her eyes squeezed shut, imagining the heavenly scene.

He caressed her forehead and whispered in her ear, "It's a quiet and peaceful day. We're in our sun-lit bedroom. The gentle cooing of our baby in the crib fills the air. We have a happy and healthy family. It's calm and perfect, just how we had pictured it."

Dhruv tried calling Mira, but she had been in Goa due to a work trip. She had rushed back and was on her way to Mumbai as soon as she heard the news of Vaanya going into labour. Both Dhruv and Vaanya's parents also took the first flight that they could.

The leftover strength in Vaanya's body was escaping. She was reaching the breaking point, as her contractions became increasingly painful with every passing second. She was slipping into unconsciousness, unable to take the pain any further.

"The baby's heartbeat is dropping," the nurse practically screamed.

"There might be a uterine rupture," Dr Kashyap announced. "She is bleeding. We'll have to take her for an emergency surgery."

"Doctor, is she going to be okay?" Dhruv's eyes searched for hope in between the tense creases of Dr Kashyap's forehead.

"Mr. Malhotra, I am going to try my best to save your wife and child. I just need you to stay calm. We'll take it from here," she said, pulling the wheels of Vaanya's portable bed out of the room, into the operation theatre.

Vaanya, don't worry. Stay strong. I'm here for you. Everything's going to be fine," he cried, squeezing her hand tight and planting a small kiss on her chapped lips.

"Dhruv..." she sighed.

"I know you're a fighter, Vaanya,", he said wiping the sweat off her forehead. "We'll get through this."

"I'll try my best. I just want you to know that I love you and this baby so much. I love our perfect little family. And I'll fight for us."

"Shh, I love you so much, I won't let you go, Vaanya. Me and this baby, our family needs you. You're going to be just fine."

"Dhruv," her voice trembled, as his hand slowly grazed off her cold, clammy palms. She got pulled into the dark room and its doors shut in front of Dhruv's helpless, puckered face.

He paced in the hallway, anxiously waiting for a word from the doctor. With numb legs and a parched throat, two hours felt like two hundred days. His dried eyes kept switching glances between the clock and the red sign on the door of the operation theatre. His lips moved in prayer as his mind kept zoning out.

At 1 a.m., Mira arrived at the hospital. Vaanya's parents had already arrived before midnight.

"Ma!" Mira ran to her mother who held her tightly and kissed her on the forehead.

The fear of losing her elder daughter reflecting in her moist hazel eyes, that she had passed on to Vaanya.

On the other end of the hallway leading up to the operation theatre, a nervous Dhruv paced across the length of the lobby.

"Jeeju," Mira tapped on his shoulder.

"Oh, hi!" He turned around to meet her eyes.

"It's going to be okay," she murmured.

"Yeah," he shot her a polite, repressed smile.

"In another half hour, Dhruv's parents showed up. The built-up tension inside of him came streaming down as tears, seeing his family. He collapsed into the chair, face buried in both his hands, and wept inconsolably.

"My brave boy," Mrs. Malhotra rubbed her son's back, trying her best to relieve his anxiety. "Think of it like a bad dream. In some time, you'll wake up and meet your baby and your wife and step into your new life, as a family. It will all be just fine."

Minutes passed like hours and hours like days. Mira went to the cafeteria to bring them some coffee. She was as scared as Dhruv, but she swallowed her fears. Anxiety kept accumulating in her body as the hands of the clock ticked away, slowly unleashing greater uncertainty with each passing second.

At three in the morning, Dr Kashyap emerged from the operation theatre with a petite, pink form of a new-born wrapped in soft white cloth held carefully in her arms.

"Congratulations, Mr. Malhotra. You're the father to a beautiful baby girl." She gave a small, half-smile and handed over the feeble, wrapped figure to him. Dhruv delicately held the fragile cotton-candy-like skin of the new-born in his gentle, warm squeeze and felt a sudden wave of overwhelming love in his heart, the kind of love he had never experienced before. He held the tiny, living breathing embodiment of their love in his bare, shaky hands and looked at the baby—with tightly shut eyes, clasped mini-fists and moist pink, brazen skin, holed up in the new safety of her Papa's arms, trying to adjust to a new world outside the dark, warm safety of her Mama's womb.

Mira was teary-eyed to see the tiny baby cocooned in Dhruv's arms. Mira's gaze fell on her face as she opened her eyes to a brand-new world.

"She has Vaanya's eyes," Mrs. Sharma said, looking at her grand-child.

Mira's throat went dry and she gathered the strength to ask, "Doctor, how's Didi?"

Dhruv shuffled nervously and shifted his attention to Dr Kashyap, his eyes again looking for hope in her dry eyes. But Dr Kashyap's face fell and her gaze fixed to the sparkling white hospital floor.

"Mr. Malhotra, can I please talk to you in private?"

Dhruv's face turned white again and Mira stood frozen on the spot. The nurse took the new-born from Dhruv's arms.

"Please come with me," Dr Kashyap spoke gently. She started walking towards her room, and Dhruv and Mira followed her.

Dhruv felt slightly relieved seeing Vaanya's favourite flowers in the room. On the large mahogany desk sat a fat bundle of files, each with the names of different patients, containing their portfolios. On the walls were various pictures of pregnant women, healthy babies, and happy mothers with their new-borns. Dhruv looked at the pictures and tried to calm his palpitating heart, still searching for the last speck of hope in Dr Kashyap's voice.

"Mr. Malhotra, as soon as the heart-rate of the baby started dipping, I was apprehensive that there might be a uterine rupture. Vaanya's uterus wasn't as strong and although it had shown good signs, somehow, our worst fears came true. It was in fact uterine rupture. It's practically a condition when the mother's uterus tears apart during labour. And I'm afraid—"

She tried to assimilate Dhruv's reaction, but he couldn't handle the medical terminology and explanations anymore. He was trying to hold on to the last flying piece of sanity inside of him. But he couldn't anymore and burst out screaming, "Doctor, my wife is okay, right?"

His voice jolted the exhausted doctor, who, after having spent the better part of the night in the operation theatre, quivered at his tone. She was scared to launch the truth upon a terrified husband.

"We performed an emergency C-section to take out the baby. It had already been over ten minutes before we could rescue her, so it was nothing short of a miracle that we didn't lose the baby. But Vaanya had already lost too much blood by then. And despite our best efforts, I'm sorry, Mr. Malhotra... we couldn't save your wife."

Dr Kashyap's words landed on Dhruv with a harsh thrust, like that of a plane suddenly crashing on the runway.

He didn't flinch. He didn't move. He didn't speak. He simply stood there, staring at a pale and sweaty doctor, who had failed at saving the love of his life.

Mira rushed outside as soon as the terrible news sank into her. She hunched over the side-walk of the hospital and vomited out the fear she had been carrying in her belly. The trauma stayed within, creeping into her. She stood up, only to hurl again, shock and anxiety, retching out of her cold, trembling body.

"Doctor, are you sure you are talking about the right patient? I'm talking about my wife, Vaanya Malhotra. She can't be dead. Could you just please go and check again? There has to be a mix-up."

"Mr. Malhotra, I can understand your shock. I am really sorry for your loss. We did the best we could. This is a rare case in which despite no prior surgeries or operations, something as tragic as this happens."

Dhruv squeezed his eyes shut and threw himself back in the chair. Disbelief dripping down his eyes, he pressed his forehead, clicked his tongue and let out a deep sigh, "This cannot happen, Doctor. Could you please just..."

"Mr. Malhotra, I empathise with you. We did all that was in our power. I am sorry."

"Doctor, could you please just... go and wake her up! Vaanya cannot leave me. Do you understand, doctor? We promised each other. To never leave each other's side, no matter what happened. And I know my Vaanya, she is not the one to break promises. She is the strongest, most invincible woman I know. Doctor, please, I am begging you, just please check again. I am sure she is okay. Right there, waiting for me."

He got up from the wobbly chair and stormed toward the door to check on Vaanya, but suddenly everything around him began spinning. The room seemed to be closing in on him, as he gasped for air and fell back on the chair. A flurry of tears escaped his eyes as he held his face in his hands and cried bitterly.

Dr Kashyap came and sat beside him.

"Dhruv, I have known you and Vaanya for the last nine months. I know my words won't mean a lot to you right now, in the face of what you're feeling, but I need you to know that before a doctor, I am a wife and a mother. Each day, I see couples come to me with hope. I see each couple for around nine months before I deliver their babies, and they thank me for helping them start their family. But I never hear from them again. During those nine months, I listen to their stories. They tell me all about their experience; their hardships and triumphs, the challenges they are facing, the small joys of parenthood and the excitement to see all that they are, manifest into another human being. To bring that life into this world. They're scared and happy. I tell them that it will be all okay and it will all be worth it. But nine months of knowing the parents, monitoring the life growing within the mother, I become a part of their journey too. So, believe me when I say that this tragedy hurts me very deeply, if not as much as you. Underneath this white coat, I am only human, as helpless like the rest of us. But as a part of the profession, I am in, I am not even allowed a moment's grief."

After a moment of silence, she continued.

"I lost my first baby on the same operating table around ten years back. Despite all the time that's passed, the pain still lingers. So, believe me when I say that I know a thing or two about loss.

"Vaanya was a strong woman, Dhruv. She fought till the end. And you are her husband, so you cannot be weak. I am sure that deep within, you too have the courage that she was made up of. I know you'll get through this. You have to. For your daughter. She is beautiful, and she has got your wife's eyes."

I withdrew into a slumber. I am in a field of bright yellow sunflowers. It's a warm and sunny morning. But I'm cold and I feel restless. I am looking for Vaanya, and I can't see her anywhere. Suddenly, I hear my name in her sweet voice, and it sounds like a summer song. She appears behind the green meadows. She is wearing a white sun dress that flows until her knees. Her hair looks scruffy, but beautiful nonetheless. Her sleepy eyes seem to carry daydreams around the corner of her lashes. A million dreams, for a million lifetimes, that I am willing to spend with her.

Her blush face and plump lips are smiling at me. She gestures to me to come close to her. I am relieved to see her. I walk toward her, but the closer I get, the farther she appears to go. I start galloping across the field, chasing her bleak shadow in the clouds. It has turned dark now. But I can see her disappearing form, and I run as far as I can.

I am short of breath, but I can't stop. Vaanya's shadow gets fainter, but something in me believes that she is right there. I will reach her, no matter what. She is mine, I won't let go of her. I will do all that it takes to close this distance between us.

My legs cramp. The sunflowers are replaced by rocky cliffs. I am running across the coastline to reach the end of the sea. I trip over the rough edges of the rocks. I try to get up, but I feel paralysed on the ground. My nose starts bleeding and I am breathing heavily. Panting and wiping off the gushing blood, I see her slipping away into the vast stretches of the ocean. I gather the dwindling energy within me to scream her holy name, to call out to her and stop her from leaving me all alone. She turns back and smiles at me. Her cheeks are flushed and she looks more beautiful than ever. She is running into the far end of the sea, I run after her. She is inches apart from me, but light-years away.

I wake up with a bitter taste of sand in my mouth. The coarse sand particles lodge into my throat and it's clogged. I can't speak. Vaanya is lying on top of me and I forget everything else. A satisfying calm lands on me. Her skin feels softer and lighter than usual. My body feels heavy, like mercury. But I am far too shaken by the moment to care about it. She kisses me gently. Her lips taste different. I try for words to come out of my mouth, but my throat closes.

I want to ask her to stay. I wish this moment gets captured in a polaroid forever. I wish to be thrown onto a different planet where time could at least move slower, if not stop altogether. I try to speak, but she silences me, placing her feathery fingers on my dry lips. She is whispering in my ear. Her voice has become more tranquil.

"I need to go," her voice washes over me like a tsunami of indescribable proportions.

I am trying to speak, but she shushes me again.

"I love you more than the meaning these words can ever carry. But you have to let me go, Dhruv. We'll be fine, I promise.

"These words and this world only limit us. What we feel and who we are transcends beyond this.

"Above this ever-changing world lies a realm of serenity, we are all but particles in this endless sea of true love. It is where you will find me again. And we will embrace, forevermore."

I try to tighten my grip around her, but her body starts dissolving into thin white dust in my hands. I try to catch hold of it, but it slips like fine sand out of my frail fists. I lay on the warm bed of white, shining sand. A thick salty teardrop scurries out of my eye. I wonder how we're all nothing but a speck of dust. A small part of the universe, being born and reborn in this world of unending episodes of joy and sorrow.

It starts to rain, as though the sky is weeping at my loss. The rain drops hit my face with impeccable thrust. I get soaked in the rainwater as it washes clean the last bit of sand particles clogged in my throat.

A disquieting voice escapes my mouth. 'Dharya!' I wake up in a jolt.

On the hospital bed, Vaanya was lying deceased. Dhruv was ten inches away from her, but she was light years away, transcending into another place. Her pale face emanated a radiant peace that assured him that it would all be okay. She had faith that he was capable of raising their daughter alone. She believed in him, in life and in death.

"I love you, Vaanya. I always will. In this lifetime and beyond," he whispered in her ears, squeezing her limp hand. He climbed onto the hard hospital bed to hold her, one last time. He could see the love of his life slipping away from his arms. He wanted to hold her tighter, and not let go, not today, not ever.

Beside the bed stood the crib of the baby. Dhruv got up to carry their new-born into bed with them. "Hi Dharya!" he said and picked her up. With one arm squeezed around her wife's lifeless form and the other linked around their few-hours-old daughter, Dhruv tried to hold his family together.

Chapter 15

Stubborn Love

I walked into our old apartment last night
Its old bricks still hold the flying fragments
Of our love with unparalleled strength
The sobs from each time we cried profusely in each other's lap
Still echo loudly across the living room hall
Our memories carved out like murals
On the worn-out, wobbly walls
Still stand the test of time
Unlike us

A strand of your dark hair lays displayed
On the cream-white satin pillow-cover
Like a rare artefact in the exhibition of our intimacy
Coupled with the muffled laughs and stolen sighs
Stuck in the folds of these crumpled sheets

But this morning, the potted dahlia
That used to stand tall and erect in the front-yard
Facing the sun in all its crimson glory

Bowed in devotion
Praying for your arrival again.

—DHRUV

"Jeeju, please come and eat something. I have brought some rajma chawal. You look so weak. You've got to start eating properly..." Mira leaned in to take a closer look at Dhruv whose hollow face was starting to pale faster than ever.

He turned around to face her and then looked away, continuing to stare out of the window. The room was considerably dark. He sat on the cold floor with a small photograph of Vaanya clutched tightly in his hands.

"I'll come outside in a while," his voice had reduced to a whisper.

Mira stood at the door for a few seconds before leaving him to check on Dharya. The third, slightly smaller room of the house that they had converted into a cute, cosy nursery for the baby still looked the same, as if nothing had changed. Vaanya had decorated each tiny corner with at most perfection during her last months of pregnancy.

The walls were painted in off white pastels and vinyl stickers. The wooden crib with soft baby pink covers and a baby monitor stood in the middle. An aqua rug lay on the floor in one corner with knick-knacks. In the other corner stood an apothecary shelf with loads of stuffed animals, soft toys, children's story books, and lullabies which they had hoarded on multiple shopping trips in Vaanya's last trimester. Vaanya would cry hysterically seeing cute babies in the store and over-stock on every tiny thing their baby would possibly need. Sky blue overalls, canary yellow baby beanie, sea-green apron and baby-pink mittens lay carefully clustered in the almirah, just how Vaanya had organised them.

Mira entered the nursery to a pair of tiny deep-brown searching eyes staring back at her from the crib. She picked up the baby in her arms and tried to sniff back the tears welling in her eyes.

For Dhruv Malhotra, pain was a shape-shifter. On some days it fell on him like snow on a glazed slippery road, blocking the tough move-over. On other days it diffused slowly like the smell of burnt charcoal in a clogged, stale room.

It started with blatant denial, which made way for a fatal numbness. He would wake up in the morning imagining Vaanya's face sleeping peacefully next to him. In the dreary December afternoons, he would walk into the kitchen expecting her to be cooking a scrumptious lunch. He would circle his arms around thin air and feel as though he was holding her from the back, as she gently stirred delicious smelling concoctions with spoons and ladles. Vaanya's sweet lavender scent lingered on the pillowcase, which he held on to tightly on nights, imagining her close to him. In the morning, his tongue tasted of her strawberry lip-balm.

Until one day, he woke up and froze in his spot, seeing her side of the bed cold and empty. That morning the pillowcase stopped smelling of her lavender scent, and his mouth only carried the stale, bitter taste of black coffee and whiskey. The white lilies on the coffee table had wilted.

Along with Vaanya's make-believe presence, left his ability to feel anything. He felt nothing but a nagging numbness as he held his daughter close to him. Her searching eyes tried to find affection in her father's distant eyes which looked at her with blank nervousness and a strange, detached paralysis.

The new-born was temporarily taken care of by Mira, who swallowed her sorrow and filled in for her sister, like a quiet promise even kept in death. Mrs. Malhotra also stepped in to help, worried for her son who kept receding into his grief-shell.

Dhruv would stay holed up in his room, collecting all of Vaanya's things through the day, and sleeping on her side of the bed holding her photograph. He lost his appetite. And soon all that was left of him was a bony framework with a face covered by a thick, untamed beard.

He'd lay out all Vaanya's belongings neatly on the bedroom floor. As his fingers traced the fabric of her clothes and the letters of her favourite books, he could feel her coming alive next to him, little by little. Pouring himself a glass of whiskey, he'd play their favourite songs and pretend to slow dance with her throughout the night. He'd read and re-read the texts, emails and hand-written notes that they had written to each other. All in a desperate attempt to hold on to the last bits of things that made him feel her presence.

One morning Mrs. Malhotra walked over to her son with a cup of hot tea.

"I know you didn't get any sleep again last night," she said.

He was sitting on the floor near the window, as he saw his mother standing over him with a look of concern in her eyes.

"I've put ginger and cardamom in this. It will help with your headache. Come on now, get up. Drink this and go take a shower."

Dhruv didn't move. He kept looking at her quietly.

"The bad dream is not ending, Ma," he finally said.

"The dream is over, Dhruv. You just need to wake up," she said, handing her son the steaming cup of tea.

After weeks of sitting in a pile of Vaanya's belongings throughout the day, distinctly playing and replaying each memory associated with every piece of article, he cased everything carefully. Mira helped him sift through Vaanya's belongings and box them carefully. They sat on Dhruv and Vaanya's bedroom floor, crying, laughing, and sharing their fondest memories of Vaanya.

"This was her favourite book," Dhruv said, holding a copy of '*All about love*' by Bell Hooks. "She gave it to me when we were dating."

"The real power of love is to transform us," Mira smiled.

"And transform it did," Dhruv shrugged and put the hardbound cover in the cardboard box.

"One time when I got dumped by my college boyfriend. Didi made me a playlist of the saddest breakup songs in the history of time, and curated a list of the sappiest movies which she would watch with me, while I cried and she'd order me a bucket of chocolate chip ice cream."

Dhruv chuckled, still holding her photo.

"Feel all your feelings, she would say. Make room for sorrow with grace. Let the grief take you to your lowest. Because once you've hit the deepest of the depths, fear just vanishes. You realise that if you've made it thus far, you've got what it takes to continue forward too. You'll be okay."

"We're always more resilient than we think we are," Dhruv smiled remembering his wife's words.

Over the next few weeks, Dhruv allowed the silent numbness to be replaced by defying anger. He was angry at Vaanya for not keeping the promises they had made to each other, the dreams they had seen together. He was mad at her for leaving him alone, in the middle of what was supposed to be the best and the most precious phase of their married life.

He was angry at his innocent daughter for having Vaanya's deep hazel eyes, staring at him, reminding him of his wife's death every day. He began accusing her of everything and immediately the anger turned into paralysing self-hate for being even remotely resentful at their innocent baby-girl, who was their only living breathing manifestation left in the world.

One evening after putting Dharya to bed, Mira went to Dhruv's room to give him some company.

"I think with Vaanya, I've also lost all the love I had inside of me." He sensed her walking in and pouring herself a drink. "I am afraid I have nothing left to give to my daughter," he said staring out the window at the pale moon, gulping down the cold bitter drink.

Mira glanced at him, and took a sip of whiskey from her glass.

"I am not sure if I can be a good father without Vaanya by my side," Dhruv continued. "We were supposed to do this together. I can't do this alone, Mira."

"No Jeeju. You can, and you will." Mira let out a deep sigh. "God gives us only what we're capable of handling. Dharya happened to you, because you are capable of giving her the love she deserves. You're capable of being the father she needs."

"I couldn't protect my wife. I had taken a vow, on our wedding, to always protect her. But I couldn't. I am afraid that I wouldn't be able to protect my daughter either. I just feel so powerless."

"I understand, Jeeju. It's a huge responsibility. But I know you're up to it. Because if you aren't, nobody can be. Don't question yourself so much. Don't beat yourself about not having done enough. You did all that you could. But at the end of the day, there's only so much in our control.

"As Lord Krishna says in the Bhagavad Gita: '*You have the right to perform your actions, but you are not entitled to the fruits of the actions.'*

"The result is not in our hands. Only the action is.

"You've been a wonderful husband to Didi and you have it in you to be a great father to Dharya. You've always done your best. And that's all we're here to do."

Dhruv took a deep breath and swallowed the entire drink in his glass. "The cosmic play," he finished her thought.

"Indeed."

"Look at you, you've grown so wise. I see your *Vipassana* course paid off well."

"It did." Mira chuckled. "And I can't thank you enough for pushing me to go for it. It was a very transformational experience for me spiritually."

"We all need a little push from time to time."

"Yeah," she paused for a moment before saying, "Jeeju, Dharya is the result of all the good karma of you and Didi. She is precious. And I know you're feeling overwhelmed but you just have to stay resilient in the face of this storm."

"But I don't know how," Dhruv turned around to look Mira in the eye.

"By practicing your faith again," she said with a definitive assurance in her voice.

Over the next few days, Dhruv started journaling religiously. His journal—an ode to the time he spent with his wife, and the entire life left unspent became his safe space that secretly carried his grief, in its creased pages. Like a cathartic ritual, every morning at 4 a.m., he would drive towards the end of the city, hike up the hill and sit on the edge of the cliff overlooking the endless sea. He'd stay there for hours, meditating, lost in his own inner world. Often, he'd be hunched over his journal writing and watching the big cherry-red sun rise from the surface of the deep blue waters.

On the morning of 31st December that year, instead of driving off to the edge of the cliff, he walked over to Dharya's room. He tip-toed bare-foot on the chilly floor and crouched over the crib to look at her angelic sleeping form, clad in white overalls. It was an eerily quiet winter morning, and he could hear her slow baby breaths. He ran his fingers on her soft skin. As his hands reached near her small pink hands, she suddenly opened up her warm fists and wrapped her tiny fingers around his index finger, and his heart filled with remorse. He scooped her up in his arms and held her close to his chest for several minutes. She peered at him with divine eyes, and he could feel Vaanya's presence close to him as he gently planted a small peck on her petite forehead.

A tear rolled down his stubbled cheek and he was taken aback by an overwhelming wave of guilt. He could see the remnants of Vaanya in his little daughter's face. He was carrying his entire world in his arms. He cried bitterly, holding her close and resolved to become the father Vaanya would have wanted him to be.

In the evening, Mira came over to drop off some things and invited them to a quiet New Year's Eve dinner at her apartment.

"It's an intimate get-together. Dinner and some drinks. That's it," Mira promised Dhruv. "It'll be a very small gathering with just Abhay and another friend from work."

Ever since Mira moved to Mumbai, she had met Abhay a few times and the instant chemistry back at Dhruv and Vaanya's wedding translated into an unexpected fling, which matured into a six-month-long relationship, going strong. Abhay had been a vital support system for Mira all this time. Rooting for her, pushing her to check on Dhruv and Dharya and being there for her by all means while she silently grieved the loss of her sister. And for her, this year Abhay had ditched his customary New Year's Eve Party at his beach-house in Goa. So, she thought it would be a nice gesture to at least cook for him and throw a small feast.

Besides, Mira didn't want Dhruv to stay indoors, wallowing and grieving even on New Year's Eve. Thus. it felt like the perfect opportunity for all of them to blow off some steam.

She pleaded with him to come, and after all that Mira had done for them, Dhruv couldn't refuse.

"Who is this other friend?" he inquired.

"Her name is Riddhi. She almost invited herself, and I couldn't say no. She had a breakup last week. So, all her plans got cancelled and she has nowhere to go."

Dhruv rolled his eyes.

"I didn't know what to say. Whatever. I'll see you tonight," she said and scurried off to start cooking a scrumptious dinner.

At 8 p.m., Dhruv arrived with Dharya. He wore a baggy jacket that made him look slightly muscular, by hiding his recent weight loss. After not having shaved for weeks, he looked sharp in his clean-shaven, neat look that brought back his boyish charm, making him seem relatively younger than his age.

"Hi Jeeju—" Mira stopped abruptly in her tracks as she saw him. He looked a lot like the old Dhruv.

"Come in," she said aloud and then whispered. "You look like yourself again..."

Dhruv shot her a half-repressed smile, and she steered Dharya's pram through the main door.

Dhruv looked around. It felt odd but nice to get out of his house and be in a new setting. Mira's apartment had a warm and cosy vibe. The dim yellow lights and plush interiors made everyone feel instantly comfortable and at home. Most of all, it didn't remind him of all his small and big moments with Vaanya, which felt like a relieving change of physical as well as mental space for him.

Abhay was sitting next to Riddhi on the couch, who immediately sprang up as Dhruv entered the room. "Hey, we're sorry for your loss," she said from the other end of the couch in a small voice that didn't sound earnest enough. She was wearing a blue winter dress with a long black overcoat and black Chanel boots. A little short and chubby, she had milky-white skin and looked at Dhruv with alluring eyes.

Dhruv pursed his lips and flashed a small uncomfortable yet encouraging smile that said he accepted their condolences. He had still not accustomed himself to the reactions of people and had not come up with a proper response if anybody brought it up.

For so long, he had seldom walked into rooms full of people alone. He always had Vaanya on his arm. Walking alone was itself daunting. Something he was unaccustomed to. To everybody else, she was dead; but to him, Vaanya's memories penetrated down to his bones and he had to remind himself that he was now alone. With these thoughts whizzing in his head, he faked a polite smile and settled himself opposite to Abhay who poured him a drink.

"It's awfully chilly for Mumbai these days," Abhay tried to engage Dhruv in some small-talk.

"Yeah, it's unusual. Apparently, everything about this year is..." Dhruv mumbled to himself while gurgling a sip of cold whiskey in his mouth.

Mira was busy laying the table.

"You didn't tell me your brother-in-law was such a snack," Riddhi went over to Mira and whispered in her ear, still ogling Dhruv.

"Riddhi!" Mira's eyes widened in disbelief. "He's my sister's widower," she couldn't believe her audacity. "And my sister passed away just a few months ago," Mira's voice almost stuck in her throat. Saying it out loud still felt unsettling. All this while, she had tried too hard to hold herself together for the sake of Dhruv and Dharya. In the process, she had forgotten how tired she was and how much she had ignored her grief.

She kept looking at Riddhi in the hope she'd understand the gravity of her remarks, but Riddhi looked like it was beyond her. She walked over to the couch and sat beside Dhruv. Mira didn't want to invite Riddhi that night, but since Riddhi was the first friend she made in Mumbai, who had gone through a break-up recently, she had nowhere else to go that night. Mira was obligated to invite her. She cursed herself for having asked her as Riddhi settled herself near Dhruv, who looked extremely uncomfortable with her moves. Mira shot an embarrassing look at him from across the room as he rolled his eyes at her.

At the dinner table, while Mira and Abhay tried to come up with casual conversation to keep everybody engaged, Riddhi kept asking Dhruv questions.

"So, what do you do?" she started casually.

"I am an investment banker," he replied softly, eating his food.

"Oh, my ex-boyfriend was also an investment banker," her face fell, and Dhruv felt awkward for no fault of his.

Abhay tried to change the subject, "So what is the new year resolution of this group?"

Dhruv fell silent; he wasn't ready to start the year without Vaanya, let alone think of resolutions.

"To strive for a finer balance between work, family and self," Mira said, trying to fill the awkward silence.

"Mine is to date hotter and more emotionally available men," Riddhi spoke, looking at Dhruv and smiling audaciously.

Abhay almost coughed up his food. Dhruv shifted in his chair, embarrassed, avoiding eye-contact with Riddhi. Mira looked at Abhay to prompt him to say something and save the situation.

Caught in a frenzy, Abhay shrieked, "Who wants more booze?"

Dhruv slid his glass for a refill. Mira pouted her lips and eyed Abhay anxiously for having nothing better to say. Abhay made a puppy face and shot her a helpless grin.

"How is the food?" Mira asked, lightening the air around the table. "I especially made this biryani for you, Jeeju," she said, passing the bowl to him.

"Yes, it's delicious," Dhruv said with a polite smile, but Mira could see him hiding his eyes. He didn't lift his gaze from the plate.

"You like biryani? What else do you like?" Riddhi interrupted, and Mira sighed, giving up on saving the dinner anymore.

"Umm..." Dhruv searched for words, but nothing came out. All he remembered in that moment was how Vaanya craved biryani during her pregnancy, as he swallowed the last morsel.

"Why don't we all play poker or something after this?" Abhay tried to digress from the topic, sensing Dhruv's discomfort.

"Yes!" Mira chimed in.

Dhruv flashed them a small half-smile to pretend to agree with the idea.

Later in the night, Dhruv slipped away from Riddhi's uncomfortable questionnaire and escaped into the balcony. He leaned against the railing that looked too low to be safe. He nostalgically glanced at the glittering Mumbai sky-line from the fifteenth floor. The entire city seemed to be made up of electric gas and metal lights. He remembered the last New Year's Eve. He had spent a whole week with Vaanya, in the Andamans, at a chic isolated cottage with a beautiful private beach.

His mind wandered off to Vaanya's gorgeous sunflower yellow bikini and the large floppy, oak-coloured hat that covered most of her face as she dozed off in between her lazy reading sessions on the beach, basking in the warm tropical sun, while he went for his rejuvenating swims. They walked along vast beaches with sparkling white sand and light blue coral waters and watched the most majestic sunsets in the evening.

He opened his phone and started flipping through the photos of their trip. Vaanya's face was always so expression-rich. He missed that. The way she looked so shocked out of her wits, scared, funny, and 'oh-so-cute' in some of the pictures. As he swiped through more pictures, another one of her holding a large cheesecake with candles on it appeared on his screen. It was the morning of New Year's Eve.

Nostalgia hit him like a speeding bus in an empty street on a Monday morning. He suddenly started missing all their New year Eves together, as he realised that this would be the first time in five years that he wouldn't be kissing her when the clock strikes twelve. His eyes got watery, but he quickly painted a faint smile on his face as Mira knocked lightly on the balcony door.

"Dharya just woke up," she said, making her way outside and pulling Dharya's pram from the adjoining bedroom.

"I've fed her," she said, and he responded with a gratifying nod.

"Jeeju, I am sorry for Riddhi. It was so embarrassing for me too. I'm really sorry."

"It's okay, come on! It isn't your fault. And anyhow, you shouldn't be apologising for anything. If there is anyone who needs to apologise, it's me."

"No, Jeeju—" Mira tried to speak, but he interrupted her in the middle.

"No Mira, let me say. It's about time. You out of everyone, knows that I haven't been myself lately. I took Vaanya's passing away to run from everything to and just stay in a mental cocoon, where I could still pretend, she was with me. But I can't run away from my responsibilities. And I don't want to, anymore. This is my life now. I have accepted it. And I am really sorry for being such a pain in the ass over the past few months."

She laughed. "No, you weren't. It's been difficult for all of us, and I think we all have our own coping mechanisms. Had didi been here, she'd have understood."

"Yeah, but she wouldn't be proud of me right now. Although I know, wherever she is, she'd understand me. She always did."

"Yeah."

"And I am deeply sorry for not seeing and acknowledging your grief. I was so consumed in my own loss that I couldn't see anything beyond that. You also lost your sister. Your best-friend. I am really sorry, Mira. I wish I could go back in time and be a better person."

"No Jeeju. You did the best you could. And I'll tell you something. I thought I could handle it, and I thought I was strong. But I'm not. There are days I just don't know how to get out of bed. But then I think about Dharya. And somehow, I find the strength," she sighed and paused for a minute before finally saying. "Didi's passing away has been a shock to all of us. And it's okay. We're all doing the best we can. And we're here to support each other. What else is family for!" She placed her hand on Dhruv's back, and he hugged her.

"No, but seriously. I have no words for all that you have done for Dharya and me all this time. I'll forever be indebted to you."

"Please Jeeju. You're embarrassing me. Dharya is like my own daughter. The word *masi* itself means, mother-like. After didi's passing, I feel that she's equally my responsibility too. Don't punish yourself for taking the time to deal with such a life-shattering loss. And I see you trying every day, to move past your grief, and show up for Dharya. That's brave," she smiled and rubbed his back.

"Thanks Mira, thanks for everything. You Sharma sisters are something else."

"Aren't we?" she chuckled and left.

Dhruv knelt to look at his tiny daughter in her pram, coiled in a sea-blue baby blanket. He ran his fingers along her pink face, and her deep eyes reflected his welled-up face hunched over her.

"We'll be okay, won't we?" he spoke softly. "Just Papa and Dharya, hmm?" After a deep sigh, he continued, "Let's make a resolution this New Year's Eve? Papa and Dharya will be each other's everything from now on."

"Pinky promise?" he held out his little finger and entangled it with her tiny one.

"Papa's sorry for everything, for all these past weeks. But you're all Papa has now. And tonight, I promise that Papa and Dharya will rock it together."

As these words fell out of his mouth, the sky lit up with fireworks. The clock struck twelve, and the Mumbai sky-line glowed with hope and love.

He looked up at the sparkling sky and picked up Dharya in his arms to show his daughter the arrival of their first new year together.

Mira and Abhay came out on the balcony to fetch the father-daughter duo. Mira kissed Dharya's forehead and whispered, "Happy first New Year, Dharya" in her tiny ears, as she tugged Dhruv's arm to drag him to the living room where the party had started, pulling him back into their new life.

Epilogue

Yesterday, I stumbled upon the dollhouse I
had as a kid
I spent my afternoons in the front porch
Building and rebuilding it block by block
With persistence, patience and love
So that my dolls had a safe space to stay in
I was all of five
But I had a clear vision
I imagined having a similar house
When I grew up
But little did I know
I'd have to build and rebuild it bit by bit
With persistence, patience and love
To make it
A home
A safe place for us to stay in.

—Vaanya

The nanny was cooking dinner in the kitchen, when the nine-year-old Dharya escaped into the balcony, enjoying the rainy August evening in Mumbai, waiting for Papa to get home. After gazing at the street for a few minutes, she saw Dhruv's car pull in. Her heart filled with delight at the sound of the revving engine, a shrill reminder of Papa coming home at the end of the day. But tonight, Dharya was surprised to see not just Papa, but a girl in a wine-coloured blouse and pencil skirt, emerge from the car. She adjusted her skirt as she got out of and then went on to give him a small side hug. Soon enough, she hopped into the opposite building as theirs, avoiding getting drenched in the rain.

In a few minutes, Dharya heard the door-knob clanking and ran towards the door to jump into Papa's arms. She decided not to bring up what she saw. They had more important things to cater to, like their rainy Fridays' tradition of spending the night baking walnut brownies and drinking hot-chocolate, while watching Disney movies on the TV. Dharya didn't ask a single question. But days later, on a crisp afternoon when Dhruv read *Goldilocks and the Three Bears*—Dharya's favourite bed-time story, to put her to an afternoon nap, she asked, "Do you still love Mumma?"

Dhruv was taken aback by the sudden question. "Yes Dharya. I do love her."

Her hazel eyes looked up at him. Reminding him of his Vaanya.

"Why this question?" he asked and paused for a moment, trying to understand what was going on in his little daughter's impressionable mind.

But when she still did not say anything, he asked, "Dharya? Did something happen at school?"

"No Papa."

"Then? Did someone say something to you?"

She was still tongue-tied.

"You can always talk to Papa. You know that, right?"

"I found your journal today," she finally admitted. "And I saw Mumma's name written in it."

Dhruv looked at her little angel. *When did she grow up so fast*, he wondered.

"Do you know it's bad manners to read people's personal things, like journals?" he said with a kind smile, that of a father whose heart ached at disciplining his child, but had to still do it nonetheless.

"I am sorry Papa," she said, with her gaze fixed to the floor. "I didn't mean to," her eyes almost welled up.

He lifted her chin up and looked at her flustered face. "You don't have to be sorry, Dharya. It's okay. It's just Papa's journal. But one should never read someone's personal things without their permission."

"Papa, why do you write a journal? And why is Mumma's name in there?" her innocent eyes were full of questions.

Dhruv took a deep breath, drawing in the strength to answer her questions. He was amazed at how bright and curious she was for her age.

"Remember when I had to travel to Singapore last month for work? And you were with Mira masi for five days?"

"Yes Papa, I missed you so much. I hated you being so far, for so many days," she said and pouted her lips.

"Exactly! You missed Papa, no? When I wasn't around?"

She nodded in agreement.

"So, what did you do? You told Mira masi how much you missed Papa; you complained to nani that why isn't Papa with me? You wrote me so many messages and called me. Remember?"

The nine-year-old tried to catch up with her father's train of thought.

"Similarly, Papa has feelings too. But grown-ups cannot always express themselves in simple words, anytime of the day. And sometimes, people who leave don't come back after a week-long trip."

"Mumma…?" Small pearls of tears had begun to clog her eyes.

"Hey…" He pulled her close to his heart. "No crying," he caught the falling tear off her eye with his fingertip before it trickled down her blush cheeks and continued, "So, some people start writing. It helps them process their feelings. And that's why, a lot of people keep a journal."

She looked at Dhruv with big, curious eyes trying to absorb everything. "So you still love Mumma, right?" She asked again.

"Yes, sweetheart."

"Then why were you on a date with the girl in the purple top?" she finally said.

Dhruv looked at her questioning eyes. Helplessness and love, both formed a lump in his throat.

He swallowed hard before saying, "Dharya, I need you to understand when I say this. I have only loved your Mumma. And I can only love her. The girl in the purple top was just a friend from Papa's office. And nothing more."

"So, you never went on a date with her?" she asked innocently.

"No," he replied with a light of sincerity in his eyes.

"Okay. But you can, in case you want to. You have my permission."

"Well. Okay ma'am." He picked her up and placed her comfortably in his lap just how she used to sleep nestled in his arms, from the ages of one to three.

"But hey, tell me how do you even know what a date is?" he asked curiously.

"When a boy and a girl go out together, it's called a date. It's basic, Papa."

Dhruv laughed at her explanation.

The next evening, Dhruv had a special surprise for Dharya.

"Where are we going?" she asked with excitement, sitting in the front-seat, carefully buckled-up playing her favourite music on the stereo.

"Patience, Dharya. You'll know when we get there."

After driving for about an hour, they finally reached what seemed to be a hilly area in the outskirts of the city. Once Dhruv parked the car, Dharya hopped out and grabbed her papa's index finger. The street was carpeted with crimson and yellow leaves of Gulmohar trees. The air smelled of the incoming autumn.

After a short walk, they entered a beautiful bakery. The smell of freshly-baked muffins and cookies made Dharya's mouth water. Behind the counter was an old lady, who had an extraordinarily kind smile. She greeted them as they walked in and handed them a special menu and a big tray of customised candy to try out.

For the next twenty minutes, Dhruv watched his little girl pick out candy as carefully as though she were picking out a wedding dress.

"This place is so great. Thank you for bringing me here, Papa. You're the best," she squealed and jumped to kiss him on the cheek, after choosing a box of half-caramel and half-milk bubble gum flavoured candy.

"But let's hurry, Dharya. You don't want to be late for the second surprise."

"Second surprise? There is more?" she asked, visibly excited.

"Yes," he replied softly with a glimmer in his eyes and a smile.

As they were beginning to leave, the old lady handed them some extra mint chocolates, saying they were 'on the house' for the most adorable father and daughter she had just met.

After bidding goodbye to the kind lady in the cafe, they stepped out for the next surprise. It was a short hike up the hill, but fortunately, they reached right on time, just before the sunset. The sky was painted in all shades of crimson and the sound of gigantic waves breaking at the rock, created a sweet symphony. And as the day-light was fading, the entire city was beginning to light up at their feet. Dharya couldn't believe her eyes. She had never seen a more breath-taking view. Her eyes widened to twice their size, as she tried to soak in the sight in one go. Dhruv looked at his little daughter beaming with joy and felt a true sense of bliss, although fleetingly. A cool breeze blew from the sea and played with their hair. He looked at her and said, "The only person I could ever go on a date with is you."

Dharya was both surprised and joyous at her father's grand gesture but still confirmed, "Is this really a date, Papa?"

"Of course, it is!" Dhruv exclaimed, and in no time the father-daughter duo was riding in a beautiful chariot, overlooking the majestic view. He pulled Dharya close and embraced her in a warm squeeze, while they both reminisced Vaanya in their memory.

Acknowledgments

First and foremost, I'd like to thank the creative power that revealed itself to me at the right time and made this piece of work come to life. Faith is a tricky thing. The more you have it, the more it's tested. But they say great things come to those who take the leap of faith, which is surrendering to the divine design. So surrender, we did.

No amount of thank you(s) would be enough for my extraordinary family and friends who have always had my back and loved me even when I have been hard to love.

My late Nanaji, our family's guiding light and backbone, without whom we all feel a little lost, for passing on his love for literature to me. I vividly remember how he used to sit out in the crisp winter sun in the backyard of our Delhi home, reading ghazals as I came home from school. A pivotal moment in my own creative journey, one in which I fell in love with words. I knew then that someday I would be writing a book.

My Nani, from whom I take lessons on difficult women, love, and resilience. Watching you be undeterred in Nanaji's final moments made me understand the meaning of commitment and what it is to love as a woman.

My Mother, my true north, and the wind beneath my wings. For encouraging me to take the leap. The formidable woman who has taught me all I know about courage, faith, and divinity. There's nobody like you, Mumma, and there never will be. All that I am and ever will be is a result of your unwavering labour of love.

My Dad may not always understand me, but that has never stopped him from letting me follow my heart. Thanks, Papa, for always extending me ample support and wisdom in moments of confusion.

My Sister, Shruti, for always trying to understand and be there for me so patiently and lovingly, even when I've been difficult to like.

Lakshay, for believing in me more than I did. For pushing me to convert a short story, I wrote for our blog years ago, 'One Rainy Evening' into a full-length novel. While the story has evolved over the years, a glimpse of it is still reflected in this book's prologue today. Thanks for always having the right words to say to me and knowing how to say them to pull me out of all moments of self-doubt. You're a godsend, and you know it. My anti-anxiety pill for a reason.

Shreya, for reading the messy first draft in 2020. You were the first true beta reader and editor of this book. Thank you for being a true friend, objective critic, and a complete cheerleader since 2015. You're one of a kind.

Jayanti, our never-ending conversations about spirituality and the universe have shaped a small but significant section of the book. Thank you for being there and helping me with specific and relevant feedback at a very ripe time in the life of this book. You make me believe in kindred spirits.

The pandemic, our former Jaipur residence, and the series of events that unfolded during that period marked a significant transformation phase in my inner and outer life that enabled me to craft the poems preceding each chapter.

The ample natural light and music in the coffee shop right across the street from my Gurgaon home. My creative sanctuary for endless editing over cold coffee for two straight months.

Taylor Swift and Lana Del Rey, two brilliant women songwriters who've made me feel seen and inspired me by giving words to some of the most inexplicable feelings we go through as young women navigating love and life. Their playlists have been my constant companions during writing sessions and have seen me through some nasty creative blocks.

Last and most important, my brilliant publishing team, without whom this book wouldn't have been able to see the light of day:

Kevin, thanks for believing in my dream and giving me the opportunity to let my voice be heard. Your passion and enthusiasm is infectious; your work ethic and ambition are truly inspiring.

Vini, who knew fate would bring us together again, and you'd be crucial in helping me get my work out. Thanks for pulling together such a flawless job on this book. And mostly for all your gracious words of encouragement and appreciation throughout the publishing process.

Vedika, your pen is sharp while your heart is open, and it shows. Thanks for investing so much time and work in this script. Every suggestion of yours has helped shape this book into what it is today. Writers are self-deprecating. We had established that early on, but our long conversations about books, romance tropes, pop culture, and trends have always left me feeling confident about my craft.

Navya, thanks for your relentless contribution throughout editing, cover ideation and proof-reading. And specially for hand-holding me through the first few developmental editing discussions when I felt like I was navigating in the dark without a compass.

Kiran, thank you for the wonderful book cover. You've brought the characters out of my imagination into real life through your art, and I couldn't be more thankful.

The entire creative team at Hubhawks, thank-you for helping me execute my ideas into tangible outcomes. I am confident that it will go a long way in making sure that this book reaches its readers.

Thank you, everyone!

Songs Credits List

1. Ain't No Sunshine (Bill Withers)
2. Can't take my eyes off you (Frankie Valli)
3. Capital Letters (Hailee Steinfield)
4. Cold Mess (Prateek Kuhad)
5. Cruel Summer (Taylor Swift)
6. Daylight (Taylor Swift)
7. Here Comes the Sun (The Beatles)
8. Hold Back the River (James Bay)
9. I've Got You Under My Skin (Frank Sinatra)
10. Kahin Toh (Vasundhara Das, Rashid Ali)
11. Keep Driving (Harry Styles)
12. Late Night Talking (Harry Styles)
13. Love in the Dark (Adele)
14. Love You Like A Love Song (Selena Gomez)
15. Nothing's Gonna Hurt You Baby (Cigarettes After Sex)
16. Perfect (Ed Sheeran)
17. Rewrite the Stars (Anne Marie & James Arthur)
18. Say Yes to Heaven (Lana Del Rey)
19. Say You Won't Let Go (James Arthur)
20. Sign of The Times (Harry Styles)
21. Sleep On the Floor (The Lumineers)

22. Somewhere Only We Know (Keane)
23. Stubborn Love (The Lumineers)
24. Stubborn Love (The Lumineers)
25. Tears in Heaven (Eric Clapton)
26. The Way I Loved You (Taylor Swift)
27. Tu Hi Hai (Ali Zafar)
28. Unsteady (X Ambassadors)
29. We Fell in Love in October (Girl in Red)
30. You Are in Love (Taylor Swift)